Buccaneer

A Dane Maddock Adventure

David Wood

Buccaneer: A Dane Maddock Adventure by David Wood

Copyright 2012 by David Wood

ISBN: 978-0-9837655-6-1

Published November, 2012 by Gryphonwood Press
www.gryphonwoodpress.com

E

Praise for the Dane Maddock Adventures

"David Wood delivers again with a fast-paced romp complete with treasure maps, hidden Templar churches and a secret organization that wants to resurrect an ancient kingdom. Fantastic!" -*J.F.Penn, author of the ARKANE thrillers*

"With the thoroughly enjoyable way Mr. Wood has mixed speculative history with our modern day pursuit of truth, he has created a story that thrills and makes one think beyond the boundaries of mere fiction and enter the world of 'why not'?"–*David Lynn Golemon, Author of Ripper and Legend*

"A twisty tale of adventure and intrigue that never lets up and never lets go!" –*Robert Masello, author of The Medusa Amulet*

"A page-turning yarn blending high action, Biblical speculation, ancient secrets, and nasty creatures. Indiana Jones better watch his back*!*"–*Jeremy Robinson, author of SecondWorld*

"Packed solid with action and witty dialogue, this rousing adventure takes a fresh look at one of the most enduring mysteries of the 20th century." -*Sean Ellis, author of Dark Trinity: Ascendant*

"A an all-out blitzkrieg of a globe-trotting adventure that breaks from the action just long enough for a couple of laughs." -*Rick Chesler, author of Solar Island*

"Let there be no confusion: David Wood is the next Clive Cussler.."–*Edward G. Talbot, author of 2010: The Fifth World*

Works by David Wood

The Dane Maddock Adventures
Dourado
Cibola
Quest
Icefall
Buccaneer

Stand-Alone Works
Into the Woods (with David S. Wood)
Callsign: Queen (with Jeremy Robinson)
Dark Rite (with Alan Baxter-forthcoming)

Apocalypse Tales
The Zombie-Driven Life
The 7 Habits of Highly Infective Zombies (forthcoming)

The Dunn Kelly Mysteries
You Suck (Forthcoming)
Bite Me (Forthcoming)

Writing as David Debord
The Silver Serpent
Keeper of the Mists
The Gates of Iron (forthcoming)

DEDICATION

Dedicated to John Blake, for always being there for us.

From The Author

Thanks for joining Dane and Bones on another adventure! As always, the plot is grounded in history, but I've taken a few liberties for the sake of the story. I hope these little tweaks add to your enjoyment.

Some readers might recall the "Name Dane's Parents" contest on my Facebook page. We had lots of great suggestions, and I won't spoil the surprise here, but I'd like to thank the people whose suggestions I used:

Cheryl Dalton, Michael Dunne, Michael R. Valentine, and Barbara Blake.

PROLOGUE

January, 1698

It was a stormy day on the Arabian Sea. Dark clouds hung low on the horizon and an angry wind scoured the decks with salt spray. William Kidd stood on board the *Adventure Galley*, surveying his prize. The merchant vessel sailed under Armenian colors, but carried French passes guaranteeing its protection, and that made it a fair game. They'd taken it with little resistance offered by its crew. If its cargo holds carried half the wealth he hoped, he would be a rich man.

"Captain, may I have a word?"

He turned to see an ashen-face Joseph Palmer standing behind him, shifting his weight from side to side and looking about as if fearful of being overheard.

"What is it, Palmer?"

"We have a problem." The sailor dropped his gaze, reluctant to continue.

"What is it? It can't be the cargo. The ship was riding too low in the water for her to be empty."

"No, Captain, it isn't that. It's the finest haul we've ever made. Gold and silver, silk and satin, and all sorts of fine things."

Kidd tried not to let relief show on his face. It would not do to reveal that he'd had even the slightest doubt. Loyalty among his crew was tenuous at best, and the dogs would bite at the first show of weakness on his part.

"So, what is this problem?"

Palmer cleared his throat and looked up at the gray sky.

"It is not a French vessel."

Cold fear trickled down Kidd's spine. The man had to be mistaken.

"It is an Indian ship," Palmer continued, "captained by an Englishman."

"That cannot be. It is under French protection. French!"

"It's the truth all the same." Palmer shrugged. "The captain of their vessel, he wants to see you."

"Then he may come and see me. I will show him all the proper courtesies." His thoughts raced. He was a privateer, not a pirate, but, after this incident, it might not be seen that way back in England. Perhaps he could reach an arrangement with this captain. "Bring him aboard."

"There's a problem with that. We tried to reason with him, but he wouldn't stop fighting. Finally, Bradinham stuck him in the gut. He's in a bad way, and I don't think he'll last much longer. He says it's important. He said he..." Palmer stopped and scratched at his chin whiskers. "What was the word? It was something like *ignore.*"

"Implore."

"That's the one." Palmer's expression brightened. "Shall I take you there?"

Kidd saw no way other than to face the problem and work his way out of it.

"Very well, sailor. Let us go."

The wounded captain sat propped up on the bed in his

cabin. His quarters were austere, not at all befitting a man of his rank, Kidd thought. Blood soaked through the heavy bandages wrapped around his abdomen, and loss of blood had drained him of any color he might have had. He forced a smile as Kidd came through the door.

"Be welcome, Captain." His voice was as thin as old parchment. "Please, close the door."

Puzzled by this courteous reception, Kidd complied.

"I understand you wish to see me."

The man's gray eyes, glassy with shock, locked on his.

"Are you a man of God, Captain Kidd?"

It was not a question he would have expected, considering the circumstances.

"Of course," Kidd replied.

"You are needed to do God's work." A series of painful coughs racked the captain's body, and red froth oozed from the corners of his mouth. "I need you to deliver something to England. It must not be lost or fall into the wrong hands." He handed Kidd a canvas bag. Inside was an ivory document case, very old and ornately carved. Bound to it was a sheet of parchment with instructions on where and to whom to deliver it.

Kidd frowned. The man's urgency indicated this was something of great value. Perhaps he could profit from this transaction.

"Captain Kidd, please listen to me." The man could scarcely manage a whisper now. His time was short. "Do not think to circumvent God's will. That way leads to ruin."

Kidd nodded. He was above such superstitious nonsense, but no harm in humoring a dying man.

"Believe me." He pulled down the neck of his shirt,

revealing a brand on his left breast. He was a hairy man, and the brand was now a pale scar, but Kidd recognized the symbol immediately.

Surprised, he took an involuntary step backward, his head swimming, and clutched the wall for support.

"It can't be," he gasped. "They are all dead!"

The dying captain managed a weak smile.

"Not quite. Not yet."

CHAPTER 1

It was like walking on Swiss cheese. Avery chose her steps with care as she wound between sinkholes and abandoned shafts. Damn treasure hunters. They'd torn the island apart over the last two centuries and for what? A legend. Then again, she wouldn't be here if she wasn't a believer.

She paused, straining to listen for any sound that would tell her where work was going on. She didn't know exactly where the crew would be, probably somewhere near the reputed location of the famous Money Pit.

It had been a long hike from the causeway. Not so long ago, you could drive onto and around the island, but no longer. The local government had taken it over and shut it down, citing safety concerns. Now, no choice remained other than hoofing it. One hundred forty acres sounded small until you had to walk across it in the blistering sun, all the while worrying that your next step would send you plunging down into darkness and whatever lay beneath.

She brushed a stray lock of hair back from her face, feeling the damp sheen of sweat and humidity that clung there. She knew she should have made an appointment, but when she'd heard the news about the new crew undertaking the search, she couldn't wait, knowing she might not get a chance like this again.

Now, if she could only make him listen.

Passing through a dense stand of the oak trees that gave the island its name, she looked out across an open space where workmen had, over the years, stripped away the native forest. There! Far across the clearing, workers milled about, setting up equipment and surveying the area. Pleased that she'd been correct about their likely starting point, she picked up the pace. She thought she saw one of the workers, a tall, dark man with long hair, turn and look her way.

Avery felt the ground give way beneath her feet. She sprang back a moment too late. Her scream didn't quite drown out the muffled snap of rotten wood shattering. She reached out, her fingers digging furrows in the soft earth as she struggled in vain to hold on to the edge of the abandoned treasure pit. She caught hold of a thick tuft of grass and, for one blessed moment, hung motionless over the void.

And then, with a tortured, ripping sound, her lifeline tore free. She battered the inside of the shaft as she slid downward, grasping for a handhold. Sharp pain lanced through her as jagged rocks sliced her palms and battered her legs. Her ankle caught on a thick root, turning painfully beneath her, but it slowed her fall enough that she was able to grab hold and loop one arm around it.

Frozen with shock, she could only gasp for breath as she gazed up at the circle of light far above her. She could have sworn she'd fallen a hundred feet, but it was more like twenty. It might as well have been a mile for all the hope she had of climbing back out. She thought of the man who had looked her way. Might he have seen her fall? Maybe, but she couldn't count on it.

"Help!" Her scream was not one of panic, but more a matter of hedging her bets. She didn't know if anyone at the work site could hear her from so far away, but it couldn't hurt to try. She considered adding, "I've fallen and I can't get up," but even her morbid sense of humor wouldn't permit it. She shouted again, this time loud enough to send a sharp, stabbing pain through her vocal cords. "I fell in a shaft! I need help."

She tried to calculate how long it would take for someone to run from the work site to the place she'd fallen. Not long. If the guy didn't show soon, she had to figure he hadn't noticed her.

Her elbow burned and her shoulder felt like it was about to be wrenched from its socket as she struggled to hang on. She managed to take hold of the root with her other arm, giving her a measure of relief. The toes of her shoes slid across the rocky wall of the pit until she found purchase on a tiny protrusion. It wasn't much, but it eased the pain in her shoulder.

What to do now? Instinct told her no one was on the way to help her. Climbing up was out of the question. Could she climb deeper? It was a crazy idea, but maybe there was a place lower down where she could safely wait for help. Twisting her head around, she took a look down into the depths of the pit.

Big mistake.

"Oh God! Oh no!" Her head swam as she gazed down at the small circle of light reflected on the water far below her. There was nothing between her and the bottom that she could hope to stand on, and she'd never survive such a fall. She closed her eyes and took three deep, cleansing breaths. The whirlpool in her head slowed to an eddy and she opened her eyes again.

Cold, harsh reality slapped her back into focus. She'd set off for the island without letting anyone know where she was going or when she'd return, not to mention she hadn't obtained permission to even be on the island in the first place. No one knew she was here.

Then she remembered her cell phone. How had she forgotten her lifeline to the rest of the world? If she could manage to get a signal down here, and she wasn't that far below the surface, she could call for help.

She let go of the root with her right hand and her body slid downward for one sickening moment, but she kept her toehold and her grip with her other arm. Fishing into the pocket of her jeans, she worked her phone free and tried to position it so she could see the screen.

Damn! It was locked. Cursing her choice of phone, she balanced it on her palm and tapped in the numbers with her thumb. 1... 7... 0... 1... Unlocked! Still working one-handed, she began to tap in the number. 9... 1...

Her foothold suddenly gave way and she screamed as she fell, scarcely clinging to the root that was now the only link between her and survival. Her cries quickly melded into a stream of curses as her cell phone slipped from her grasp. She watched its luminescent screen as it tumbled through the air, landing with a pitiful splash in the water below.

Now, to quote her father, she was screwed like a Phillips head.

"Drop something?"

The voice caught her off guard and she almost lost her grip. Down below, a diver smiled up at her. He had short, blond hair, blue eyes, and an easy smile. She recognized him immediately. So this was the famous Dane Maddock. It certainly wasn't the way she'd planned on meeting up with him. Nothing like making a good first impression.

"What are you doing down there?" Despite her predicament, Avery couldn't keep a tone of annoyance from her voice. Couldn't he see she was holding on for dear life?

"My friend and I were exploring a channel under the island when this fell in front of me." He held up her phone.

At that moment, another diver surfaced. This man had a shaved head and skin the color of dark chocolate. He looked at Maddock, who pointed up at her.

"Hey girl, what's up?"

"Me, obviously," she snapped.

"Well, you ought to know the water is only about five feet deep here and the bottom is solid rock. You definitely don't want to let go."

"No, really?"

"Sorry," Maddock said. "Willis loves to state the obvious. How are you doing up there?"

"Hanging in there." Just then, the root gave a little, dropping her a few inches. Her cocky façade dissolved in a girly shriek that, as soon as she realized she wasn't plummeting to her death, at least not yet, turned her face scarlet.

"I'm coming up to help you," Maddock said. "Don't you let go."

Avery gave her head a tiny shake, fearful that greater movement would dislodge her for good.

"You can't climb that!" Willis protested.

"Sure I can. You just get back as quick as you can and bring Bones with some rope. I radioed as soon as I saw her, but I doubt they got the message." Maddock had removed his air tank and was already feeling the wall for handholds as he gave instructions.

Avery wondered if "bones" was some sort of climbing gear or rescue device. She couldn't think of any reason for Willis to bring actual bones, unless they were going to rescue her with some weird voodoo magic.

"Yeah, I heard it." Willis tapped his mask. "Sweetheart!" he called up to her. "You know how to do a cannonball?"

"Yes." Avery's voice was so small she doubted he could hear her.

"Cool. If you slip, and I ain't saying you're going to, do a cannonball. Whatever you do, don't straighten your body out. Got me?"

Avery nodded, not wanting to consider the possibility that she might fall, but grateful for the advice. She stole another glance down and saw that Maddock had already covered a good ten feet of the wall.

"What are you? Some kind of spider?"

"Nope, just a SEAL." Cords of muscle stood out on his shoulders and arms, showing the strain of the climb, but his expression and voice were relaxed. "So, how does a nice girl like you find herself hanging around in a place like this?"

"I just felt like dropping in," Avery grunted. It was crazy to be bandying words with this guy like they were clever college kids, but it kept the fear and discomfort at bay. Her muscles cramped and she was losing feeling in her hands. She couldn't hang on much longer.

"Did Crazy Charlie hire you?" Maddock asked as he hooked his fingers in a cleft in the stone so shallow Avery couldn't even see it.

"I don't know anyone by that name. I was actually coming to..." The root slipped again, this time accompanied by a cracking sound. Avery was too frightened to cry out. She just hung there, gasping for breath. Her foot found a tiny fissure and she pressed her toe into it, more for the comfort it afforded her than the weight it bore.

"I'm almost there." Maddock was maybe ten feet away now, but he looked like he was moving in slow motion. He was never going to get to her in time.

The sound of her rapidly beating heart pounded in Avery's ears. She was keenly aware of the sensation of abraded flesh against smooth wood, cold sweat running down the back of her neck, the smell of brine in the damp pit, and the crack of the root giving way.

And then Maddock was there. He drew a sinister looking knife and jammed it into a crevice just as the root finally snapped.

Avery felt only a momentary lurch and then a strong arm had her around the waist. She looked into Maddock's eyes, so like the sea, and her panic subsided.

"I've got you. But if you can get your fingers into that crack right there, it would help."

She looked up and realized his knife bore most of their weight, though he still had small footholds. She couldn't believe he'd made it up here, but time to marvel would come later.

She worked her left hand into a crevice, and draped her other arm around Maddock. She looked at him, uncertain what to say. She'd expected to dislike him, but now she wasn't so sure.

"How are you holding up?" Maddock asked, his thickly muscled arms trembling and his knuckles white.

"That depends on how much longer you can hang on." Avery struggled against the urge to look down.

"Are you kidding? I'm in this for the long haul."

Avery forced a smile and felt herself slip a little bit. "I'm sorry about this. It's not the way I intended for us to meet."

"So you don't spend your days hanging around pits

with strange men?"

Her fingers slipped again and she wondered, for a moment, if she should just let go. This was all her fault and it wasn't fair for Maddock to go down with her. Literally.

"Did somebody say hanging?" Just then, a rope dropped down alongside them. "Don't worry. It's not a noose."

"Bones!" Maddock exclaimed. "It's about time you got here."

"Talk about ungrateful. Now, how about you and your new friend take hold of this rope before you both fall?"

Avery reached out, slipped one arm through the loop, and grabbed hold of the rope. She started to rise and, next thing she knew, strong hands lifted her up and onto solid ground

Her rescuers were tough-looking men. One, a stocky man with short brown hair, introduced himself.

"I'm Matt," he said. "This is Bones."

Bones stood well over six feet tall, with striking Native American features, and a mischievous twinkle in his dark eyes. He wore his long, black hair pulled back in a ponytail, and his t-shirt displayed a giraffe with a speech bubble that read, "Moo! I'm a goat."

"Maddock's got to go back down for his air tank and other crap," Bones said. "He'll meet us back at headquarters, if you can call it that."

"Okay." Avery could barely find words. She was still freaked out about her near death experience and she was exhausted from the ordeal. "Are you part of Mister Maddock's crew?"

"He's my partner. Or I'm his. It gets a little confused at times. And don't bother with the 'Mister.' He just goes by Maddock." He raised an eyebrow. "You got a name?"

"Avery Halsey," she replied. "Sorry, I'm usually much friendlier."

"I hear you." Bones took her by the arm and guided her toward the work site. "What are you doing out here anyway?"

"If you're Maddock's partner, then I have a business proposition for the two of you."

Bones didn't break his stride or even look at her, but threw his head back and laughed.

"Did I say something funny?"

"No," he said. "It's just, we get that all the time."

A motley group awaited them at the work site. The two who stood out to her were both Native American. One was an attractive young woman with the body of an aerobics instructor. Avery wondered if she was Bones' girlfriend, and found the thought raised a pang of jealousy. Whatever. She'd known the guy for all of two minutes.

The other was a man of about sixty. Unlike Bones, he wore his long, silver-streaked hair down, with a black leather headband holding it back. His weathered face was handsome and, like Bones, mischief danced in his eyes. He wore a coat and tie, blue jeans, and cowboy boots.

Bones introduced the man as his uncle, "Crazy" Charlie Bonebrake, and the girl as his sister, Angelica, or Angel for short. Now that she saw them up close, the family resemblance was unmistakable.

"Glad to see you're okay," Angel said. Her handshake was firm, almost manly in its strength, but the air about her was distinctly feminine, though with a touch of tomboy.

"We had no idea anyone was coming out to the site," Crazy Charlie said, a touch of disapproval in his voice. "If we hadn't gotten Willis's call, we'd never have known.

"I still can't believe I fell. I've been coming to this island since I was a little girl. I know better than to let my mind wander."

"So, what brings you here?" Charlie crossed his arms and waited for an answer. The transformation was immediate, as his expression went from warm and inviting to cold and calculating in a flash. Two men moved in to flank Avery on either side. What was going on?

"You need to chill, Uncle." Bones stepped in between them. "She's here to see me and Maddock.

Charlie considered Bones' words before dismissing his men with a jerk of his head. He looked at Avery a moment longer.

"All right, then. Just be sure to let us know before you visit the work site again. For safety reasons."

Avery nodded. She doubted that safety was Charlie's primary concern, but she couldn't very well argue with him. After all, she'd just demonstrated the perils of wandering the island alone. Still, what was with the thugs? Just treasure hunter paranoia, she supposed.

"I understand. Sorry for coming unannounced."

"I'll leave you to the kids, then." Charlie winked at Bones, patted Angel on the shoulder, and left.

"Gotta love old folks," Bones said. "They never forget you were once five years old."

"Maybe if you didn't still act like you were five," Angel said in a scornful tone. She turned to Avery. "Let me look at your hands." She gave them a quick inspection before leading Avery to a nearby tent where she cleaned and bandaged them. Maddock arrived just as they were finishing up.

"So, you never told me what you were doing here," he said without preamble.

"I came here looking for you." Avery bit her lip. "It's about your father and his research."

The color drained from Maddock's face. He looked at her, nonplussed. It was an odd expression for a man who, minutes before, had bravely scaled a wall to rescue her.

"I'm sorry. I don't know much about his research, and he's been dead for years."

"Please." She felt a lump forming in her throat. "I wouldn't ask if it weren't important. Could we, maybe, meet somewhere and discuss it, at least?"

Maddock and Bones looked at one another, as if each were reading the other's thoughts. Finally, Bones gave a shrug and nodded.

"All right," Maddock said. "No promises, but you name the time and place and we'll be there.

Chapter 2

"Oh, come on." Avery balled her fist and pounded the dashboard of her Ford Ranger. She found the loud thump satisfying. Not so satisfying was the hot air that continued to pour out of the vents. She supposed punching the dash wasn't air conditioning repair 101, but it was her only option at the moment. She'd just have to roll down the windows and deal with it.

Springtime in Kidd's Cross with no air. This would do wonders for her hair. Was she fated to look like a slob every time she and Maddock met?

Already imagining rivulets of sweat pouring down her back, she pulled into the parking lot of the Spinning Crab, narrowly missing a drunk college kid who reeled into her path. He shouted and gave her the finger, but froze when their eyes met.

Avery rolled down the window as she guided the little pickup into the nearest empty parking space.

"Let me guess," she called to the dumbstruck young man. "You're telling me I'm your number one professor."

The boy grinned sheepishly.

"Sorry Miss Halsey. I guess I had a couple too many."

"Don't forget you've got an exam coming up. I think it would be a good idea for you to impress me, if you get my meaning."

The young man nodded and hurried away amid the good-natured ribbing of his friends. Considering the quality of his academic performance so far this semester, Billy Dorne wasn't likely to impress her or anyone else with his brilliance, but maybe the dunce would at least crack a book.

She killed the engine and checked her hair and makeup in the rear-view mirror. Not as bad as she'd feared. She just needed to get inside before she started sweating like a pig.

"All right, Avery," she said to herself as she climbed out of her truck. "You know what's at stake. Time to sell this baby."

"Ave, what are you doing here?"

"Rodney, what a surprise." Avery turned to face her ex-boyfriend and his idiot friends. Now, as ever, she wondered why she'd ever consented to a single date with the man, much less four months of dating. Actually, she knew why. She was a lonely girl working in a college full of academics with sticks shoved so far up their... Anyway, Rodney had been a distraction. He was handsome and uncomplicated.

He was also a bully. She hadn't seen it at first but, once she spotted the signs, she put the brakes on the relationship. In her mind, it was over. Rodney, however, didn't see it that way.

"You really shouldn't be coming alone to a place like this," he said, folding his thick arms across his chest and smirking. "Drunk guys everywhere. You never know when you might run into someone with bad intentions." He grinned with pride, as if he'd made a brilliant joke. Behind him, his buddies, Carl, Doug, and Reggie, guffawed.

Don't encourage the buffoon, she thought.

"I'm not alone. I'm actually meeting someone. Now,

if you'll excuse me." She tried to move past him, but Rodney blocked her way.

"Meeting somebody?" Rodney's voice rose an octave as the idiot chorus behind him began to *ooh* like a bunch of twelve year-olds. "One of those Einsteins from your work? You'd be safer going in there alone."

"It's none of your business who I'm meeting. Now, get out of the way. I've got an appointment and you're going to make me late."

"Cancel it." Rodney's voice was suddenly cold. "Me and you should go somewhere and talk."

"We have nothing to talk about. Now get out of my way." She tried to keep her voice calm, but she frustration welled inside of her. She hated this feeling of helplessness. She couldn't make Rodney move and she wasn't about to leave. She couldn't. This meeting was too important.

"Watch out Rod. She'll call the cops on you, man," Reggie crowed.

Avery hoped she wasn't blushing. Rodney's father was the sheriff of Bridge County, and his son used that relationship as a shield. Rodney worked as a bouncer at a local club and had abused his position too many times to count. He took pleasure in humiliating, and sometimes seriously injuring, bar patrons. Any other employee would have been terminated, even prosecuted, several times over for such conduct, but everyone tiptoed around Rodney.

Sick of standing there, she tried to brush past him, but he grabbed her by the arm and held her tight.

"Sorry we're late." The strong voice cut across the chatter, and everyone turned to look at the speaker. It was Dane Maddock, followed by Bones and Angel. He clearly understood what was happening. "Are we interrupting something?"

"Yeah, you are," Rodney said, releasing his grip on Avery. He turned and looked down at Maddock, who stood a few inches shorter, and smirked. "Why don't you step off?"

"I never miss an appointment," Maddock said, stepping closer. "Give her your number. Maybe she'll call you, but I doubt it."

Avery tensed. She'd felt a momentary relief at Maddock and Bones' arrival, but Rodney and his friends outnumbered her would-be rescuers, and they all loved to brawl.

"I'm not gonna tell you again." Rodney thrust out his chest and took a step toward Maddock.

"Good. I'm getting tired of the sound of your voice." If Maddock was at all fazed by Rodney, it didn't show.

"Your breath is pretty stank, too," Bones interjected. "I can smell you from over here."

Tension crackled in the air. A few patrons had come out front to watch the inevitable fight. Avery's eyes flitted from one man to the next, wondering who would throw the first punch.

Surprisingly, it was Angel.

Bones' sister pushed her way past Reggie and held out her hand to Avery. "Let's go inside." She smiled and gave Avery a reassuring nod.

"Mind your business." Doug, the third of Rodney's cast of stooges, grabbed her roughly by the upper arm.

That was a mistake.

Faster than Avery would have thought possible, Angel lashed out, and Doug cried out in pain as she crushed the bridge of his nose with the back of her fist. His hands came up to protect his face, and she punched him in the gut, and followed with a knee to the groin. As he staggered a few steps, she kicked him in the side of the knee.

Everyone flew into action. Rodney reached for Maddock, who sidestepped and struck back with a barrage of crisp punches that sent the larger man reeling.

Reggie was slow to react, drawing back his fist just as Bones drove an overhand right into his temple. Reggie looked like a marionette whose strings had been cut as he flopped, rubber-legged, to the ground. Carl took one look at his fallen friend and ran.

Bones stepped over Reggie to help his Angel, who had leapt onto Doug's back and was choking him. Red-faced, Doug wobbled toward Bones, who smiled and delivered another one-punch knockout.

Angel rolled free as Doug slumped to the ground, and came up cursing.

"Damn you, Bones! That one was mine." Her face, so beautiful only moments before, burned with a dark fury. "You've got to cut that out."

"You should have finished him sooner," Bones said, still smiling. Angel made an obscene gesture at him, then they turned toward Maddock.

"Quit playing with him, Maddock!" Bones called. "I'm hungry."

Maddock was still peppering Rodney with punches and easily avoiding every attempt to take him down. Rodney's face was a mask of red; he was bleeding from his nose, mouth, and from cuts above both eyes. Maddock winked at Bones as he ducked a wild punch, then struck Rodney on the chin so hard that Avery swore Rodney's feet came off the ground.

His eyes rolling back in his head, Rodney fell into Bones' arms. Bones slung Rodney over his shoulder like a sack of potatoes and turned to Avery.

"Car or dumpster?"

It took her a minute to understand what he meant.

"That's his truck over there." She indicated a battered pickup truck on the other side of the lot.

Bones dumped the semi-conscious man into the bed of his own truck.

"Anyone else need a lift?" he called to Reggie and Doug, who had regained their feet but clearly wanted no part of him, Maddock, or even Angel. They cut a wide berth around the trio as they made their way to Rodney's truck, fished the keys from his pocket, and drove slowly away.

"Now that we got that out of the way," Bones said, offering her his arm, "let's eat. I worked up an appetite."

Avery suppressed a grin as she hooked her arm in his and allowed him to escort her toward the entrance. She froze halfway there.

"We might have a problem."

"What's that?" Bones asked as Maddock and Angel fell in either side of them. "Don't tell me that anal probe is your boyfriend."

"He is... I mean, he was. But it's not that. His dad is the sheriff here."

Maddock and Bones exchanged knowing looks.

"It's cool," Bones said.

"But he might make trouble for you. He's the reason Rodney gets away with so much."

"We don't run from bullies," Maddock said, "even ones who wear a badge. Besides, if we leave, that makes us look guilty. If daddy shows up, we'll deal with it then."

Maddock held the door for her and Angel, then stepped in and closed it in Bones' face.

"They're like kindergarteners sometimes," Angel said, rolling her eyes.

"Well, they are men," Avery said, eliciting a

knowing chuckle from Angel. "I have to ask. Where did you learn to fight like that?"

"It's sort of my profession," Angel said. She looked a little embarrassed as she explained that she was a professional mixed martial arts fighter, and was, in fact, in line to fight for the bantamweight title.

"That's awesome," Avery said. "How did you wind up working with these two?"

"Oh, it's just a little vacation for me." Her eyes flitted toward Maddock, who stood talking with someone at the bar, and her face fell. "Besides," she continued, her expression quickly back to normal, "I live to annoy my brother. He's such a loser."

"I heard that." Bones had caught up with them. Ignoring the sign that read "Please Wait to Be Seated," he sat down at a table with a view of the parking lot and flagged down the first waiter who passed by.

"Dos Equis for me and my friend, who'll be back in a minute," he nodded at Maddock's empty chair. "Nothing for this girl," he indicated Angel. "Indians can't hold their liquor, you know."

The young man looked thoroughly befuddled.

"Just kidding, bro. Get them whatever they like. Oh, and another thing." Bones took out his wallet and handed the young man a twenty. "Keep an eye out for me. If any cops or angry dudes who look like they just got slapped around show up, let me know."

Maddock came back, a grin on his face. Bones gave him a questioning look, but he shook his head. Avery wondered what he was up to, but that wasn't her biggest concern.

They lapsed into an uneasy silence while they waited for their drinks. Maddock clearly wasn't going to broach the subject, and Avery had been nervous enough without wondering when Rodney's dad would show up. When her rum and coke arrived, she took a healthy gulp, hoping to find some liquid courage there. Maddock seemed like a good man, after all he'd saved her twice, but when she'd mentioned his father, his blue eyes had turned to ice. There was something cold and hard inside him that made her distinctly uncomfortable. She sighed. There was no help for it. He was her best hope.

"I guess," she began, "we should get down to business."

CHAPTER 3

"I'm all ears," Dane said. Truth was, he had a feeling he knew exactly what Avery wanted to discuss, and he wasn't eager to talk about it.

"It's about your father's research."

Dane kept his expression blank. It was exactly what he'd expected.

"Specifically, Captain Kidd." Avery must have seen something in his eyes because she hurried on. "Understand, I'm not some nut job or amateur treasure hunter. I'm an associate professor. I teach at the local community college. Captain Kidd is my area of professional interest."

"Seems like an odd thing to build your profession around."

"I have my reasons." A shadow passed across her face, but it was gone as quickly as it arrived.

"What's so weird about researching Captain Kidd?" Angel asked. "Isn't it his treasure we're searching for on the island?"

"We're investigating the so-called Money Pit, that's all." Bones said. "We're not necessarily looking for something Kidd left behind."

"Kidd's treasure is a legend," Dane said, "and a farfetched one at that. He buried a few chests on an island down south but, other than that, there's no reason to believe he had more to hide than that. If he had, he would have used it to bargain his way out of prison before they executed him.

"I think that's exactly what he did." Avery's gaze grew hard. "I've done extensive research on Kidd, much of it I've kept secret, and probably will continue to do so until I decide I can trust you. But believe me when I tell you I have evidence that he did, in fact, have a treasure of immense value, and he tried to use it to buy his freedom."

"Didn't work out for him, did it?" Bones took a swig of beer.

"No, but the important thing is, he did have a treasure of immense value."

"How do you know?" Dane couldn't keep the doubt from his voice.

"I told you, I've done extensive research, more anyone who's studied Kidd or the island."

"That might be but, if you want my help, you've got to convince me."

"Your father believed it."

Dane shifted in his chair. She was probably right, but that didn't make it true.

"Did you know his father?" Angel asked.

Avery's face reddened and she looked down at the table.

"He's familiar to me. He and I followed the same trails in our research."

"Dad enjoyed his pirate research, but it was a hobby, that's all. I doubt he took it seriously." Dane took a long, cold drink of Dos Equis to cover the brief wave of sadness that washed over him. His parents, Hunter and Elizabeth Maddock, had died in an auto accident years before, and he still found it hard to talk about.

Avery sighed and brushed a stray lock of blonde

hair out of her face. She looked down at her hands, eyes narrowed. When she looked up again, her expression was resolute.

"Captain Kidd hid clues, probably maps, in four sea chests. Your father owned one of these chests."

Dane raised an eyebrow.

"That's true, or at least he believed it belonged to Kidd. We don't have it anymore, though. He donated it to..."

"The New England Pirate Museum." Avery completed the sentence. "I've already examined it." She saw the confusion in Dane's eyes and hurried on. "I found a hidden compartment. Inside was a brass cylinder where a document could have been rolled up and hidden inside."

"But it was empty?" Dane asked.

"Afraid so." Avery nodded. "I think your father found whatever was hidden inside before he donated the chest to the museum. In fact, I'm fairly certain of it."

"What makes you so sure?" Dane wanted to dismiss her claim out of hand, but his instincts told him she was reliable.

"Around the time he donated the chest to the museum, he wrote seeking permission to explore the island." She paused, probably waiting for Dane to object or question her, but he remained silent, so she went on. "He indicated that he had new evidence that could be authenticated if need be."

"I guess they turned him down?" Angel asked.

"Yes. Around here, you have to throw a lot of cash around to get anywhere." Bitterness cast a dark shadow across her face. Then, something seemed to click into place and she looked at Bones, eyes wide. "No offense intended toward your uncle."

"Get real." Bones waved the apology away. "We

have no illusions about how Charlie does business."

"Anyway," Avery said, visibly relieved, "I don't know if your father didn't have the money or simply was unwilling to play the game."

"Maybe a little of both." Dane shrugged. "I'm sorry to have to tell you this, but I looked through my dad's research shortly after he died, and there was nothing like what you're talking about."

Avery hesitated. "Could I examine his papers? Perhaps there's something you missed. I mean, you probably weren't searching for a clue to Captain Kidd's treasure when you were going through them."

Dane considered that. Sorting through those books and papers would dredge up memories he'd buried long ago. Besides, while Avery was correct— he hadn't been looking for anything in particular when he went through his father's research, he was certain something like an authentic document from Kidd would have caught his eye.

"Captain Kidd's sea chests hold the key to unlocking the secret of Oak Island. I'm certain of it."

Dane rested his chin on his fist, thinking it over.

"If need be, I'll take you to the museum and show you the secret..." She froze, staring over Dane's shoulder.

Dane turned around to see a stout police officer of late middle years standing behind him. He was blocky with gray eyes and hair to match. The calm detachment with which he eyed the people at Dane's table said, *I own this town and everyone knows it.* Rodney's battered face peeked over the man's shoulder. He spotted Dane and whispered something to the officer, who nodded and approached the table.

"Good evening." The man's gravelly voice held no emotion. He took a chair from a nearby table and sat down. "Miss Halsey." He nodded to Avery, whose face reddened as she whispered a soft hello.

"My name is Charles Meade," he said to Dane and Bones, ignoring Angel. "I am the sheriff and, as such, it is my duty to keep the peace." The man's calm demeanor and articulate speech took Dane by surprise— he'd been expecting an older version of Rodney.

"Everything's peaceful around here," Bones said, his tone easy.

"That is gratifying." Meade steepled his fingers and his gaze turned flinty. "But I understand that was not the case only a short while ago. I need to see your identification, please."

Dane, Bones, and Angel all produced identification, but Meade declined Angel's proffered driver's license with a flick of his index finger.

"Only the gentlemen, please." He examined the licenses. "Dane Maddock and Uriah Bonebrake," he pronounced, like a principal calling unruly students into his office. Dane saw Avery glance at Bones when Meade read his name. Bones hated his birth name. "You are a long way from home, gentlemen."

"That's not a crime, Sheriff," Dane said. "As I'm sure you're aware."

"But aggravated assault is a crime, Mister Maddock. As I'm certain *you* are aware. I don't know what your relationship is with Miss Halsey, but I can assure you I do not condone beating up ex-boyfriends."

Avery started to argue, but Meade silenced her with a cold glance.

"You and your friend provoked a fight with my son. Were it not for the presence of his friends, his injuries might have been even worse."

Now it was Dane's turn to quiet Avery. Meade

thought the game was his, but Dane held the trump card. He had to play it just right, though.

"I assume you've taken statements from witnesses?" Dane said.

"Of course." Meade smiled, leaned back in his chair, and folded his arms across his chest.

"Witnesses other than your son's friends, I mean,"

Meade shifted uncomfortably in his seat.

"They all tell the same story. Rodney and Miss Halsey were talking out their differences. You interrupted, my son spoke rudely to you, and the two of you attacked him. His friends pulled you off, both of them sustaining injuries in the process."

"Well, allow me to retort," Bones said, quoting a line from his favorite movie, *Pulp Fiction.*

"Did your son and his friends tell you he was manhandling Avery?" Angel snapped, cutting across Bones' rebuttal with one of her own. "I tried to get her away from him, and was forced to defend myself when one of his friends grabbed me. Or do you condone violence against women in this county?"

"That is not the story as I heard it." Meade's voice remained calm but Dane did not miss the annoyed glance he shot at Rodney, who, beneath his mask of bruises, wore a guilty expression. "Can you produce witnesses to support your version of events?"

"You've got four witnesses sitting right here," Bones said. "Two of them decorated veterans of the United States Navy."

"You're not in the States, Mister Bonebrake. In any case, your ribbons and medals hold no sway in my county." Meade looked around the table. "Do you have any unbiased witnesses who can support you?"

"You know everyone in this county is afraid to testify against Rodney," Avery said," because they're afraid of you."

"I'll take that as a no, then," Meade said. "I'm afraid I'll have to ask you gentlemen to come with me. Please know I have deputies waiting outside should you resist." His smile indicated he welcomed the thought.

"You're an elected official, aren't you, Sheriff?" Dane asked. The question stopped Meade as he rose, his bottom hovering a few inches above the chair.

"Why do you ask?"

"I take it you have not yet reviewed the security video."

Meade eased back into his chair.

"The video confirms our story. The owner was kind enough to make a digital clip of the incident and email it to me. I'd rather not post it online and send links to the local news outlets." From the corner of his eye, Dane saw Rodney shuffle away from his father, who had gone stock-still. "Let's be realistic," Dane said. "We both have the power to make trouble for each other, but why bother." He hardened his voice. "I've been in all kinds of battles, Sheriff Meade, and one thing I've learned; it's better to avoid them whenever you can."

Meade was intelligent enough to see reason.

"Clearly I was misinformed. But next time you have a problem with someone, let the authorities deal with it. That is our job, not yours."

Angel looked like she was itching to make a sarcastic comment, but Dane nudged her under the table.

"We will," Dane said. "Thank you for hearing us out."

Meade nodded to the ladies and beat as fast a retreat as dignity would permit.

"I can't believe him!" Angel said. "Like it's so easy to stop and call the cops when some guy's got his hands all over you."

"We let him save face," Dane explained. "That way, maybe he'll stay out of our hair."

Angel thought for a moment, then nodded. "You know, you're a lot smarter than Bones gives you credit for."

Dane grinned and called the server over for another round of drinks. Their meals arrived, and they passed an easy hour of beer, seafood, and conversation. Angel, who had joined Crazy Charlie's island work crew at the last minute, steered the conversation away from Kidd's treasure, asking about the history of Oak Island and its fabled Money Pit.

"It all goes back to 1795," Avery began, when a young man found an old block and tackle hanging above a depression in the earth. This area was thick with pirates back in the late seventeenth and early eighteenth centuries, and kids around here grew up hearing stories of buried treasure. So, the young man came back with some friends and they started digging. Within a few feet, they hit a layer of flagstones. Not a layer of natural rock, but actual, hewn stones. They kept digging, but kept hitting wooden platforms at regular intervals. That, plus the pick marks on the sides of the shaft made it obvious to them they were dealing with something man-made."

"Now the story rings a bell," Angel said. "I hadn't put that particular legend together with our project. Bones was always more into legends than I was. If I recall, since that first discovery, treasure hunters have tried to excavate the shaft but, no matter how deep they go, they just hit more platforms."

"Correct. And the pit keeps flooding," Avery said. "The island is filled with underground channels."

"Which is where we come in," Bones said. "Charlie

wants us to locate every channel we can find and see if any appear to be man-made."

"Which they don't," Dane added.

Bones nodded. "He also wants to see if they can be sealed and the water drained out."

"No one's tried it before?" Angel asked.

"They have, but they've always failed." Avery shook her head.

"So why keep trying? It sounds like an impossible task. Has anyone found a single bit of treasure?" Angel's brow was knotted and she pursed her lips. "Have we signed up for a wild goose chase?"

"A few things have been found over the years." Avery stiffened and raised her voice. "Seafaring-related artifacts, bits of gold chain, parchment, and, of course, the stone."

"What stone?" Angel asked.

"A stone inscribed with strange symbols," Dane said. "The message was translated as *'Forty Feet below two million pounds are buried.'* Its authenticity is questionable, though."

"I have more evidence than that," Avery said. "Accounts no one else has seen. I know there's something down there." She turned to Dane. "That's why I need to see your father's research." She held his gaze. "I'm not a quack treasure hunter. This has been a scholarly endeavor for me from the start. My colleagues haven't taken me seriously, but I'm right on the verge of proving them wrong. I've got everything I need to publish except..." She fell silent and looked down into her half-empty mug of beer.

"Except proof," Dane said. Avery nodded and looked up at him again. Dane saw the pleading in her eyes. "I don't want to get your hopes up," he sighed. "I've been through Dad's papers, and there's nothing there. But I'll take another, closer look. If there's anything at all that might help you, I'll give you a call."

"I suppose that's as much as I could have hoped for," Avery said glumly. "Thanks."

Dane went out of his way to avoid looking at Bones. He knew what his friend was thinking, but Bones was wrong. This was not the beginning of another of their crazy adventures.

CHAPTER 4

The door to his parents' vacation cottage overlooking Mahone Bay felt heavier than usual as Dane pushed it open. Sensing his mood, Bones and Angel slipped past him like shadows to their respective rooms. At Bones' suggestion, they'd seen Avery home safely before returning to the cottage for the night.

For a moment, he considered leaving his father's research where it lay and telling Avery he'd checked, but the coward's way out was not for him. This reminder of his parents' death was something he'd have to face.

In the kitchen, he slid the microwave oven from its cabinet and grinned. Leave it to his father to ignore the seascape painting in the bedroom, where any normal person would hide a safe, and put it behind a kitchen appliance instead.

He opened the safe and withdrew a fat envelope. He hadn't touched it since shortly after the accident. Leaving the safe open and the microwave on the counter, he moved mechanically to an armchair by the fireplace, and emptied the contents of the envelope onto the coffee table.

It was much as he remembered: printouts of articles, scans of documents, and a thick sheaf of notes written in his father's elegant, yet masculine hand. He let out a low chuckle as he recalled, as a teenager, trying to imitate his father's signature on a bad report card, only to be forced to own up to the bad grades and the failed forgery.

Along with the stack of research, a smaller manila envelope held brochures of museums and other pirate-related sites his father had visited, and loose bits of paper with notes jotted on them. Last was a small, leather-bound print of Edgar Allan Poe's story, *The Gold-Bug.* Fitting, he thought, as it told the story of a search for Captain Kidd's treasure. He turned it over, surprised to discover that the book looked brand new. This was not some old volume his father had taken notes in. He opened it to the middle and flipped through a couple of pages, then turned it over and gave it a shake in case anything was hidden inside, but no luck.

He set the book aside and started with the pile of research. The first several papers were various Kidd biographies, peppered with handwritten annotations. He read through them and found nothing new or unusual, certainly no references to Oak Island or the Money Pit.

He laid them on the table, rested his elbows in his knees, and buried his face in his hands. This was a waste of time. He was putting himself through this for nothing. In fact, he'd been foolish to stay here at all, where reminders of his father were everywhere and his presence seemed to hang in the very air. The weight of an unbearable burden of sadness pressed down on him. He should have stayed in the travel trailers Crazy Charlie had set up for the crew, and where Willis, Matt, and Corey were bunking.

He sensed movement behind him and a pair of gentle hands rested on his shoulders. He looked up to see Angel smiling sadly at him, sympathy shining in her eyes. She kept her silence and, for that, he was grateful. He gave her hand a squeeze and indicated that she should sit down.

She dropped into the other armchair and picked up the papers he had been examining. Understanding dawned on her face as she scanned them.

"This can't be easy for you. I remember when my grandmother died. Seeing to her affairs and taking care of her things wasn't so painful for me. That just felt like work. It was the personal things, you know. Letters she'd saved, pictures of me she'd written my name on. It was all too... real."

Dane nodded.

"I can do this for you, Maddock. There's no reason you should have to dredge up painful memories."

"It's okay. I've been avoiding this place and these papers for years. Besides, I told Avery I'd do it."

"How about some help? Two of us can get through it faster than one."

"All right." He shrugged. "You know what we're looking for: clues to a treasure on Oak Island. I don't think a document old enough to be a clue from Kidd himself would have escaped my notice the first time I went through this stuff, so keep an eye out for anything that looks like a scan or copy of something older."

They set to the task, working in companionable silence. Occasionally, Angel would call his attention to a mention of treasure or the island, but they found nothing like what Avery was looking for.

The night wore on and he found that, the deeper he delved into his father's research, the more academic the endeavor became. His malaise melted away as he focused his thoughts on the subject. It was interesting, but shed no light specifically on the Oak Island mystery. By the time he finished reviewing his share of the material, he found himself eager to take a look at the rest. Angel, too, was eager to keep going.

When both sets of eyes had passed over every paper, he was forced to admit defeat. Whatever Avery was looking for, had it even existed, was not here.

"Sorry, Maddock." Angel gave him a quick hug.

"Thanks for getting me through it. Avery's going to be disappointed, but it was a pipe dream anyway." He gathered the papers and returned them to the safe, but held on to *The Gold Bug*. Perhaps a bit of pleasure reading would help him relax.

Retiring to his room, he dropped down on the bed, opened the book, and froze. There, on the first page, was an inscription from his father. The date was December 25 of the year his parents died. This was to have been Dane's Christmas gift. They had lost their lives only a few weeks before the holiday. His father must have written this shortly before his death.

Dane,

I know you think my search for a pirate's treasure is a fool's game. Perhaps, by the end of this book, you will wish to join me on this adventure.

Dad

He closed the book, dropped it on the floor, and turned out the light. He'd always, perhaps a bit childishly, believed his dad's pirate research to be something from which Dane was excluded. But now... He rolled over and stared out the window, his mood as black as the night.

Rodney cursed and shifted in his chair, trying to find a comfortable sitting position. He was battered and bruised, and was pretty sure he had at least one fractured rib. He'd get his revenge on that Maddock guy, but that wasn't foremost in his mind at the moment.

He'd only caught snatches of the conversation Avery had with those jerks, but he'd heard enough. Captain Kidd had a treasure and he'd hidden the clues in old chests. Now, the treasure bug had bitten Rodney, and he was determined to be the one to find whatever it was Kidd had left behind.

Like many locals, he'd done his share of poking around on the island in his youth, but gave it up as hopeless. So many treasure hunters had excavated Oak Island that no one knew which pit was the original. Besides, he lacked the knowledge and equipment to carry out a proper search but, if he could find something definitive, a treasure map, maybe, he was sure he could get help in that area.

He looked at the monitor screen and his shoulders sagged a little. He'd never been much for research, or anything related to education, for that matter. Classes were just hoops to jump through so he could play football, wrestle, and meet girls. Tonight, he was wishing he'd paid a little more attention in school.

He'd tried the obvious research sites, searching for any mention of Captain Kidd's sea chests, with no success. He'd felt a momentary thrill when he found an account of Kidd burying a treasure on some place called Gardiner's Island, but read on only to find the treasure had been recovered shortly thereafter and used as evidence in Kidd's trial. The more he searched, the more discouraged he became.

Finally, he stumbled across a website that focused on the Oak Island mystery. Navigating to the forums, he was pleased to see an entire section dedicated to legends about Kidd's treasure. It took him a few minutes to figure out how to use the search function, but he got there in the end. He typed in "Kidd chest maps legend" and hit the enter key.

Nothing.

Finally, he overcame his revulsion at the thought of being a big enough loser to actually join an internet forum. He created a sufficiently masculine username, HotRod69, and made his first post.

does anyone know anything about a legend where captain kidd hid maps or clues inside sea chests

He stared at the screen, waiting for a reply, but to no avail. After ten minutes, he went to the kitchen for a beer and two pain relievers, but returned to more disappointment. What the hell? People were logged in to the forum. He could see the number of users online down at the bottom of the page.

And then he remembered the circular arrow at the top of the browser. He didn't remember what it was called, but Avery had shown him how to click it to update the page back when he'd been following a football game he'd bet on, and wondered why the score wasn't changing. Proud he'd figured this out on his own, he clicked the button and was happy to see he'd gotten a reply.

Do you mean the Gardiner Island treasure chest?

He gritted his teeth and banged out a harsh reply.

no idiot i dont

That shut the guy up. A few minutes later, he

received a private message from a user named "Key."

Not familiar with a sea chest legend. Where did you hear of it?

Frustration at this idiot wasting his time dueled with pride at actually knowing something that, apparently, no one else did. This was a new, heady experience for him, and pride quickly won out. He typed a reply.

I know a researcher who found one of the chests

Key's reply was immediate.

Who?

Rodney didn't like the question. For one, it was none of the guy's business. What was more, it made Rodney seem less important if he was simply passing along information someone else had given him.

don't matter do you know about it or not??

He added the second question mark to show he meant business. He waited for Key's reply, but none came. Returning to the forum, he was puzzled to discover his post was gone. That was weird. He re-typed his initial message, posted it again, and watched the screen. Two gulps of beer later, the screen flickered and the website vanished, replaced with an error message.

"What the hell?" He banged his fist on the desk, spilling his beer all over his keyboard and lap. Upending the keyboard over the wastebasket, he drained the remainder of the foamy liquid, then rubbed it on his shirt. It didn't help. The keyboard was dead. Using the mouse, he refreshed his browser a few times, only to get the same error message. The website was down.

He shook his head. Just his luck. Maybe it would be up and running again in the morning. In any case, he wasn't beaten. If web searches didn't pan out, he'd simply have to try another tactic. As he settled into bed, he vowed he'd find a way to get to that treasure before Avery and her new friends did. And he didn't care what he had to do to get it.

CHAPTER 5

"One more quick dive and we knock off for lunch."
Bones squinted up at the midday sun that hung high
overhead. "Maybe for the day. I'm hungry and I'm
bored. This whole thing is a wild goose chase."

Dane nodded. He'd called Avery this morning and
gave her the news that there was no clue among his
father's papers. The disappointment in her voice was
palpable, but she'd thanked him and asked him to
contact her if he found anything. So far, nothing they'd
seen today gave him any reason to believe he'd have
any good news for her.

Every channel they'd explored had been natural.
Not a hint of chisel marks or anything that would
indicate human hands had altered it in any way. Each
time they finished exploring a passage, Charlie set a
crew to sealing it off. Dane thought this was a waste of
money and effort. The island sat on what was very
much like a giant sponge. The hope of eventually
sealing off all the waterways beneath its surface
seemed futile to him. But, Charlie had the resources to
make it happen, and remained undaunted by the lack
of discovery. He bounced around the island, inspecting
the work sites and keeping up a steady stream of
encouragement.

"How long do you think Charlie will keep us at it?"
Dane sat down on *Sea Foam's* side rail next to Bones. "I

know he can afford it, but I feel a little bit bad taking his money."

"Don't." Bones grinned. "If he doesn't give it to us, he'll just spend it on his latest bimbo girlfriend. Anyway, he'll keep us working until he can prove to the local authorities that the pit's a hoax, or a natural formation."

"What?" Matt stood nearby, making ready to dive. "You mean we're not here to find a treasure?" He looked affronted.

"I mean Charlie always has a backup plan. If we find the treasure, great. If we prove there never was a treasure, he's already laid the groundwork for building a pirate-themed casino on the island."

"And by laying the groundwork, you mean greasing the palms of local politicians," Dane said.

A knowing grin was all the answer Bones gave.

"So, who's got tunnel seventeen and who's going to inspect the next stretch of shoreline?" Dane asked.

"It's you and Matt in the creepy, dark tunnel this time," Bones said. "Me and Willis get the easy duty."

"Are you sure about that?" Matt asked.

"Yep. I checked the schedule and everything." Bones exchanged evil grins with Willis, who had joined them at the rail.

"Maddock, you never should have delegated that job to Bones," Matt said. "Somehow, the Army guy keeps getting the crap duty."

"Seems fitting," Bones said, leaning away from Matt's playful jab.

"All right, y'all better get going," Willis called. "Don't be mad, now. Nothing but love for you."

Dane rolled his eyes, pulled his mask on, and flipped backward into the water.

The cool depths enveloped him and he swam

through shafts of green light, headed in toward the channel they'd labeled number seventeen. The entrance was well hidden in the midst of large, jagged rocks where the surf's ebb and flow surged with relentless force. He led the way, swimming confidently through the perilous passage.

A few feet inside the tunnel the light melted away. Dane flipped on his dive light, setting the passageway aglow. Like all the others they had explored, the passage was wide enough for a man to swim through comfortably, the way irregular, and the rough edges worn smooth over time. This time, though, something immediately caught his eye.

A groove, two inches thick, had been carved up each side of the entrance and across the bottom. There was no way it was natural— the lines too sharp and straight, the groove almost perfectly square. His first thought was someone had slid planks into this groove to form a cofferdam.

"Matt, do you see this?" he asked through the transmitter. The long-range communication devices were state-of-the-art, and came courtesy of Charlie's generosity.

"Yeah. Looks like someone tried to block this channel. Pirates?" He said the last in a comic, throaty growl.

"Or treasure hunters. Charlie isn't the first to try to dam up the channels under the island."

"You, my friend, are no fun."

Grinning behind his mask, Dane led the way into the passageway, which ran back only about forty feet before it made a sharp bend to the left and came to a dead end.

"That was easy," Matt said. "We'll check this one off the list and be back on deck, drinking a cold one, before

Bones and Willis drag their soggy carcasses back."

"Hold on." Dane played his light slowly up and down the wall that blocked their way. He saw immediately that it wasn't like the sides of the passage. Instead of a smooth, regular surface, a pile of rubble blocked their way. A thorough inspection revealed an opening at the top, and darkness beyond.

"Think we can make it through?" Matt moved alongside him, reached out, and gave the topmost rock a shove. It gave an inch. "I think we can move it."

Dane nodded and together they worked the stone, which was the size of a small microwave oven, free, and let it fall. Matt vanished from sight as a cloud of silt roiled in the water.

"There's no current carrying it away," Dane observed. "I don't think this tunnel goes much farther."

"Then there's no point in wasting time waiting for things to clear up. Let's keep working."

Three large stones later, they had cleared a space large enough for one man to swim through. After securing one end of a strong cord to a length of branch that jutted up from the pile of rubble, Dane went in first. He held on to the rope in case he lost his way and moved slowly due to the limited visibility, not wanting to injure himself or damage his equipment on an unseen snag. As he cleared the pile of debris, he felt a tug on the cord and knew Matt was behind him.

As he had predicted, the passage did not extend much farther, perhaps another forty feet, before it came to another dead end. This time, it wasn't a pile of stones blocking their way.

"Holy crap!" Matt's voice was dull with disbelief.

The twin beams of their dive lights shone against a wall of stone, and a carving of a Templar cross.

Chapter 6

Morgan plucked the phone from its receiver on the first blink. Her sisters never answered immediately, thinking it a subtle way of showing they had more important things to do than to take a telephone call. She brooked no such nonsense. She was a firm believer in immediate, positive action in all things, even the smallest.

"Yes?"

"Locke is here, Ma'am. He wishes to speak with you if you will consent."

"Of course." She hung up the phone, closed the file folder she had been reviewing, and stared expectantly at the door, which opened a moment later. Jacob knew her philosophy on wasting time, and made a point not to do so. He appeared in the doorway, his shaved, black head gleaming in the artificial light, and his broad shoulders filling the door frame. He gave her a respectful nod and stood aside for Locke.

The two could not have been more different. Where Jacob, formerly of the Elite Royal Marines, was built like a bull, the tawny-haired Locke was lean like a puma and moved with the deadly grace of one of the big cats. Formerly of MI-6, his whiskey-colored eyes shone with intelligence. Every member of her personal staff was an asset, mentally and physically, and he was her top man.

"Ma'am," he said without preamble, as was always her expectation, "we have a potential lead on the Kidd chests."

She felt her entire body tense. Locke often surprised her with information, but nothing of this magnitude.

"How strong a lead?"

"We can't be certain yet. Someone in Canada posted a query on a message board. He claims to have been tipped off by a researcher who gave him the location of one of the chests. An agent in the area is following up on it as we speak."

"A message board? I assume the post is gone?"

"We actually took down the entire site. We'll restore it, the post in question deleted, of course, after we've investigate the claim. Could be a crackpot." He sounded doubtful.

"For three centuries we have suppressed every mention we could find of these chests. It is not something one would accidentally stumble upon." She turned in her chair and gazed out the window. Truro lacked the size and bustle of London, and she liked it that way, but the modern world intruded here too. There was too little appreciation for the old ways, and old powers. "I want you there. Depart as soon as possible."

"As you wish. Should I wait until after your training session?"

"Jacob can train with me today." Morgan turned around just in time to see the ghost of a smile play across Locke's face. Jacob hated their training sessions. He was averse to striking a woman, which was a fatal weakness Morgan exploited to its full extend. Locke had no such compunction, but this task was more important.

"There is something else." His hesitation was so brief that none but Morgan would have noticed. "A potential complication."

"What?" Her word cracked like a whip as suspicion sent hot prickles down her spine.

"Two others viewed the post before we eliminated it. I traced the ip addresses. One is an American from a small town in the south. A bit of a nutter who blogs about Bigfoot and aliens and the like."

"Erase him and his internet presence." Morgan would not accept even the tiniest risk of the legend of the chest spreading across the internet.

"Already done," Locke said. "It was a house fire. Truly, those so-called mobile homes are veritable death traps."

"Very good. And the second person to see the post?"

"That one is problematic. It took a great deal of doing, but I traced the source to Germany. BÜren, to be precise."

Morgan froze. "Wewelsburg?"

"I cannot say for certain, but..." Locke shrugged.

"Herrschaft," Morgan whispered. "We must assume they have the same information we do." Her eyes met Locke's. "We *will* get there first."

"It will be as you say. Anything else before I go?"

"No, that will be all."

Morgan returned to her desk as Locke saw himself out. She performed a series of calming mental exercises to slow her racing heart, opening her eyes when she was, once again, her serene, rational self.

She gazed at the family portrait on the far wall. How unlike sisters they looked—Tamsin, a raven haired beauty, Rhiannon, with her coppery tresses and emerald eyes, and Morgan, a blue-eyed blonde. They were not sisters by blood, only distant cousins, but they were bound by something deeper. How she longed to call the assembly and deliver the news that a chest had been found. Soon, perhaps, she would be able to do just that. But not until it was in her possession. To tip her hand too soon would be an unnecessary risk. Her position at the top of the order was strong, but she was not immune to the machinations of her Sisters.

She struggled to return to her work, but her duties as director of the British History Museum suddenly seemed mundane, even trivial, in light of what her people might soon uncover. Rock-hard discipline overrode any distractions, and she made quick work of her list of emails and telephone messages. She then took a half-hour to compose a carefully crafted opinion piece for *The Times* in which she questioned, but did not criticize, the Prime Minister's position on a key budget item.

Since being elevated to the leadership of the Sisterhood, she had used her connections to gradually raise her public profile, carefully crafting the image of one who took great pride in her nation's heritage and fought for its history without being perceived as backward. Though never presenting herself as having any interest in politics, her name was already being bandied about as a candidate for Parliament, even Prime Minister. Her aspirations, of course, were higher.

By the time she'd sent her submission to the editor, she could no longer curb the flow of energy that coursed through her. She buzzed Jacob.

"Close the offfice and meet me in the fitness room."

"Yes, Ma'am." He almost managed to cover his tone of resignation. The fitness room was never fun for him.

Smiling, she tapped in a code on her telephone

keypad and watched as the painting on the far wall, "Le Morte D'Arthur" by James Archer, slid to the side, revealing her private collection of weapons. Morgan's eyes swept lovingly across the sharp, gleaming blades and angry spikes. She excelled at hand fighting and with firearms, but medieval weaponry was her true love. She selected a long sword and held it out in a two-handed grip, savoring its weight and balance. With a step and a twist, she sliced a whistling arc through the air. Yes, this was the one.

She caught sight of her distorted reflection in the blade. Like this image, the world did not yet see her for what she truly was, but they would. Oh yes, soon they would know.

CHAPTER 7

Dane drifted in for a closer look at the cross. He shone his light across it and saw a thin circle carved around the image.

Matt ran his fingers across the surface of the carving, his fingers gently probing the recess.

"Careful," Dane warned. There was something odd about it, but he could not put a finger on it.

"I think I can get a grip on it." He shoved his fingers into the groove and twisted.

"Matt! No!" But Dane's warning was too late. The stone circle rotated a quarter turn and, with a whooshing sound like a drain opening, the stone vanished, pulling Matt's arm into the wall.

Matt shouted and struggled against the force of the water that was being sucked into hole. Dane grabbed hold of Matt's arm but, before he could pull him free, he heard a hollow thud and Matt's cry of pain burst through the transmitter.

"My arm!" Matt yelled.

Dane directed his light into the hole and saw, to his horror, that a section of wall had come down, crushing Matt's arm and trapping him. The smooth, regular edge of the stone told him in a single glance that it was not a natural rockfall.

"A booby trap," Dane said. "Hold on." He called into the transmitter. "Bones, Willis, Corey, you guys copy?"

Nothing.

He made a second attempt and again got no reply.

"We're too deep under the rock." Matt's voice was thick with pain. "You've got to get closer to open water if they're going to hear you."

"I don't want to leave you here." Dane knew Matt was right, but he hated to leave an injured man behind.

"What? You think I'm scared of the dark? I'm a Ranger, not some girly SEAL."

Dane grimaced. "All right. How much air do you have?"

"It doesn't matter. Just go." There was just enough light that Dane could see Matt glaring at him through his mask. "I'll watch my air supply. If you aren't back when it gets to ten minutes, I'll cut my arm off and swim the hell out of here. Now go." Matt closed his eyes and leaned his head against the rock wall.

Dane swam with desperate fury, all the while calling for his team members. He squeezed over the pile of rubble and, with powerful kicks, zipped back up the passageway toward open water. He had just caught a glimpse of light when one of his calls finally got a response.

"Yo, Maddock, what's keeping you? We're done." Bones said.

"I need you guys here quick. The tunnel was booby-trapped. Matt's stuck and he's hurt. Bring pry bars.

"Roger." Bones and Willis spoke on top of each other as each acknowledged Dane's message.

"Corey, you call for help."

"Already on it," came the reply.

Dane gave Bones and Willis a quick description of the underwater tunnel, then turned and headed back down the passage. When he reached Matt, he feared the worse. His friend sagged limply against the wall, his trapped arm supporting his weight.

"Matt, you still with me?"

"Yep," came the weak reply. "I'm *hanging* in there. Get it?"

The next few minutes seemed to stretch into hours as Dane watched and waited for help to come. He worked at the stone that pinned Matt's arm down, first with his bare hands, then with his knife, but could not budge it. He knew it was futile, but Matt needed hope to strengthen his resolve. All the while, Dane kept up a steady stream of encouragement until Matt told him to shut the hell up and go look for the others. Just then, a glimmer of light appeared, and two dark shapes swam into view.

"His arm is trapped under a stone block. You guys pry it up." Dane instructed. "I don't know if he has the strength to pull himself free."

"That's what you think," Matt growled, rising up and placing his free hand against the wall. "You guys just get me loose."

Bones and Willis worked their pry bars into the open space beneath the rock and heaved. The rock moved, but no more than a centimeter. The two men tried again, groaning from the strain, and it budged a little more. Matt pulled back, roaring in anger and pain, but his arm scarcely budged.

"Again!" Dane barked.

They continued to work at the stone. Dane took Bones' knife in one hand, his own in the other, and used both to help lever the rock upward. The effort was tiring them rapidly and none of them had much air left.

"Cut it off." Matt gasped.

"No way." Willis said. He and Matt were tight, and he seemed be taking this accident as a personal affront.

"It's not going to work." Matt's voice was barely discernible. "We're all going to run out of air soon. Just do it."

"We'll give it one more try," Dane said. "When we lift, you pull with all you've got."

"That's not much, but okay."

Dane counted down from three and they all lifted one last time. Dane's muscles burned and the strained grunts and groans of his team rang in his ears.

"Now, Matt!" he shouted.

Matt threw himself into the attempt and his arm gradually slid free of the trap.

And then he collapsed, folding onto himself like an accordion.

Dane dropped the knives and grabbed hold of his friend, yanking him free of the trap just as the stone crashed back into place. Together, they hauled their semi-conscious comrade up the tunnel and out to their waiting boat.

Dane bandaged Matt's crushed arm while Corey piloted them to shore, the sound of approaching sirens telling them help was on the way. By the time they got him to shore and into the waiting ambulance, Matt was alert, though in tremendous pain.

"You guys don't worry about me," he said. "And don't let those asshole pirates beat us. Finish the job."

"We'll talk about it at the hospital," Dane said as the ambulance doors closed. He turned to his crew. "We're done for the day. Does Charlie know what happened?"

Corey nodded.

"Good. We'll head to the hospital and we can talk about it more while we wait."

"I'm telling you right now," Bones said, "I want another crack at that tunnel."

Everyone gave him a quizzical look.

"I got a look inside just before the stone fell. I don't know what it is, but something is back there."

There it was again. A flicker of shadow, like someone moving past the back window. Rodney muted the television, rose slowly from his chair, and headed to the back window. Squinting against the afternoon sunlight, he scanned the back patio, but saw nothing. Weird. He was working later, so he'd had only one beer. Must be his imagination.

He returned to his chair, a cracked leather number he'd bought cheap at a garage sale, and reached for the remote.

"Do not move." The voice was cold and hard, but carried a hint of a pansy British accent.

Still pissed about being jumped by that Maddock guy and his friends, Rodney sprang to his feet, whirled about, and flung the remote in the direction he'd heard the voice. It flew through empty space and shattered against the wall.

He saw a blur at the corner of his eye and something struck him a hard blow in the temple, followed by a flurry of kicks and punches so lightning-fast he hardly knew what was happening. The next thing he knew, he was flat on the ground, knee buckled, head ringing, ribs screaming, and fighting for breath. Someone bound his wrists and ankles with cable ties. He twisted his head around and caught sight of his captor.

They guy was not what he expected. He looked like a banker, clean shaven and dressed in a coat and tie. The only odd thing about his appearance was the pair of latex gloves he wore.

And the razor he drew from his breast pocket.

Rodney gasped, the relief of the sudden intake of breath failing to overcome his abject terror.

"What do you want?" He hated the way his voice squeaked and the hot, damp feeling in his crotch as his bladder released. "I'm broke, man, but take what you want."

"What I want," the man said in a voice like a schoolteacher in an old movie, "is information."

"I don't have any information. Ask anybody."

"On the contrary, you do indeed." The man knelt and pressed the flat edge of the razor against Rodney's cheek. "Tell me what you know about Captain Kidd's sea chests."

"What?" *How did the guy know about that?* "I don't know what you're talking about."

The man flicked his wrist and a line of hot fire blossomed on Rodney's cheek. He was too shocked to cry out.

"This will go much easier for both of us if we do not lie to one another. To encourage you to be truthful, I will cut something off each time you lie, or attempt to hide something from me: ears, fingers, toes eyelids, lips."

Rodney whimpered and tried to squirm away, but the touch of cold metal on his eye socket froze him in his tracks.

"In the interest of fairness, I shall, of course, be truthful with you. You posted a query on a message board last night, asking about the legend of the Kidd chests. You also indicated that a researcher gave you this information. Now, tell me what you know."

"I heard that Captain Kidd hid treasure maps in his sea chests."

"Good. That wasn't so hard, was it? What else do you know?"

The man's friendly tone chilled him almost as much as the razor. It was like the guy did this every day. He racked his brain, trying to remember exactly what he'd overheard.

"There's one in a museum."

"Which one?" The man's voice was sharp as the crack of a whip.

"I don't know which one. Aren't they all the same?"

"Not which chest, which museum, you imbecile."

"The New England Pirate Museum, or something like that." He didn't mention Avery's connection to the chest. She might hate his guts, but he still felt like he ought to protect her. It was the closest thing to a brave act he could manage in what might be the rest of his very short life.

"Excellent. You're doing very well. Now, do you know the locations of any other chests?"

"No. Only the one."

"Anything at all? Rumors, legends?"

"No. I swear." he pleaded. He wanted desperately for the man to believe him. Maybe if he realized just how little Rodney knew, he'd let him live. "That's everything."

"Very well. Now, I need to know from whom you learned this information."

He couldn't give the man Avery's name. He just couldn't.

"I heard somebody talking in a bar."

The man sucked his teeth and gave his head a disapproving shake. With a deft movement, he sliced Rodney's ear and held the bloody gob of flesh, his earlobe, out for Rodney to see.

"I told you to hide nothing from me. You might have been given this information in a pub, or bar, as you put it, but you know the person who told it to you.

What is he or she called?"

"Maddock!" Rodney blurted the first name that came to mind. "Dane Maddock. That's all I know about him."

"Very good. I appreciate your honesty."

Rodney relaxed. Whether the man killed him or let him live, at least it was over.

"I now have the unfortunate duty of confirming your honesty. That requires a more severe test of your veracity. We shall start with your thumb, I think."

The man stuffed something into Rodney's mouth, which made it very hard to scream.

CHAPTER 8

"All right! Let's dam this baby up!" Charlie rubbed his hands together and grinned, the lines on his face crinkling. He paced to and fro along the rocky bluff overlooking tunnel seventeen, his exuberance lending a youthful bounce to his step. The prospect of solving the mystery seemed to have taken twenty years off of him.

Dane had to smile at the old man's excitement. Matt's arm was broken in several places but, given time, he'd heal. Once his recovery was assured, Matt had maintained his insistence that Dane and the crew finish what they'd started. He further vowed to be back on the job the minute he was released from the hospital.

After spending much of the night at the hospital, Dane, Bones, and Willis gone back to work. They returned to the passageway and made a failed attempt at opening the trap, after which they used GPS to chart the twists and turns of the tunnel, though their signal crapped out before they got to the area behind the wall. Charlie's plan was to block up the passageway, pump the water out, if possible, and drill down directly into the chamber. It was far from the craziest thing the man had tried in his lifetime.

"I'm telling you, Charlie, I don't know what I saw back there," Bones said. "Not trying to shoot you down, or anything, but it might not be anything big."

"You're full of crap, boy." Charlie dismissed Bones' words with a gesture like shooing a fly. "Why would anyone put a booby trap in front of a chamber unless they had something they wanted to protect?"

"To be a douche?" Bones volunteered

"Bah! All the evidence says that tunnel's important. They didn't carve a Templar cross at the chamber entrance for no reason. And, you said yourselves, it looks like someone dammed it up."

"How did searchers manage to miss it all these years?" Angel asked. "There have been, what, thousands of people looking for the treasure. You'd think someone would have found it by now."

"They've all been focusing on the Money Pit," Dane said. "There probably haven't been too many skilled divers experienced in marine archaeology who've explored these channels." He looked out across Smith's Cove, where a single boat plied the waters, a white dot on the gray horizon. "Those who did could easily have missed this particular passage, or found it, but were fooled by the debris blocking the way. Matt and I almost missed it."

"Well, you boys found it and that's what matters." Charlie clapped his hand on Dane's shoulder, his grip strong, despite his age. "We are going to be the ones to finally solve the riddle. I just know it."

"How long do you think it will take to dam up the tunnel?"

"Should be finished this afternoon. Then we'll start pumping the water out and see what happens." He looked like he was going to say more, but something out on the water caught his eye.

Dane turned to see a police boat drift up to shore. Two uniformed deputies sat inside. The pilot gave a curt nod, but that was all. They gave neither an indication of landing the craft, nor leaving.

"Wonder what the hell they want." Charlie scratched his chin. "They'd best leave me alone. I've got work to do."

"Maybe they heard about Matt's accident and came to check things out?" Angel said.

"Then why don't they get out of the boat?" Charlie kicked at the ground with his booted foot. "Meddling government types is what they are. Can't let a simple businessman go about his work."

"Uncle, you are hardly a simple businessman," Bones said.

The sound of an approaching vehicle cut off Charlie's retort. They all looked toward the road in surprised. It had been closed long before their arrival and had fallen into a state of disrepair. The trucks that delivered Charlie's equipment were the only traffic they'd seen.

Dane's instincts told him something was not right, and he keenly felt the absence of his Walther. He hadn't felt there was a reason to be armed on the island, so he'd left it back at the cottage. The impulse fled as quickly as it had come, and he suddenly understood the reason for the police boat.

"I think we're about to be paid a visit by the local authorities," he said.

"What for?" Bones frowned.

"I guess we'll find out."

A police cruiser appeared around a bend in the tree-lined road and coasted to a stop near where they stood. Two deputies climbed out, exchanged nervous looks, and approached Dane and the others.

"They look scared." Bones grinned, his eyes alight with ill intentions. "Should I mess with them a little?"

"Hell no!" Charlie snapped. "This is my work site. Play your games somewhere else, young man."

"Yes, Uncle." Bones actually managed a respectful tone, so unlike his normal manner.

The deputies fanned out as they drew closer and stopped ten feet away. One, a short, attractive woman with fair skin and brown hair, rested her hand on her sidearm. Her partner, a tall man with wavy brown hair and a moustache, spoke first.

"We're looking for Dane Maddock and Uriah Bonebrake." He fidgeted and ran a hand through his hair.

"You found them." Dane's mind raced. What did they want? He and Bones hadn't done anything wrong, but getting entangled with the police, especially outside one's home country, was not a good thing. "What can we do for you?" He and Bones took a few steps away from the rest of the group.

"I'm deputy White,"the dark-haired man said. "This is Deputy Boudreau. The two of you are wanted for questioning."

"Okay, shoot." Bones smiled and managed not to make it look predatory.

"We'll need you to come with us."

"Are we under arrest?" Dane kept his tone easy.

"Not yet," Boudreau snapped. She glanced at his partner and blushed as he gave a quick shake of the head.

"You don't have to come with us," White said. "I can tell you, though, if you don't, our orders," he nodded toward the boat, "are to make sure you don't leave the island until the sheriff obtain warrants for your arrest.

"All right," Dane said. "Can I ask what you're going to question us about?"

White shrugged and forced a sympathetic smile.

"It's not allowed. Sorry."

It was a short ride to the sheriff's department, but it felt longer thanks to Bones' need to fill every silence with annoying snatches of song or conversation. When he broke into "Achy Breaky Heart," Deputy Boudreau whirled around and promised to gag him and put him in the trunk if he didn't shut up. Bones winked at Dane, clearly pleased he'd gotten under the deputy's skin, but Dane was grateful for the peace and quiet.

They were taken to separate rooms, and left to simmer for a good twenty minutes before a man in slacks and a blazer, a single button straining to hold back his paunch, entered.

"I'm Detective Williams of the Kidd's Cross Police Department," he said, dropping heavily into a folding chair on the other side of the table where Dane sat. He paused, perhaps waiting for Dane to introduce himself in turn, but gave up after ten seconds of silence. "I understand you know a Rodney Meade."

"The name sounds familiar, but I can't place it."

Williams raised his eyebrows. "The two of you had a fight two days ago. Ring a bell?" He folded his arms, rested them on his belly, and leaned back in his chair.

"The sheriff's son. Sure, I remember."

"I understand the two of you were fighting over a girl."

"Are you telling me you haven't already reviewed the incident report and the security footage?" Dane took pleasure at the sight of the man's obvious discomfort. "Or did the sheriff sweep it under the rug?"

"He declined to make a report due to a lack of evidence." Williams cleared his throat and sat up straight. "I'd like to hear your version of the events."

"What did you hear from the sheriff?"

"I already told you what I heard..." Williams bit off

the sentence, his face now beet red. Clearly he'd just realized he was answering Dane's questions instead of the other way around. "I'm investigating a crime and I'm asking you for an answer."

"I'll be happy to give you one, detective." Dane folded his hands and rested them on the table. "But you'd do better to forget fallible eyewitness testimony and simply get a copy of the security tape from the owner of The Spinning Crab. I'll be happy to wait while you go get it."

"I want to hear your version of events."

"Detective, I'm sorely tempted to say nothing at all and make you do the detective work you should have done already, but I know how small towns operate and I'm sure you're doing the best you can, so I'll indulge you. Rodney assaulted a young woman, and one of his friends put his hands on another young lady who was part of my group."

"And you decided to beat him within an inch of his life for it?" Williams snapped.

"Actually, my friend fought back against the guy who was trying to manhandle her, and that's when Rodney and his other buddy started swinging. Like I said," he raised his voice and held up a hand to forestall the argument he could see Williams was about to make, "don't take my word for it. Check the video and decide for yourself."

"So he messed with your girlfriend..."

"Acquaintance," Dane corrected.

"...and started a fight. I suppose you were pretty mad at him. Maybe wanted to get back at him?"

"For what?" Dane couldn't stifle a laugh. "Detective, I'm sorry for how this sounds, but those guys got what was coming to them and they didn't leave a scratch on any of us. As far as any of us are concerned, it was over as soon as the fight ended."

"Fine. Let's suppose I believe you." Williams opened a file folder and made a show of inspecting the contents. "Where were you yesterday between the hours of two and eleven p.m.?"

That was an unexpected question, but Dane had an easy answer.

"At the hospital. One of my crew was injured on the job. We stayed with him until well after midnight."

"Can anyone verify that?"

"My entire crew and maybe some of the hospital staff. There's a nurse there with frizzy gray hair and crazy eyes who wouldn't stop hitting on me. I'm sure she, at least, remembers."

Williams actually cracked a smile.

"I know her. Sorry to break it to you, but you're not her first." He took a deep breath and let it all out in a rush. "You realize I can check hospital security video to confirm your story?"

"I'm counting on it," Dane said. "I'm guessing something bad happened to Rodney."

"You could say that." Williams closed his folder. "Give me a few minutes." He pushed himself up from his seat and lumbered to the door. "Can I get you anything to drink?"

"No thanks." Dane hoped the abrupt ending to the interrogation, if it could be called that, and William's sudden bout of courtesy were good signs.

Williams returned twenty minutes later. He opened the door and leaned inside. "How long do you plan on being in town, Mister Maddock?"

"Until the job's finished. I don't know how long that will be."

"All right. You're free to go." Williams didn't seem angry or upset. Whatever follow-up he'd done seemed to have persuaded him that Dane was not responsible for whatever had happened to Rodney.

"I'll need a lift back to the island. Are the deputies still here?"

Williams' expression darkened for a moment. "It would be better if I drove you. The deputies are..." He shrugged.

"Out for my blood?"

"Maybe not your blood, but they want a pound of flesh from somebody, and you two were the prime suspects."

Dane took note of the past tense and nodded.

Williams guided Dane and Bones out of the station. As they exited through the front doors, they heard shouting and turned around. Sheriff Meade, apoplectic, was struggling to escape the clutching arms of the three deputies who held him back.

"You killed my son!" he cried.

"My partner's going to talk to him," Williams said, ushering Dane and Bones out the door.

"A horse tranquilizer might help," Bones said.

Williams smirked and shook his head.

"So, Rodney's dead." Bones made it a statement, not a question.

"Very." Williams' expression grew grave. "Until we find the killer, I suggest you two steer clear of the sheriff. He's a powerful man and he can be a dangerous enemy."

"That's fine," Dane said. "So can we."

Williams stopped and looked at them each in turn. "I believe you."

CHAPTER 9

"They have one, Ma'am." Jacob's expression was studiously blank. He never said so, but he disapproved of this exercise.

"Very well. I'll be down there shortly."

Her phone rang as Jacob was closing the door. It was Locke. "Yes?"

"We found the chest and it was empty."

Though Locke had delivered the news exactly as she preferred— swiftly and succinctly, like a clean cut, she still felt a momentary thrill followed by a sagging disappointment. She'd been so certain.

"So it was another false trail." She hated the hollow sound of her voice.

"You misunderstand me. The secret compartment was there, but someone must have gotten to it first. I've secured the chest so our people can examine it, though I doubt they'll find anything. I took a few other items of no great value and ransacked an office as well. No need to call attention to the chest."

"Very good." Her head spun and her heart raced. So Kidd's story was true. She'd never doubted it, but this was the closest thing to definitive proof they'd found.

"I know it isn't the news you hoped for, but at least we have a path to follow."

"Who took it?" An overwhelming rage filled her, and she wanted nothing more in the world than to have the responsible party right there in front of her, where she could put her hands around his neck and choke the answer out of him.

"I don't know yet." How could Locke remain so calm? *"But the chest was donated by a man called Hunter Maddock. He told the museum he believed it belonged to Blackbeard."*

"A cover story," Morgan spat.

"Possibly. Or, he truly did not know what he had, and was ignorant of the compartment."

"In which case, whatever was hidden inside could have been removed by someone at the museum." The wheels of Morgan's mind were turning at a rapid clip.

"Or it was removed before the chest came into Maddock's possession." Locke completed her thought, as he often did.

"Pursue all angles." Morgan's flare of anger was settling into a cold fury. "Investigate the museum. Acquire it if you must. Our New York branch could stand to expand its reach."

"Yes, Ma'am. The budget for this acquisition?"

"At your discretion." She would not have given anyone other than Locke such a free rein. "Find this Hunter Maddock and wring the truth out of him. I don't care how you do it. If he doesn't have the clue, find out from whom he obtained the chest."

"He is deceased, with only one living relative. A son, a military type and a bit of an odd bird."

"How so?"

"He is a treasure hunter of sorts and his name is associated with some sensational rumors. It also seems that someone at a high level of the American government has worked very hard to hide information about him, though I can find no evidence that he has worked in any official capacity since he left their

military. I know he is well-trained and keeps company with similar men. He would be difficult to kill or capture." He paused. Two eternal seconds of silence dragged past.

"What is it?" Morgan snapped. Locke knew better than to waste time.

"I can't be certain, but it appears he is on Herrschaft's list."

That was a surprise. What were the odds that an American civilian would have run afoul of the German sect of the Dominion? Morgan frowned, considering this new detail.

"In that case, perhaps an arrangement can be reached," she mused. "The enemy of my enemy, as they say."

"I will consider all angles."

"Is there anything else?"

"There is yet another treasure hunting expedition underway on Oak Island. Probably the same sort of misguided buffoons as always. Should we investigate?"

"Yes. As you say, it is not likely to amount to anything, but if it does, take control in any way you see fit." Morgan ended the call, pocketed her phone, and walked to the window.

Modron was her personal retreat. Built in the style of a medieval castle, it stood atop a lonely tor in Bodmin Moor. It was well off the beaten path, surrounded by a dense wood planted two centuries ago by her many-greats grandmother and cultivated by later generations, providing her the solitude she craved and the privacy she required.

She looked down onto the grounds, where a tidy formal garden gave way to acres of forest. The vast grounds were protected by a variety of security measures designed to keep intruders out... and other things in.

She espied movement among the trees, a brief glimpse of gold and green, and then it was gone. She smiled at the sight. She would have enjoyed a walk in the forest right now, but she should not keep Jacob waiting. The exercise would be a satisfying release after Locke's call.

From her private study, she descended a narrow, winding stone staircase. There was no light here, and each step carried her deeper into the darkness, a fitting twin for her mood.

The stairway emptied into a square room. To her left, a heavy oaken door barred the way. Suits of armor stood sentinel in each corner and, to her right, arched windows flanked a floor-to-ceiling tapestry depicting a scene from the Battle of Ager Sanguinis. She glided behind the tapestry and her hand went automatically to the trigger stone.

The door swung open on silent hinges, revealing a jarringly bright room. Built in an octagonal shape, it was thoroughly modern, from the soft, blue carpet, to the fluorescent lights, to the high-definition television set high on one wall. In contrast, a medieval-looking rack of weapons lined the wall to her left: swords, long knives, a mace, a morning star, and staffs of varying lengths and thicknesses.

Jacob stood watch over a handcuffed man in his late twenties, who scowled at her when she entered. Morgan looked him up and down. He was tall and solidly built, and the scarring on his knuckles indicated he'd done his share of fighting. Dark stubble dusted his shaved head and cheeks. He wore sagging blue jeans, jack boots, and a West Ham United football jersey.

"So who is she, then?" he growled. "Why'd you bring me here?"

"Why are you here?" Morgan echoed. "That is an excellent question, for which I shall give you an honest answer." She accepted a black leather portfolio from Jacob, opened it, and flipped through the contents.

"Richard MacKenzie, originally from Liverpool, late of Falmouth" she read. "You came to our attention because you beat your girlfriend two weeks ago."

"Them charges didn't stick, now, did they?" He grinned, his crooked, beige teeth gleaming like jagged fangs in the artificial light. "If you're one of them bizzies you can just bugger off and let me go on my way."

"You set a car on fire during the riots," she continued, "and you have an impressive list of criminal offenses."

"That's not all that's impressive about me, blondie." He moved his hips suggestively.

"I do not see here that you have a job, or have ever held one." She cocked her head and waited for a reply.

"See now, I've worked here and there." His smug grin flickered. "It's hard, you know. Not many jobs to be had."

"You have never held a job for which you earned a salary or paid income taxes."

"So what if I haven't? That's not a crime now, is it?"

"You are a parasite, Mister MacKenzie. Britain has provided you with support for your entire life, yet you repay her by preying on good and decent people."

"Most of them wasn't decent, Miss. No more than me, anyhow." His grin was back.

"Give me one reason I should let you leave here alive, Mister MacKenzie."

His face turned beet red and he trembled, not with fear, but rage. "Bollocks. You ain't going to do nothing to me." The man was either too arrogant or too lacking in imagination to understand he was in her power.

"Let us try again. If you ceased to exist at this very moment, give me one example of how Britain would be the worse for it."

"Piss off!" If his hands had not been cuffed, Morgan was sure he would have attacked her right then and there. Good!

"Nothing, then? Because I can think of several ways in which your death would improve our country immensely." She sniffed. "Not the least of which would be the absence of your foul stench."

"Let me go or I'll..." He glanced down at his handcuffs.

"What? You'll hit me, like you did to your girlfriend?" She nodded to Jacob who produced a key and removed MacKenzie's cuffs. "That is exactly what I want."

"What?" The confusion in his eyes was comical.

"I want to fight you, Mister MacKenzie. You may use any of the weapons you see here." She nodded to the rack. "I shall be unarmed. If you fight me and win, Jacob will drive you home and give you one hundred pounds for your trouble. Should you lose, you may still walk out of here."

"What if I don't want to?" He looked all around the room, searching for a way out. "There's some kind of trick here. Let me go."

"If you do not fight me, Jacob will shoot you and bury you in the moor."

"You're out of your mind." He took two steps toward her and froze, recognition dawning in his eyes. "I've seen you before. You've been on television and whatnot. Just wait until I tell my story. Somebody'll pay me nicely for it."

Jacob glanced at her and she smiled.

"Fight me, and you will be free to go and tell your story to anyone you like." In one swift movement she closed the gap between them and slapped him across the face. The loud crack and sharp sting felt good. "Hit me." She struck him again, this time with a closed fist.

Richard reeled backward, pressing a hand to his split lip. He raised his bloody hand, eyes filled with disbelief.

"You crazy bitch!"

He swung a wild right cross that Morgan easily ducked. She sidestepped and drove a fist into his side where his ribs ended. He grunted in pain but managed another swing, which she ducked. This time she drove a roundhouse kick to the inside of his knee and followed with a right cross to his nose. Her fist struck home with a satisfying crunch.

Richard flailed blindly, trying to grab hold of her, but she was too fast for him. Another kick to the knee and he stumbled to the floor.

"You fight like a Frenchman," she hissed. In an actual life and death situation she would have finished him, but this was something else entirely.

Richard found renewed strength and, with a roar, leapt at her. He almost managed to grab hold of her, but she sprang to the side and he crashed into the wall. Now, mad with rage, he went for the weapons. He grabbed a longsword and charged.

Morgan easily eluded his clumsy strokes and feeble thrusts. It was not long before he began to tire— he struggled to keep the sword aloft, and his breath came in ragged gasps. Summoning the last of his strength, he raised the sword and rushed in for a vicious downstroke. Morgan dodged and drove a roundhouse kick into his unprotected middle. The breath left him in a rush, and he dropped to one knee. Knowing he would offer no further meaningful resistance, she delivered an axe kick to the back of his skull.

It took Richard ten minutes to recover whatever wits he had at his disposal. Jacob wiped the blood off from his face, congratulated him on a "bloody good fight" and offered him a glass of water. He sipped it, staring daggers at Morgan.

"I'll show you out if you're ready," Jacob said.

"Where's my hundred pounds?" Richard snapped.

"You didn't win." Morgan said. "But you do get to leave here alive."

Richard didn't bother to argue. He lurched to his feet and followed Jacob out.

Jacob returned a few minutes later. "I assume you want to watch." His voice was as dull as the look in his eyes.

"Of course," Morgan said. Her eyes turned to the television on the wall. Jacob turned it on, revealing a wide-angle shot of the formal garden. Jacob zoomed in on Richard, who was limping toward the wood. "Your disapproval saddens me, Jacob." Morgan kept her eyes on the screen as she spoke.

"I don't mind the fighting," he said. "These blokes all deserve an ass whipping, and you're more than fair about it. But this..." He gestured at the screen. "I just don't know."

"We are culling the flock. Can you honestly say our nation would be better off with him and the others alive?"

Jacob shook his head.

"Besides, the children need to hunt. It is their nature." She smiled as the feed switched over to a camera in the wood. Richard was already jumping at every sound. He sensed danger.

"I would respectfully argue it is their training, not

their nature, Ma'am."

"Centuries of breeding and, yes, training have made them what they are today. Perhaps it was not in the nature of their ancestors, but it is their nature. It amounts to the same thing."

"True," Jacob said. "Let me know when you wish for me to press the button."

They lapsed into a tense silence as they watched Richard move into the depths of the wood. Things were about to get very interesting.

A branch rustled somewhere behind him. Richard spun around, sending a new burst of pain shooting up his injured leg. He hadn't taken a licking like that since school. The bitch must be some kind of soldier or spy or something. He'd be well shut of her and this damn forest.

He didn't like it out here. He couldn't properly say he knew anything about the outdoors, he was a city lad after all, but this place was all wrong. It felt unnatural. The trees weren't planted in rows or anything, but it had an orderly feel to it, as if everything were laid out according to a plan. And there were no bird sounds, only the occasional rustle of something heavy moving through the treetops or scuffling along the ground.

He quickened his pace, not entirely certain where he was headed. The black fellow had told him to keep going straight ahead and he would find a gate that opened onto a path leading into town. Richard had been too out of sorts to ask the name of the town or how, exactly, he was to get back home, but he didn't much care. He just wanted away from this place. And when he got home, he'd call one of those reporters who made their living exposing public figures, march right back to this place, and show the world what a nutter the woman was. He'd make her sorry she'd crossed him.

This time, the sound came from his left, and he saw a flash of movement. So there *was* something out there. Now he knew for certain he wasn't imagining things, but he'd have preferred his own paranoia to what he had just seen. It wasn't much— only a glimpse of a mottled hide of dark green and gold or orange, he couldn't be sure, covered in a lattice-work pattern of raised ridges. What the bloody hell was it?

He veered off to his right and quickened his pace, hoping he would not lose his way. There were more sounds now, coming from every direction, and moving closer. He scanned the ground for a stick, a rock, anything he could use as a weapon, but the forest floor was clean; another thing that lent to its unnatural feel.

A noise right beside him made him jump. With a scrabbling and scratching like sharp claws on a wooden surface, something climbed the tree where he stood. The thick trunk blocked the thing from view, but he caught a glimpse of a scaled tail vanishing into the leaves up above.

So complete was his panic, he was scarcely aware of the warm, wet feeling as he soaked his boxers. Clutching a belt loop to keep his pants from sliding down and tripping him, he ran blindly. Limbs slapping his face, he bounded like a pinball from tree-to-tree.

From somewhere close by, he heard a low moan that he realized was coming from his own mouth. He'd heard that sound many times in his life, always from someone he'd robbed or beaten up. It was the sound someone made when they finally realized they were powerless to stop what was about to happen to them. Now, it was finally his turn.

He broke through a thick tangle of brush and suddenly he was flying. He cried out in shock and flailed his arms as he hurtled through the air and, with an icy shock, plunged into darkness. Down and down he went, certain this was the descent into hell.

Then his feet touched something solid, and he realized he had fallen into water. He pushed up, but his booted feet held fast in the soft muck. Panic, which had momentarily faded, rose anew, and he struggled to break free. He worked his way out of one boot, then the other, only to have his baggy jeans tangle around his knees. He tried to cry out and got a mouthful of water for his trouble. Choking and thrashing about, he opened his eyes and saw a glimmer of light up above. He'd never get there. It was too far.

Somehow, all the fear and panic washed away in the face of his inevitable demise, and he was able to think again. He stopped his flailing about, slipped out of his jeans, and swam for the surface. Light and blessed air seemed to dangle tantalizingly out of reach as he kicked and paddled with every drop of his remaining energy. He clenched his jaw and fought the impulse to breathe. Just a little farther.

And then he broke the surface and pulled in a loud, rasping breath. Sweet air filled his lungs, and even the overcast England afternoon seemed bright and sunny after the depths of the pond and the darkness of the forest. He struck out for the shore, which was only a few meters away, hauled himself up onto the steep bank, and rolled over onto his back. He was dead tired, but he was alive.

It was only after he'd caught his breath that he remembered why he'd run pell-mell into the water in the first place. What had happened to the things that had been following him? Were they still there?

He rolled over again and looked up to where the sloping bank met the edge of the wood. He saw naught but trees and scrub, and relaxed.

And then a gray green snout poked out the undergrowth. It was only there for a moment, but it was enough. Robert whimpered and scrambled crablike along the shore. He had to get away.

He had gone perhaps ten meters when a high pitched tone, almost above hearing, rang out. It hung in the air for the span of two heartbeats, and then... nothing.

He looked all around. Had it been a signal of some sort?

And then he raised his head.

Something detached itself from a treetop and drifted down toward him. As it drew closer, he realized just how big the thing was, and were those... wings? He was frozen in place, stupefied by the sight. It couldn't be.

But it was.

And then the world exploded all around him, and he found his voice long enough for one bloodcurdling scream.

CHAPTER 10

"I'm afraid pumping the water out of the passageway isn't going to work." Charlie looked like he'd been sucking lemons. "We've been at it for hours and the water level hasn't gotten much lower."

"It's not unexpected," Dane said. "This island is like a sieve."

"Somebody sealed that tunnel up once before, and all they had were primitive tools compared to what we've got. This is crap."

"That was a long time ago, Charlie. New cracks could easily develop over two centuries."

"You're probably right," Charlie agreed. "You know what? Screw the drilling! We're going straight for the chamber and, when we break through, you diver boys can do your stuff."

"We're not certain of the location," Dane said. "You have our best guess, and that's it."

"I'll take your best guess every day of the week and twice on Sunday. Now, if it was Bones doing the guessing..." Charlie made a face.

Dane laughed. There were some significant differences between Bones and Charlie, but they both had a long sarcastic streak that he appreciated.

The old man gave him a wink and headed over to give his crew their new instructions.

Dane checked his watch. It was late afternoon, two

days after the discovery of the underground chamber, and progress was stalled. He and the crew had continued surveying the shore, but they hadn't found any more underwater tunnels like this one. One more day and boredom would set in in earnest.

No sooner had the thought crossed his mind than his phone vibrated. It was Avery.

"Maddock, I've got some weird news."

"Okay." What news could she have that would be of interest to him?

"Your father's chest was stolen from the museum."

"Seriously? When?"

"Two nights ago. The same day Rodney was murdered."

Dane pondered this new development.

"You don't think the two are related, do you? Unless you let Rodney in on what you knew about the chest."

"Of course I didn't tell him anything, but who knows how long he was lurking out of sight that night at the Spinning Crab? He might have heard me telling you about the chests." She lowered her voice to little more than a whisper. *"Rodney was an ass and, frankly, I'm not surprised someone killed him. But he was the kind of guy who gets knifed in a parking lot, not tortured."*

"Tortured?" Alarm bells were going off in Dane's mind. "What do you mean?"

"I'm not supposed to know this, but one of the deputies is an old friend. They cut off his ears, his fingers, his eyelids. All kinds of crazy stuff you think only happens in horror movies."

"Somebody wanted information."

"Right, and believe me when I tell you, Rodney had no information in that head of his. None."

In spite of the grisly news, Dane couldn't stifle a

grin at Avery's dry sense of humor. Then a thought occurred to him that wiped the grin from his face.

"Do you think he gave them your name?"

"I've been wondering that very thing." Her voice was tight. *"I think they would have come after me by now if he had. At least, that's what I keep telling myself."*

"Is there any place you can go, anyone you can stay with, where you can hide out for a while?" He didn't know why he was bothering with the question. He already knew how this conversation was going to end.

"Maybe." Doubt tinged her voice. *"Classes ended today and I'm not teaching this summer, so I suppose I could leave town, but what if they found me? I'm not a helpless Barbie girl, but I don't think I could do much against professional killers."*

"You can stay with us. Gather what you'll need and I'll send Bones to get you." Dane wanted to kick himself. Why must he always try to rescue the damsels in distress? He had to admit, he had no romantic interest in Avery, but he felt an odd affinity for her. In the few hours they'd spent together, she'd seemed to really get him, and understand his way of thinking. He liked her and didn't want to see her get hurt.

"I don't want to be any trouble. You guys have work to do and I'm sure Bones doesn't want to chauffeur me around."

"Trust me. The dive work is done for the moment and a bored Bones is an annoying Bones. He'll be happy to get off the island and I'll be glad to not listen to his grumbling."

"All right, then. Thank you."

He had just hung up the phone and was about to go find Bones when two sheriff's department cars pulled up to the work site. Deputies White and Boudreau climbed out of one, while Sheriff Meade, grinning ear to ear, and a tall man in an expensive suit exited the other.

"What the hell is this?" Charlie had noticed their new visitors and come to stand beside Dane.

"Charles Bonebrake?" Meade didn't wait for a reply to his question. "I have an order here for you to cease operations and leave the island." He held out a document which Charlie snatched.

"You mind telling me what this is all about?" He scanned the document, his countenance growing darker as he read.

"A man almost lost his life on your job site. The local authorities need to conduct a safety inspection, after which time, the Bailyn Museum will be taking over the project."

"The hell they will! I've got a permit!"

"Which has been revoked, effective today." Meade's grin grew predatory, his straight, white teeth gleaming in the sunlight. "I'll need you and all of your equipment off the premises by five o'clock."

"That's impossible," Charlie snapped. "We're in the middle of a job here. It's not that easy just to pick up and walk away."

"It's a thousand dollar a day fine for trespassing."

"Pocket change." Charlie's grin matched that of the sheriff.

"And you'll be arrested for criminal trespass and your equipment impounded." Meade tucked his thumbs into his belt and rocked back on his heels, awaiting Charlie's next protest. Behind him, Boudreau looked pleased and White uncomfortable. The third man's expression was one of polite interest.

"Why is the museum taking over the project, Sheriff?" Dane knew the truth, the sheriff blamed him for Rodney's death and this was payback, but he was curious what the excuse would be.

"Indian artifacts have been found on the island. We need qualified researchers to do a complete archaeological survey before any other work can proceed. Since they're going to be doing the survey, it's more expedient for them to follow up on any leads you might have."

"Son, the only Indian artifact on this island is me." Charlie's voice and demeanor were serene, which meant he was already working on a plan. The old man never surrendered, but he knew when to make a strategic retreat.

"On the contrary," Boudreau said. "I found this arrowhead just lying on the ground when I got out of the car." She held up a leaf-shaped, fluted projectile point.

"That's a Folsom point." Dane hadn't heard Bones approaching. "And it's obsidian, so it's from the American southwest. If you're going to pull a scam, at least try not to make yourself look like an idiot."

Boudreau's face reddened, but she was undeterred.

"In that case, I'm sure the museum will be interested in determining how it got here."

"Oh, I think we all know how it got here," Dane said.

"We're wasting our time with these ignoramuses," Charlie said. "I'll give my men their marching orders. Bones, you and Maddock tell your fellows to clear out until I take care of things." He stalked away, muttering, "*When I buy somebody, he stays bought.*"

Dane noticed that the man in the suit do a double-take at the mention of Dane's name. Now, he approached Dane and offered his hand.

"Dillon Locke. I'm with the Bailyn Museum in New York." The man had a strong grip and he looked Dane square in the eye as if he were trying to read Dane's thoughts.

"You're a long way from home, Mister Locke."

Locke laughed. "I'm a bit of a vagabond. New York is home for now, but I fear I'll never lose my accent." His smile faded into an earnest look. "I'm sorry about this, mate. This was all arranged between the local authorities and someone at the museum with a higher pay grade than mine." He shrugged.

"You're not buying this charade, are you?" Bones asked.

"I'm just here to do my job." Locke shrugged. "The arrowhead was absurd, I'll grant you that, but I promise I've no interest in local politics. We'll do our best to continue the good work you've done here." His eyes fell on the drilling apparatus Charlie's crew was already disassembling. "Looks like you're on to something over here."

"A dead end," Dane lied. "We thought there might be something in this spot, but we were wrong."

"A shame. Sorry if this is an insensitive question, but is there anything at all you can tell me that might guide our search?"

"Give up and go home. There's nothing here but legends." Dane hoped his words sounded sincere rather than spiteful. True, the museum wasn't at fault, but he wasn't going to give this Locke fellow a bit of help.

"Too bad. Hopefully the museum won't keep me on this wild goose chase for too long." He bade them good day and left.

"If that guy's an academic, I'm a ballerina." Bones glowered at Locke's receding form.

"I don't think you're in danger of having to wear a leotard any time soon," Dane said. There was definitely more to Locke than a simple museum employee. "Since we've got some free time on our hands, I think we should see what we can find out about the Bailyn Museum."

CHAPTER 11

Dane stretched out on the sofa in the living area of his parents' cottage, feeling the bone-wearying fatigue that had plagued him since the sheriff had shut them down. He hated to think they'd wasted their time, but what did they have to show for their work? One injured crew member and a chamber they hadn't managed to penetrate. He despised failure.

He was tired, but sleep eluded him. There was too much on his mind.

He opened his eyes and rolled over onto his side, and his gaze fell on *The Gold Bug.* He'd read a few pages, but not gotten very far. Might as well give it another go.

It was the story of a man who had to decipher a cryptogram in order to find a treasure buried by Captain Kidd. It wasn't the best book he'd read, but it held his interest to the final page. And what he found there made his heart lurch.

Beneath the words *"The End,"* his father had written another personal message.

"So, what do you say? Are you in?"

After the inscription, an arrow pointed to the edge of the page. The next page was blank, with another arrow, beneath the words

"Keep going!"

He flipped to the back page cover and was disappointed to find it blank. He was about to toss the book on the floor and try and get some sleep when he saw it. The dust jacket was taped to the cover, and peeking out from underneath it was a thin, wax paper envelope, with a yellowed sheet of paper inside.

"Bones!" he shouted, springing to his feet. "Get out here now!"

Seconds later, Bones burst through his bedroom door wearing only a pair of boxer briefs and holding his Glock. Moments later, a bleary-eyed Avery came stumbling out of the bedroom Dane had given over to her, while Angel, not wearing much more than Bones, scrambled down the stairs that led to the loft where she was bunking.

"What's wrong?" Bones had needed only a glance at Dane to realize they weren't in danger, and had lowered his pistol.

"What's wrong is, I'm an idiot. Look!" He held out the book for Bones to see what he'd found.

Bones whistled.

"What is it?" Angel was pressed up against him, one hand resting lightly on his shoulder. Dane's eyes drifted to her taut stomach that her tank top didn't quite cover, and quickly tore his gaze away, cursing himself for ogling his best friend's sister. He glanced up to see if Bones had noticed, but Bones was checking Avery out, and making little effort to hide it.

"I think it's whatever was hidden inside the sea chest. My dad left a note in this book inviting me to help him search for a treasure." Under any other circumstance, he would have felt a lump in his throat and found it difficult to continue, but excitement and a measure of discomfort at Angel's closeness, served to distract him. "It was supposed to be a Christmas gift, but he never got the chance to give it to me."

"He wanted *you* to help him find the treasure?" Avery's voice held an odd note he couldn't quite define.

"I'm his son, and treasure hunting is what I do." He shrugged. "Anyway, everybody grab a chair and let's check this thing out."

"I'm just glad you woke me for a good reason," Bones said. "I was dreaming about a Victoria's Secret model."

"Which one?" Avery asked.

"I don't know. They all look alike to me."

With the utmost care, Dane worked the envelope free of the tape that bound it to the book cover, and removed its contents. There were two items inside: a sheet of stationery covered in symbols, and another sheet, folded, yellowed with age.

"Want me to do that?" Avery spoke in hushed, reverential tones. "I have experience with old documents."

"Sure," Dane slid it over to her.

"Give me a moment." She hurried into her room and returned with a pair of latex gloves. "I was going to color my hair," she explained. Dane didn't miss the way her eyes flitted toward Bones and her cheeks reddened a touch. "This is more important."

A silence borne of anticipation fell as they watched Avery go about her delicate task. When the sheet was finally spread out before them, they all broke out in grins.

"It's the island," Bones said.

It was an aged map of Oak Island, rendered in exquisite detail. It alone would have been an exciting find, but there was more.

"X marks the spot." Angel gave Dane's arm a squeeze. "That's the place you and Matt found, isn't it?"

"Looks like it," Dane said. "We can't say for sure, since it's probably not to perfect scale, but I think it's the same place."

"And check this out! There's a way in." Bones indicated a dotted line leading from a different location on the island to the chamber.

"It starts on land, so it's unlikely to be an underwater channel," Dane mused. "Unless it's become flooded over the years. That's a possibility."

"I know where this is!" Avery exclaimed. "I can lead you right to it. If the sheriff will let us back on the island, that is."

"That's not going to happen," Dane said. "He said he's going to arrest anyone who wasn't gone by the end of the day. No way he lets us come back."

"What are we going to do?" Avery was on her feet, fists clenched. "We have to get to that secret passage before Locke drills into the chamber. That won't be long!"

"Chill," Angel said. "You forget who we've got on our side."

"She's right." Bones rocked back in his chair, hands folded behind his head. "Maddock and I are experts getting into places we're not invited."

"Only because you were never invited to any parties in high school," Angel jibed.

Bones' obscene gesture was half-hearted at best. He loved the adrenaline rush of anything dangerous, and was clearly focused on finding a way onto the island. "You've got to figure he'll have deputies guarding the road that leads to the island, and, maybe, a boat patrolling the coast, though I doubt it. He thinks he's beaten us, so he'll probably be lax."

"Don't count on it. His ego is huge, but he doesn't miss a detail. We'd better plan on two boats, and a patrol on the island as well." Avery cupped her chin and narrowed her eye as she stared at the map. "We'll have to go in at night without lights or a motor. Kayaks?"

"You've got a good head for this sort of thing," Bones said. He gave Avery an admiring smile and she blushed.

"I love kayaking!" Angel exclaimed. "Let's rock this!"

"Hold on." Dane held up his hands. "Avery's right about going in at night, but any kind of boat is too risky. Besides, I want to do this tonight. Bones and I will swim it."

"No!" Avery shouted and sprang to her feet. "You can't do that."

"We're pros," Bones said. "We've done the same thing hundreds of times, and trust me, the stakes were much higher. Worst that can happen here is we get arrested and Charlie bails us out."

"I need to go too." Avery clenched her fists until her knuckles were white. "I have to show you the way in."

"I'm sure you can tell us all we need to know ahead of time," Dane said. "Show us on the satellite images."

"It's cool, Avery. We've got this." Bones reached out to take her hand but she snatched it away.

"This is my project. I'm the expert. Besides, I've done plenty of diving. I can handle it."

"You wouldn't be able to keep up if we ran into trouble." Dane said. "Look, I've been on plenty of treasure hunts and I know how you're feeling." Avery shook her head and, too late, Dane remembered that you should never tell a woman that you know how she feels. "If the circumstances were different, I'd have you right there with us, but this is just one of those times when it needs to be me and Bones. Only me and Bones." He said this last to Angel, who made a pouting face that sent a shiver down his spine. He looked back at Avery, trying to ignore how warm he suddenly felt. "I'm sorry, but this is the way it has to be."

"Besides," Angel said to Avery, "this is Maddock's treasure hunt. His father left it for him."

"You don't understand." Avery whispered as a solitary tear trickled down her face. "He was my father too."

CHAPTER 12

Dane sat, dumbfounded, gazing up at Avery, who seemed almost as shocked by her words as he was.

"I'm sorry," she mumbled. "I've been trying to figure out a way to tell you. This wasn't how I wanted to do it."

Dane looked from Angel, who was likewise speechless, to Bones, who frowned, and then his face split into a broad grin.

"I can totally see it!" He pounded his fist on the table, threw back his head, and laughed. "The hair, the eyes, the thing you both do when you're thinking hard. I should have figured it out."

"How?" Angel asked.

"Our father," Avery said, settling back into her chair and studiously avoiding Dane's gaze, "spent a lot of time here. Sometimes he was with his wife, but other times he came alone. He and my mother had a fling; two ships meeting in the night and all that. They didn't carry on any sort of long-term affair, but he sent money every month and made sure I had everything I needed. He even helped me with college." Her eyes grew moist. "Once every summer, he would spend a few days with me. We'd always do something related to his pirate research. I suppose that's why I chose my the career path I did."

"So, this is more than an academic pursuit," Angel

said. "This is personal."

Avery nodded.

"Say something, Maddock," Bones urged.

"Sorry, I'm just shocked. I never..." He trailed off, lost in dark thoughts. He'd never dreamed his father would lead a double-life.

"Let's leave these two alone," Bones said to Angel. "I think they've got some talking to do." He rose from his seat and headed out the back door onto the deck. Angel gave Dane an encouraging smile and followed her brother out the door.

"I'm not lying." Avery said after a lengthy silence. "I'll take a DNA test if you want me to."

"I don't guess I want that." Dane said. "Bones is right. It's kind of obvious once you know what to look for. How long have you known about me?"

"All my life. I don't mind telling you I've hated your guts for as long as I can remember. You got my dad fifty one weeks out of the year. I got the leftovers. And now, after all the times he and I spent researching Kidd's treasure, I find out It was you he wanted to share it with." Her tears flowed freely now, but her eyes shone with resentment.

Dane nodded, unable to summon any words of comfort. He couldn't blame her for feeling like she did.

"So, how do you feel about me now? Still hate me?"

"I haven't made up my mind yet." Avery managed a tiny laugh. "You're bossy as hell and you don't listen to anyone but Bones. That much I've already figured out."

"I'm not bossy, I'm decisive." He grinned. "And I do listen, it's just that everybody else is wrong most of the time."

"We really are an awful lot alike. Creepy." Avery wiped her eyes with the back of her hand. "So, what else do we have in common? Are you as unlucky with the ladies as I am with the guys?"

"Maybe." Before he realized what he was doing, he was telling her about his wife, Melissa, and her tragic death; a subject he studiously avoided even after all these years. Then it was on to his ex-girlfriend, Kaylin, and, finally, his current sometimes-girlfriend, Jade. "Things just aren't working out between us. Sometimes I think Jade and I are too much alike, you know?"

"I've got to hand it to you, Maddock. I never suspected you had that many words in your vocabulary, much less you were the kind of guy who would talk relationships for ten minutes straight." She reached out, tentatively, and took his hand. It was a good feeling: companionable and comforting.

"That's the longest I've ever talked to anybody about relationship crap," he said, knowing he sounded a bit too much like Bones. "Is this typical sibling conversation?"

"Don't ask me. I'm new at this too. Are we good?"

"Yeah," he said after a long pause. "I think we are. It's still weird, though."

"Totally," she agreed, slipping her hand from his grasp.

"How about we bring the two peeping Toms back inside and let's make a plan for getting to whatever Dad wanted us to find?"

Bones and Angel were making no effort to hide the fact that they were watching Dane and Avery through the window. When Dane motioned for them to come inside, they bounded through the door like children headed to recess.

"This is so cool!" Angel said. "Now I have somebody who can understand what I go through with this assclown." She glared at Bones, who feigned innocence and his heart.

"Time's short. Let's get to work," Dane said.

"Bossy," Avery said to Angel in a confiding tone. "I just told him about that."

"They don't listen," Angel said in a mock-whisper. "You have to learn how to push their buttons to get what you want. I'll show you." She smiled at Dane, eyes sparkling, and winked.

Once again, he found himself feeling uncomfortably warm, and hurried on.

"It's going to be me and Bones going in. You get it, right?"

Avery gave a grudging nod.

"What can you tell us about this spot on the map?" Dane asked.

"We'll have to compare it against contemporary maps and photos." She couldn't hide her guilty expression. "I lied. I have no idea what spot on the island this correlates to."

Dane buried his face in his hands. "Why me?"

"Just kidding. I know exactly what this spot is."

Bones and Angel burst out laughing and Angel high-fived Avery.

"Fine," Dane sighed. "Fill us in."

"The spot here is in the swamp." She pointed to the mark that denoted what they presumed was the entrance to the passage. The swamp was a triangular body of water that virtually cut the island in two.

"I thought the swamp had been investigated and dismissed as a possibility," Dane said.

"Sort of. Back when portions of the island were privately owned, someone tried to drain it. As the water receded, he found what looked like a wooden shaft rising up out of the water, but when they investigated it further, it turned out to only be a few feet deep. He gave up his efforts to drain it any further.

After that, there were disputes over the swamp between the different people and groups who owned parts of the island. Eventually, the government took control and, since then, the swamp has been ignored."

"Do you think this map is pointing to that shaft?" Bones asked. "If we have to dig, there's no way."

"It's not. Look here." She pointed in turn to six circles. "These indicate the locations of huge granite stones that form what we call the Oak Island Cross. The width of the cross," finger hovering millimeters above the aged map, she traced the line, "is 720 feet, with the center stone perfectly centered. The distance from the center stone to the bottom of the cross is also 720 feet, and 360 to the top. Everything is perfectly proportioned except for this one." She pointed to a circle between the middle and bottom stones.

"That's the entrance," Angel whispered.

"This stone ought to be halfway between the center and bottom stones, but it isn't. Researchers have always wondered why it alone is disproportionately spaced. Now we know." Avery looked around the table, her expression triumphant.

"Is it in the swamp?" Bones asked, leaning down for a closer look.

"It juts out into the water," Avery said. "I'll bet there's a hidden passage underneath it."

"What if the stone is covering the passage? They'll never be able to move it." Angel pursed her lips and tugged at her earlobe. It was one of her little habits that made Dane smile.

"I guess we'll find out." Dane's eyes drifted to the bottom right corner of the page. "What are these symbols?" A tiny block of glyphs, triangles, circles, squares, some incomplete or slashed through with diagonal lines, had escaped their notice.

"They look like the same glyphs that can be found on the stone that was discovered in the pit back in the 1800's." Avery gave the symbols a long, appraising look. "This uses some of the same symbols, but it's a different message entirely. No wonder no one has ever been able to make sense of it!" She sprang from her seat and hurried into her bedroom, returning shortly with a battered briefcase.

Dane's eyes widened when he saw the case. "I remember that." It had belonged to his father. Dane could recall being surprised when Hunter Maddock had returned from one of his research trips with a shiny, new briefcase instead of his beloved old one.

"Dad always had this with him whenever he visited," Avery explained. "When I was little I used to like to play with the clasps. As I got older, I guess I came to associate it with the good times we had together. He gave it to me on my sixteenth birthday. I hope it doesn't make you feel weird."

"It's cool. He told me the airline lost it. I'm glad it's still around."

"Anyway," Avery said, opening the case and extracting a folder, "here are some possible translations of the original stone. Maybe they can help us figure it out."

"What about this?" Angel held up the other paper that had been in the envelope. "It's got a bunch of those weird symbols plus a code." She flipped the paper around for the others to see.

"That looks like the cipher in *The Gold Bug*," Dane said, reaching for the book that lay forgotten on the table. He flipped to the pertinent page and turned it around for the others to see.

"No way!" Avery's eyes grew wide. "Do you think Dad translated the runes, and then encrypted them?"

"Definitely." Dane was certain of it. "He would have thought it added to the fun and made it more secure in case the wrong person stumbled across it. Besides, to the average person, it looks like a long math problem."

"Do either of you know how to break this code?" Bones asked. "Because I hated Calculus."

"I'll bet there are plenty of Gold Bug decryption sites online," Avery said. "Bones, want to grab my laptop?"

"Only if you sit on my lap top." Bones had scarely gotten the words out when Angel hit him over the head with *The Gold Bug*.

"Get the computer, you creep."

Ten minutes later, they had their translation.

"Shaft south," Bones read. "Tunnel divides. Lower shaft. Third tunnel north. Upper shaft."

"What do you make of it?" Angel asked.

"I think there are a maze of tunnels in this part of the island," Dane said, "and these are directions for navigating them." He looked up at Bones. "You up for a swim?"

Bones grinned.

"Let's do it."

CHAPTER 13

"That doesn't look like a deputy to me." Bones kept his voice so low that Dane could scarcely hear him over the gentle ebb and flow of the surf. They were a scant twenty yards from shore, floating in the dark waters of the bay under a moonless sky.

"You're right," Dane agreed. The causeway leading to the island had indeed been guarded by the sheriff's department— White and Boudreau to be exact, and they'd swam unseen past a patrol boat anchored offshore. He imagined another boat guarded the island's far side. But the man who stalked the shore of Oak Island was nothing like the deputies. He was tall, lean, and prowled the coastline like a predator on the hunt, his eyes taking in everything around him. Despite the quiet night and calm surroundings, he was clearly on alert.

"Let's slip right past him for old time's sake," Bones said.

"Maybe, but we'll give him a minute and see if he moves on."

They watched as the man continued on his way, eventually disappearing around a bend. Dane and Bones didn't wait, but swam for the shore, their powerful kicks driving them through the water like torpedoes locked onto their target. They hit the shallows, slipped their fins off and tucked them into dive bags— they'd need them again soon.

There was no need to speak. They'd done this so many times Dane had lost count. His eyes took in everything to the east, while Bones scanned the island to the west. At first glance, all appeared clear, but then the smallest of glimmers caught his attention. The scant starlight flashed off a badge as Sheriff Meade himself strode out of the forest.

Dane needed only to incline his head a fraction of an inch to indicate the man's presence. Bones scowled and nodded once. Moving as one, they submerged and worked their way along the coastline, moving in the opposite direction.

They emerged in a pool of darkness on the rocky beach a stone's throw from the swamp. Meade had positioned himself on the sea wall that separated the swamp from the beach. The sheriff stood with his thumbs in his belt, gazing out at his patrol boat.

Dane led the way, creeping wraith-like through the deepest shadows and noiselessly moving through the undergrowth that surrounded the swamp. He paused when he reached the edge of the brackish water. Here they would have to cover ten feet of open ground before reaching the swamp. He glanced at Meade, who had not moved, and then back to Bones. It was unlikely the sheriff would spot them, but Meade just might be mad enough to take a shot at them.

Bones held up a fist, thrust his chin in Meade's direction, and gave Dane a quizzical look. The question was clear— *Want me to knock him out?*

Dane shook his head. He wanted to slip in and out with no one the wiser. If they harmed the sheriff, the finger would point either to them or to Charlie and his crew. They didn't need that. Besides, this way was more fun.

After slipping back into his fins, Dane stretched out on the ground and slithered forward, keeping his eyes on Meade, who shifted his weight, but continued to gaze out at the bay. He aligned himself with the stone that marked their destination, and entered the swamp. The water, warm after chill of the bay and the night air, enveloped him as he vanished into its dark depths. Visibility was almost zero, but he navigated the tangle and muck with ease. Finally, he arrived at the stone, Bones sliding up beside him.

Now would be the most precarious stage of the operation. They didn't know what they might find when they surfaced. For all Dane knew, someone might be standing above them when they emerged from the water. Also, they'd need light to inspect the area around the stone.

Slowly, like a sodden log drifting upward, Dane rose up until his mask broke the surface of the water. He immediately looked for Meade, and felt the shock of cold surprise to see the sheriff facing them. Reflexively, he reached for his Recon knife, not that it would do any good at this distance, but, as his fingers closed on the handle, Meade turned away again.

The sheriff unhooked his radio and spoke into it.

"You boys awake out there?" So the boat crew *was* on his mind. Dane couldn't make out the garbled reply, but it must have been a question or a complaint, because Meade barked out a sharp retort. "It doesn't matter if you haven't seen anything. We're keeping this place sealed tight."

As the sheriff continued his tirade, Dane seized the opportunity to turn on his waterproof flashlight and sink down beneath the water at the place where the stone vanished beneath the surface.

He saw nothing but mud.

Unwilling to give up, he scrubbed at the silt, stirring up a muddy cloud. He was about to give up when his fingertips scraped on coarse rock. He kept working until he had uncovered a stone, two feet square, with a cross carved in its surface. Remembering Matt's accident, he inspected it closely. Unlike the seal on the booby-trapped opening he and Matt had found, this cross was sunk deeper in the stone and was wider on the inside than at the surface. It was like it was made to grip.

He considered for a moment. He was convinced this stone had to be removed in order to gain access to the passage shown on the map. But what if it was another trap? Somehow, he didn't think so. This passage was marked on the map while the other was not, thus indicating that this one was the way in. The directions telling them which passages to take were likely the safeguard on this end. He'd have to take a chance.

Dane had taken hold of the stone with both hands when Bones, who was keeping watch, grabbed him by the shoulder. He raised his head out of the water and looked around. Meade was still talking on his radio, but someone else was approaching. It looked like the same man they'd seen patrolling earlier.

They'd have to hurry. Meade might be useless as a guard but Dane felt certain the other guy was of a higher caliber. Speaking in the lowest tone possible, he gave Bones a hasty set of instructions, and the two of them sank beneath the surface, took hold of the stone, and pulled.

It did not budge.

Dane surfaced and stole a glance back toward shore. Meade had spotted the approaching figure and was walking in his direction. Neither had spotted the intruders in the swamp.

Submerging again, he made a corkscrewing gesture, indicating they should add a counterclockwise turn this time. They tried again, pouring all their strength into the effort. Dane felt the burn from his hands all the way to the base of his neck as he strained against the rock. Finally, as if something had broken free, the stone rotated a smooth quarter turn and stopped with a hard knock of stone on stone. In the silence, it sounded like an explosion, and he dared another look above the surface.

"Fisher," Meade greeted the approaching man. "Quiet night?"

"So far," Fisher replied in an accent twin to Locke's. "Of course, anyone could have slipped past while you were waffling on with your mates out there and we'd never have heard."

Meade started to say something but, just then, a burst of sound that Dane recognized as a drill filled the air. Locke and his crew were already trying to break through to the chamber. On the positive side of the ledger, the noise should cover any sound they might make removing the stone.

He and Bones set to the task, and worked the stone free of its socket just as the sounds of drilling ceased. This time there was no whooshing sound, as the passageway they had uncovered was already filled with water. They lay the stone aside and Bones forged ahead. Dane was just about to follow when a glimmer of light up above caught his eye. Someone was playing a flashlight across the surface of the water directly above him! The mud and debris they'd stirred up made it impossible for anyone to see him, but it would be obvious, even to as dim a bulb as Meade, that something or someone was down here. And when they investigated, they'd find the underwater passageway.

The thought had just occurred to him when a bullet sliced through the water inches from his face. These guys weren't messing around. Adrenaline surging through him, he plunged into the passageway, wondering what they would find, and how they would get out again.

"What the bloody hell is going on here?" Locke called as he trotted up to the shore of the swamp. Sheriff Meade leaned against one of the boulders that formed the so-called Oak Island Cross, staring down at Fisher, who was waist deep in the water, shining his light all around. "I heard a shot. Who fired?"

"It was your man here," Meade said. "I don't know how you do things at your *museum*, but we don't take pot shots at everything that moves."

In the reflected light of Fisher's torch, Locke could see the sheriff's scornful sneer.

"Remind me to put up a sign reading *Trespassers Will Be Shot On Sight*," Locke said. "Because that is precisely what will happen to anyone who invades my work site.

"I'm the law around here, not you people." Meade's back was ramrod straight and his voice trembled with anger. "I don't care who you've bribed. I will take you to jail."

"Of course you will." Locke gave the man a tight smile and turned to Fisher. "What concerns me is, in shooting at a muddy swirl and not a target, you might have alerted potential intruders that they have been spotted."

"Nobody came out of the water," Meade said. "It was probably a beaver."

"A beaver." Locke could not keep the sarcasm from his voice. "As a professional law enforcement officer, that is your assessment of this situation?"

Meade grimaced but had no reply. Just then, Fisher called out.

"I've found something. Hold my torch." He handed the light to Meade, who shone it where Fisher indicated. Fisher took a deep breath and vanished beneath the dark surface, emerging ten seconds later clutching something to his chest. He staggered to the bank and set the object on the ground and Meade turned the beam of the torch onto it.

The circle of light revealed a stone disc with a Templar cross adorning its surface.

"God in heaven," Locke whispered. "Someone has found it!" He produced his own torch and shone it on the boulder, where his sharp eyes immediately caught something Fisher and Meade had not noticed. "There's an outflow of clear water coming up from underneath the stone. See what's there."

Fisher swam for the stone, vanished from sight, and resurfaced moments later.

"There's an underwater tunnel down there," he sputtered, water streaming down his face.

"You're certain it's a tunnel, not a chamber?"

"I think so," Fisher gasped. "I couldn't see well, mind you, but it looked like a long, narrow tunnel."

"Good. I want divers down there immediately." He rested his hand on the grip of his Browning HP Mark III. Meade noticed and frowned. "Sheriff, please put your people on high alert and resume your patrol. I will see to things here."

Meade didn't bother to argue. He returned Fisher's torch, unhooked his radio from his belt, and walked away, barking orders as he went.

Locke gazed down at the Templar symbol. Finally, after centuries of searching, they were close, and no intruder was going to stand in the way...

...or live through this night.

CHAPTER 14

The darkness in the underwater passage was absolute, and Dane moved forward cautiously, keeping one hand on either side of the tunnel. He wasn't worried about running into anything in front of him; Bones would encounter any obstacle before Dane did.

He estimated he'd gone twenty feet when a light blinked on in front of him. Now that they were well away from the entrance, Bones had turned on his dive light. Dane followed suit, revealing a tunnel identical to the others they'd surveyed.

He caught up with Bones and they swam side-by-side, following the passageway as it curved to the right and angled downward, gradually narrowing. Bones fell back, letting Dane scout ahead. Just as the way was growing uncomfortably tight, they came to place where the main shaft continued forward, while a wide passageway branched off to the left and another, much narrower, broke off to the right. The first direction in the map had been "shaft south." Dane checked the compass on his dive watch, and confirmed that the tunnel to the right would take them south.

This passageway, though narrower than he would have liked, was straight and its walls worn smooth, and they made good time as they penetrated its depths.

Dane's confidence in the map's directions grew as they came to a divide. One shaft led up and to the left, the other almost straight down.

Tunnel divides. Lower shaft, he thought as he took the lower passage. This tunnel corkscrewed at a dizzying rate before angling back up again. Now thoroughly confused, he checked his compass and confirmed they were once again heading east.

The first tunnel they passed branched off to their right, leading south. The next clue was *"third tunnel north,"* so they kept moving. It was odd, as the chamber they sought lay somewhere to the south. Dane was suddenly grateful they hadn't stumbled across the entrance to this chamber on their own. Without the directions, they'd be lost, and who knew if more booby traps could be found in some of the other shafts?

Soon they came upon three tunnels in a row on the north side of the passageway, and Dane halted. Now they had a problem. Did the directions mean "take the third north-facing tunnel," or did they mean "at the third tunnel, go north?" He looked at Bones, who shrugged, then pantomimed a coin toss. Dane grinned, motioned for Bones to stay back, turned, and moved to the third tunnel.

He inched forward, looking for anything that might indicate the presence of a trap. The walls here were irregular, and his light cast deep shadows on the pitted ceiling. He drifted forward, fingertips touching the bottom in case he had to arrest his forward motion on short notice.

He had gone no more than ten feet when he caught sight of a row of dark, jagged rocks looming up above like the teeth of a giant shark. The beam of his light flashed across them and he realized they were not stone at all, but rusted iron points like spear heads. He grabbed onto the nearest outcroppings and pushed, trying to shove himself out from under the spikes.

One of his handholds was solid, but the other gave way, rotating forward with an audible clack. He yanked his hands back and twisted as the iron spikes crashed down. One grazed his forearm, tearing his suit and slicing through flesh. He was scarcely aware of the pain. Instead, he was imagining what would have happened had he been even a moment slower in getting out of the way. Being pinned to the bottom of the tunnel for eternity was not his idea of fun.

He felt a hand on his ankle and looked back to see Bones behind him. He gave his friend a thumbs up and crooked his finger toward the second tunnel; the one he'd passed up. Bones nodded and retreated from the passageway.

Dane was about to follow when he had an idea. He took hold of the lever he had first mistaken for a stone, and pulled back on it. With a hollow grinding sound, the spikes slowly retracted into the ceiling. No need to narrow the choices for anyone who might follow behind.

The other tunnel, the one he'd bypassed, looped around and led south. This, Dane's instincts told him, was the direction in which the passage lay. Minutes later, they emerged in an underground cavern. As they shone their lights around, his heart lurched.

This was no simple underwater cave— it was a chamber of some sort. The walls on either side were carved with scenes of knights in action, and the vaulted ceiling was supported by ornate columns. Dane had the feeling he'd seen carvings like this before, or, at least, carvings much like these.

Against the opposite wall, three steps led up to a small altar, behind which, six crosses in circles formed a larger cross on the wall itself.

Bones tapped him on the arm and directed his

attention to the center of the floor. Bones' light illuminated a great seal, ten feet across, showing a temple and encircled by the words "Cristi de Templo." Now he understood.

The seal was one of the ancient symbols of the Knights Templar!

Bones shook his head, and Dane knew what his friend was trying to say: *No freaking way!*

Dane had to agree. He and Bones took out their digital underwater cameras and quickly took pictures of this strange room. As he worked, Dane could not help but wonder what was the purpose of this place? It was reminiscent of a traditional Templar church. Had it been a center of worship which had to be abandoned when it flooded? But that didn't make sense. There was no evidence that the Templars had ever lived here. Why build a church on the other side of the Atlantic? And how did the Money Pit fit in?

And then it hit him. There was another direction they had yet to follow.

Upper shaft.

Amazing as it was, this chamber was not the end of the journey. But there were no shafts leading out, save for the one through which they'd entered. Where to go now? Beneath the seal? That wouldn't make sense.

He took another look around, searching for a clue. He looked at the walls, the columns, the altar, the cross...

The cross!

The circles that formed it were very much like the stone seal that blocked the entrance to the secret passageway. Furthermore, it was laid out in exactly the same proportions as the Oak Island Cross! He signaled for Bones to follow and swam to the uppermost circle.

Bones clearly understood what Dane was thinking

because he immediately set his fingers into the grooved edge of the cross and turned. The circle spun but, this time, did not come free. Instead, it rolled sideways into the wall, revealing a dark tunnel beyond.

Dane and Bones exchanged glances. He imagined they were thinking the same thing. *What if it closes behind us... or on us?* Nothing they could do about it. He shrugged and entered the tunnel.

There was no sign of them. Fisher cursed the minutes they had wasted getting prepped for the dive. Worse was Locke's ire at Fisher letting someone slip past him and into the swamp. He knew it would do no good to point out that the sheriff had been guarding the swamp, with more of his own people anchored just offshore, so he held his tongue. The only thing that would make this right would be for him to find the intruder, or intruders, and take care of the situation.

He held his pneumatic speargun at the ready. Thirty centimeters long, it could be carried in a holster and fired double-barbed steel shafts with deadly power and accuracy at short range. It could not be purchased on the open market, for it was not made for fishing, but for killing. He swam with reckless abandon, eager to put his weapon to good use. Behind him, Baxter, Penn, and Hartley followed, all armed and ready.

They came to a place where the tunnel split into three. He made a quick signal and the divers fanned out. Hartley shot up the left passage. He was, perhaps, the most enthusiastic of their group. He was always spouting his theory that Francis Bacon was the true author of Shakespeare's plays, and the proof lay hidden beneath Oak Island. Baxter, a tall, lean fellow took the narrow shaft in front of them, and Penn took the one on the right.

Hartley was the first to return, shaking his head and making a dismissive gesture. One dead end.

No sooner had the thought crossed his mind than a dull rumble sounded from the passage in front of them, and a cloud of debris spewed forth. Fisher didn't need to look in order to know what happened, but he had be sure.

Twenty meters down, the tunnel ended in a heap of rubble. Only Baxter's foot, swim fin dangling from it, jutted out. Fisher reached out and gave the foot a squeeze, but no response. Baxter was gone. His mood grew blacker at the loss of a good fighter, even if the man did crap on a bit too much about how much he loved Russell Crowe movies.

Retreating from the cave-in, he and Hartley took the tunnel Penn had scouted. They caught up with her at another split. Here, one tunnel went up, the other down. Hartley took the upper passageway, this time with a touch more caution after Baxter's accident. Penn took a similar approach to the lower tunnel.

Seconds stretched into eternity as Fisher fretted over their slow progress. And what if their quarry had gone down the passageway that was now caved in? What if they found a way out on the other side? He was just ruminating on this new, unhappy thought, when he heard a sound like a bowling ball rolling down the lane. The sound grew louder and, with a thud, a massive stone ball lodged in the entrance of the passage Hartley had taken. Fisher tried with all his might to dislodge it, but the rock held fast. He thought of Hartley trapped in the tunnel, and hoped there was a way out on the other side.

His heart beat like a snare drum and the blood

coursing through his veins set up a roar like a hurricane in his ears. Now he knew the truth. What happened to Baxter had not been an accident. This place was a death trap, and he had no choice but to try and make it through.

Once again, he followed behind Penn. The woman was a zealot, perhaps a bit too blindly devoted to Morgan, though he'd never say that aloud, but she either had good instincts, or was very lucky. Perhaps her good fortune would help them carry the day.

This passageway took him round in a descending series of circles before ending at a juncture where a single tunnel broke to the right. He frowned. Penn should have stopped here and waited for him, but she was nowhere to be seen. He decided to continue along the main tunnel a little farther, eyes peeled for traps. A bit farther down, he came upon a series of shafts leading off from the main tunnel. No sign of Penn. He was about to go back and investigate the first tunnel he'd passed when something caught his eye— a trickle of something dark drifting out of the last shaft. Heart sinking, he went to investigate. Two meters down the shaft, he found Penn.

She lay pinned on the floor by thick iron spikes. Her arms and legs were contorted in a grotesque tableau. She had lost her mask, and her eyes stared blankly upward, her face frozen in a mask of agony.

A black rage descended on Fisher. He no longer cared for booby traps, treasure, or Locke's wrath. He wanted revenge.

This tunnel opened into a smaller chamber, circular, like a turret. A double-line of repeated symbols spiraled down from the peak of the domed ceiling, where an odd, wedge-shaped pattern was carved, running all the way down to the floor. The seal at the center of this room showed two knights riding a single horse— another Templar seal. To their left was the trap that had injured Matt's arm. To their right stood another stone altar, but this one was not empty.

A wooden casket, two feet long, sat atop the altar. As Dane swam closer, he could see it was coated with some sort of resin that gave it a glossy sheen and had protected it from who knew how many years of immersion. Like many ancient caskets, it was shaped like a split log: wide and flat at the bottom, rounded on the top half. Its hinged lid appeared to be sealed with lead.

Dane reached out and gently took hold of it, fearing all the while that the wood would crumble at his touch. It did not. Emboldened, he lifted it. It was deceptively heavy. Either the casket was lined with lead, its contents were extremely heavy, or both.

Despite the dim light and the dive mask, he could see excitement shining in Bones' eyes. They were about to solve the riddle of Oak Island. He put the casket in a mesh bag and hooked it to his belt as an added precaution, though he'd have to carry it. Now, to get out of here unseen and unscathed.

He turned to make for the exit tunnel, hoping it had not closed behind them, when a beam of light sliced through the water. Someone had caught up with them.

CHAPTER 15

Dane and Bones drew their Recon knives, extinguished their dive lights, and moved to either side of the passageway that led back to the underground church. Any small ember of hope that the unseen person did not know they were there was doused when something silver flashed through the water and embedded in the limestone wall. Whoever was out there had a spear gun.

Their only hope was to take their pursuer unaware as he entered the chamber. Of course, they'd need to be quick and luck would have to be on their side. The intruder's dive light cast a faint glow— just enough that Dane could see Bones swim to a spot above the passageway and cling to the wall Spider-Man style. Good thinking. Their adversary was likely to to the sides and down before looking up; an instinct honed by life outside the water.

They waited in near-darkness and absolute silence. Energy coursed through Dane, every nerve on edge. It was amazing how alive he felt when possible death was near. Danger brought everything into focus.

Seconds passed, then minutes. Nothing. The guy was waiting for them to make a move, and who could blame him? He had the projectile weapon and the full length of the tunnel to take shots at them. It would be like a carnival game to him— Dane and Bones were sitting ducks.

Dane glanced up at Bones who shook his head and tapped his pressure gauge. Their supply of air was limited. Right now they had sufficient reserves, but it wouldn't last forever, and only a fool let his tank get close to empty. They were screwed.

He racked his brain for a possible solution. Going down the tunnel was out of the question unless they had something they could use as a shield, which they did not. He wondered if the top of the altar would work, but dismissed the thought immediately. He couldn't get anywhere close to it without placing himself in the line of fire. Besides, it wasn't wide enough to provide suitable cover. What they needed was a way out.

And then he remembered the booby-trapped shaft he and Matt had discovered. If they could get through, they could make their way out to the shore, and to open water. He swam to the blocked shaft, turned on his light, and inspected the space closely.

The shaft was three feet square and sealed off by a solid stone block. He already knew it couldn't be pried up, but he remembered the iron spike trap they'd encountered and the lever that sprang and released it. Besides, he had to believe that whoever constructed this chamber would have left themselves a secondary exit in the event that the tunnel leading to the temple collapsed.

The ornate bands carved in the wall angled past on either side of the shaft. Dane gave them a close look, all the while wondering when their stalker would show up and start shooting. He pressed on anything that resembled a button, but to no avail. And then his hand passed over a carving of a chalice. This particular image was raised farther than those surround it, and the top of the cup was scooped out. Dane hooked his fingers inside and pulled.

The chalice tilted forward and, with a scraping sound made to seem all the louder by the silence in the chamber, the stone block rose.

He signaled to Bones, who swam over. Dane released the chalice and the stone remained in place. But would they trigger the trap again by swimming through? He inspected the shaft, searching for anything that would spring the trap, but he saw nothing.

Without warning, the block fell again with a resounding crash. Bones held up ten fingers and shrugged. *Ten seconds?* Keeping one eye out for the man with the speargun, Dane pulled the lever again and watched the stone rise. He counted down and, twelve seconds later, the trap sprang.

So that was the trick. You could open the trap from the inside, but you had twelve seconds to make it through. The shaft was only a couple of feet. They could do it.

Just then, the light in the tunnel winked out, followed an instant later by the pink of another spear against the wall. Their pursuer's patience was at an end. He was coming for them.

Bones brandished his knife and made to swim for the tunnel to meet the attack, but Dane grabbed him by the arm. Bones understood the reason a moment later when another projectile sliced through the water. The man wasn't taking any chances.

Dane pointed to Bones, then to the tunnel as he yanked down on the lever. Bones knew him well enough not to argue, but dove through before the stone came crashing down.

Time was almost up. Dane turned out his light, plunging the chamber into inky darkness. He pulled the lever and, relying on instinct and sense of direction, shoved the casket through the shaft as the stone was still rising.

A light blinked on behind him and another spear whizzed inches past his face. He knew it would take the man a few seconds to reload, but he was already on his way through. He felt Bones take hold of his arm and yank him through as the trap fell again. Something yanked at his foot as he tried to swim down the tunnel. For a moment, he thought his foot was trapped, but then he realized his fin was caught. He wasted no time working his foot free and swimming down the passage with the speed and grace of a one-legged frog. Bones, carrying the casket, was well ahead of him.

Dane figured it was only a matter of time before the lever that released the trap was discovered, but their enemies would be waiting for them to emerge in the swamp, not on the shore. He hoped.

A small circle of light swam into view overhead. This was the spot where Charlie's crew had tried to pump the water out of the tunnel. Charlie's crew! They had sealed up the end of the tunnel before beginning the pumping. He and Bones had almost found themselves in a dead end.

He flicked his light on and off to get Bones' attention, and pointed to the opening. It was their only option. Bones stared for a moment, then seemed to catch up with Dane's train of thought.

Dane went first, wondering what he'd find waiting when he stuck his head out of the hole. He treaded water, listening for any sound that would warn of danger, but he heard nothing, not even the rattle of the drill. Locke's crew must have stopped working when they became aware of his and Bones' presence. Figuring there was no time like the present, he hauled himself out onto solid ground.

No one was about. Breathing a sigh of relief, he helped Bones out of the hole and, breathing the sweet, night air, they crept into the trees, moving away from the work site and the swamp.

On the north side of the island, they hid in the shadows beneath an ancient oak tree and assessed the situation before hitting the water. By the time they came ashore more than a mile away from the island, they were both spent.

"It's been a long time since our training days," Bones panted as they made their way to the place, far from shore, where they'd arranged to meet Angel and Avery.

"I can't say I miss the six mile swims," Dane said. They emerged on a hill overlooking a dirt road. Down below sat Avery's car.

It was empty.

CHAPTER 16

It took every ounce of Locke's self-control to keep from pacing. He waited at the edge of the swamp, impatience battling with eagerness. More than once he considered putting on dive gear and going in himself, but that would not do. He was in charge and needed to act like it.

He consulted his watch for at least the tenth time. What was keeping Fisher and his team? Having only begun operations the previous evening, they'd not yet had the opportunity to investigate the warren of tunnels beneath the island. For all he knew, his people were navigating a veritable maze. And then there were the intruders. Who were they? Were they armed? There was too much he didn't know.

He was about to check his watch again when Fisher appeared. To Locke's surprise, he didn't emerge from the swamp, but from the direction of the drilling operation. The look on his face told him the news was not good.

"Report," Locke snapped, his harsh tone a concession to his mood.

"It's a death trap down there. The tunnels are like a honeycomb and whoever built this place added a few nasty surprises. I lost everyone." He took a deep breath and looked away.

"Tell me the rest." The back of Locke's neck

warmed with his rising anger.

"There is a church down there, clearly built by the Templars. Behind it, I found a hidden chamber." He paused, stiffened, and swallowed hard. "The intruders got there first. Whatever was in that chamber, they took it."

"How did they get away?" Locke bit off every word. Calm on the outside, his insides quaked with rage.

"I thought I had them trapped, but the Templars built in an exit. The lever that opened it was hidden and I had to search for it. By the time I made it through." He shrugged.

"Where are they now?"

"They made it to the surface. I tried to track them, but they left little sign. I finally found a few tracks on the north side of the island. I think they swam for it."

Locke grabbed his radio, ordered his men to scour the island, and instructed the sheriff to send both of his boats to the island's north side. It was clear from Meade's tone that he did not appreciate taking orders from a civilian, but Locke couldn't care less. Even as he put his forces in motion, he knew it was too late. He would have to admit his failure to Morgan.

Who could have done this? Who had the skill to infiltrate the island, move like shadows through armed and alert guards, navigate the underground tunnels, and swim to freedom? Almost as soon as the question crossed his mind, he had the answer.

Maddock!

A commotion coming from the direction of the causeway drew him from his thoughts and he looked up to see two of his men escorting a handcuffed woman toward him. Two of Meade's people, White and Boudreau, followed closely behind.

"This is our prisoner!" Boudreau shouted. "You

can't just take her. We want to see the sheriff about this."

"Who is she?" Locke asked as he looked the prisoner over. She was an athletic-looking woman, dark of skin, eyes, hair, her lovely face at odds with the stream of vulgarity she spewed as she yanked at her bonds. She managed to land a kick to the knee of the man who held her, almost sending him to the ground.

"Our people picked her up along the coast road. We were told to be on the lookout for anything suspicious," White explained. "She was looking out over the water like she was waiting for someone. She had a car parked nearby."

"I wasn't waiting for anything," the girl snapped.

"You were just sitting on the shore, in the middle of the night, doing nothing at all?" Locke took a step closer. "Or were you waiting for someone? Dane Maddock, perhaps?"

"Who the hell is that?" She looked like she wanted to bite his face off.

Now he could see she was Native American, and something clicked into place.

"You are with that fellow who was running the operation here before we took over."

"I don't know what you're talking about you poncey..."

Fisher stepped forward and drove a fist into her gut. Surprisingly, she absorbed the blow and grinned.

"Is that all you got?"

Fisher tensed, but Locke put a stop to his foolishness with a wave of his hand.

"Enough." Everyone fell silent, even the Indian girl. He turned to the deputies. "Something of value was stolen from the island tonight, and I suspect this woman is an accomplice."

"We'll take her to the jail." Boudreau took a step toward the prisoner but Fisher blocked her. "Step away from me." Her hand went her weapon but, just then, Sheriff Meade returned.

"What's this now? We have a prisoner?"

"You do not have a prisoner, Sheriff. I do." Several of his men had gathered round. All were well-armed and obeyed orders without question. As the Sheriff and his deputies became aware of their presence, Locke could see the fire in their bellies flicker and die. "Get my helicopter ready. We're leaving."

"To the museum?" Fisher asked.

The idiot! Locke tried to silence him with a glare but to no avail. "I can question her first, if you like."

"No." Would he have to choke Fisher to get him to shut his mouth? Clearly, the ordeal beneath the island had rattled him, but that was no excuse.

"Wait a minute, Mister Locke." Sheriff Meade swallowed hard, took a deep breath, and went on. "I understand you have the support of some important people, but the law is the law. I cannot allow you to take this woman away. She..."

Locke stared him into silence, then stepped so close he could see the one silver hair in the man's left eyebrow. The sheriff stood his ground, but he worked his jaw nervously.

"Sheriff, you have two choices." He raised his index finger. "You can set your people back to guarding this island so my museum staff can continue its work here undisturbed, and we shall remain friends. Or," he raised a second finger, "you and your two deputies can take out your sidearms and attempt to stop us. I would prefer we we remain friends, and I would consider it a great personal favor if you permitted me some time alone with this woman before I return her to your custody."

For an instant, he thought Meade would go for his weapon, but the sheriff thrust his hands in his pockets instead and stalked away.

"Have her back to me by morning," he said to no one in particular. The deputies sent twin withering looks in Locke's direction before following Meade.

"Are you sure you don't want me to question her?" Fisher asked when they were out of earshot. He turned to watch the young woman being led away.

Locke turned and punched Fisher in the jaw. The man crumpled to the ground.

"What was that for?" he mumbled.

"Stupidity," Locke said. "You speak of interrogation in front of the man whose son you tortured and killed only a few days ago?"

"He's too dumb to put it together," Fisher said, still holding his jaw.

"You don't know that. In any case, your special brand of questioning gained us no new information and added a complication. Between that and tonight's fiasco, I no longer trust your judgment."

"I'm sorry. I always give everything I have to the cause."

"Morgan will decide whether or not to accept your apology. For now, I want everyone out of here except the museum staff. They may continue their research just as we planned. You will remain here as security until your fate is determined."

"I'll see to it immediately." Fisher wobbled to his feet and staggered away.

Locke shook his head. Fisher's failure notwithstanding, Morgan would consider this Locke's responsibility, and it was. Morgan could temporarily be assuaged by the news of the temple beneath the island, but he would have to produce results soon or she would grow impatient. Perhaps this girl could help him bring things back into balance.

CHAPTER 17

Where could they have gone? Dane looked around, but there was no one in sight.

"Maddock?" A voice called from the woods. "Bones? Thank God." Avery appeared from the shadows and hurled herself into Bones' arms.

Dane raised an eyebrow and Bones shrugged.

"What happened?" Dane asked.

"Angel's been arrested. I went over to the shore to look for you and, when I came back, they were putting her in their patrol car. I feel like I should have tried to stop them, but what could I do?"

"Nothing," Bones reassured her. "They would have taken you in too." He looked over the top of Avery's head and scowled. "Let's go get her. Meade and his crew have pushed this too far. They can't just take my sister in on some bogus charge."

"I know," Dane said. "First, we need to get out of here in case they come back. Then we'll figure out the best way to handle this."

Avery handed him her spare set of keys and, only then, did she notice the casket they'd recovered from the island. She looked at him in surprise and excitement.

"It's sealed shut. We'll take a look at it when we're somewhere safe. Bones, you ride in the back and keep the casket with you. If we get stopped, you might have to slip away."

"No problem," he said.

Dane took them on a route that led up the coast, away from town and, he hoped, the sheriff's patrols. As he drove, he fought to suppress the rage that boiled inside of him. Right now, all was forgotten except the thought of Angel locked in a jail cell. He wanted to go in, guns blazing, and rescue her. He had a vague picture in his head of carrying her out through the front doors, action hero style, and laughed inside at the image. Where had this sudden hero complex come from?

As rational thought took hold, he considered their options. He and Bones were on the sheriff's radar, and likely wouldn't get anywhere if they showed up at the jail. Besides, they were in a foreign country. What she needed right now was bail money, a good attorney, or both.

"We need to call Charlie," he finally said. "He's got money and connections we don't have. If we show up there, we might get arrested too."

Bones considered that for several seconds before acquiescing. "Yeah, Charlie's the man for the job. He can take care of getting her out while we follow up on this." He tapped the casket.

"The mystery's solved," Dane said. "That casket was the only thing on the island. Once it's opened, that's it."

"Hardly," Avery said. "There were three chests. Three treasures. I don't think Dad planned on quitting after only one. He'd follow it all the way to the end."

"You know how it goes with us, Maddock." Bones leaned forward and rested his chin on the back of Avery's seat. "The first thing we find is never it. There's always more."

"Yeah, I know." Dane chuckled. "You can't blame a

guy for wishing for a quiet life."

"I'm not even going to comment." Bones sat quietly for a minute, then suddenly burst out laughing.

"What's so funny?" Avery asked.

"Angel's going to be pissed when she finds out we started without her. She's been dying to go on another of our little adventures."

"Do you do this sort of thing often?" Avery looked from Bones to Dane, who grinned ruefully

"You have no idea."

They contacted Charlie, who assured them he would take care of Angel, as well as send a couple of his men to the cottage to collect everyone's remaining belongings. They didn't provide him with any details of what they had discovered beneath Oak Island, but assured him the search was over and encouraged him to pack up his crew and return to the States as soon as possible. By the time they rendezvoused with Corey and Willis, who met them aboard *Sea Foam,* they had filled Avery in on all the details of the hidden Templar church. She was fascinated and couldn't wait to see the pictures they'd taken, but was even more eager to see what was hidden in the casket.

While Willis piloted the boat toward international waters, Dane, Bones, Corey, and Avery gathered belowdecks. Using small chisels, Dane worked at the seal until he freed the lid. He paused and took a long look at the others. This was the moment he relished—the edge of revelation.

"Stop titillating us and open it already," Corey said.

"Dude, you said *tit.*" Bones elbowed Corey, who winced and rubbed his arm.

"Are they always like this?" Avery cast an annoyed glance at Bones and Corey.

"What did I do?" Corey complained.

"Never mind," Dane said. "Masks on and we'll do this." When they had all donned surgical masks, Dane took hold of the lid and lifted it free.

The inside was stuffed with a tangle of string brown material.

"Coconut fiber," Avery said. "It was used for packing material. They even found some in the Money Pit."

Dane reached a gloved hand inside and pushed the fiber aside to reveal a dagger with a dark, mottled blade and a gleaming white handle. He looked up to see Avery holding the casket lid in trembling hands, and Bones and Corey looking over her shoulder.

"Carnwennan." She turned the lid so Dane could see the Latin word carved on the inside. The word was unfamiliar, but the look in her eyes told him it was significant.

"And what is that?" he asked.

"King Arthur's dagger." She leaned in for a closer look. "He had three legendary weapons: Caliburn, which we know as Excalibur, Rhongomnyiad, his spear, and Carnwennan, his dagger."

"Wait, so we've just found proof that..." Bones began.

"King Arthur was an actual, historical figure?" Dane finished. His mind was numb with shock. He'd expected to find treasure beneath Oak Island, but not this.

"It was one of the legends associated with Oak Island, but probably the most far-fetched one of them all." Avery's voice trembled.

"But why would somebody try to kill us for it?" Bones asked. "I mean, it's a huge discovery, but there's got to be more."

Dane withdrew the dagger and held it up to the

light. The blade was made of a substance unfamiliar to him. It was mottled gray, its surface covered in a hexagonal grid of alternating light and dark metals. The blade was honed to razor sharpness, and the butt was translucent, almost black, like obsidian.

As he gazed at it, the handle began to pulse with a dull, bluish white glow that gain strength with every beat.

"What is it doing?" Avery took a step back as if it were a venomous snake.

Dane didn't reply, but removed his hand from the hilt and, carefully holding the knife by the blade, held it up to the light. The pulses came faster, the light more intense until it shone so bright that Dane had to avert his eyes, and a low hum filled the room.

And then it stopped.

The hilt no longer shone, but it glowed a brighter white than before. Pinpoints of light like tiny galaxies sparkled deep in the handle and butt, and threads of blue flickered around the hexagonal patterns on the blade.

"It's like it absorbed energy from the light," Avery said. "I've never seen anything like it."

"We have." Bones grimaced.

Dane examined the dagger closely, carefully running his finger along its length. There was something odd about the way the butt was made. It was concave on the bottom and flattened out so that it did not quite conform to the dimensions of the hilt. Frowning, he pressed his thumb into the recess. Nothing. Then he gave it a twist.

The dagger vibrated and his vision swam for a split second.

"What the hell?" Bones said.

"Maddock! Where did you go?" Avery sounded

panicked.

"I'm standing right here."

"No way." Bones reached out awkwardly, as if he were playing Blind Man's Bluff, and grabbed Dane by the forearm. "He really is here," he marveled.

"But... how?" She gaped at a spot a few inches to Dane's left.

"What are you two talking about?" Dane looked back and forth between the two of them. If it were only Bones, he'd figure it was a lame joke, but Avery appeared rattled.

"Dude, you're invisible." Bones' matter of fact tone was void of humor. "One second you were there and then you were gone."

"It must be the dagger." He explained what he had done, and what he had seen and felt.

"The stories are true," Avery whispered. " Legend says Carnwennan had the power to cloak its owner in shadow. It really does make you invisible."

Dane turned the butt back and, once again, the room swam for an instant.

"He's back!" Bones said. "Here, let me see that."

Dane handed him the dagger and, a moment later, Bones vanished.

"I don't feel anything," Bones' voice said from nowhere. "Am I really invisible?"

"Yes, but we still recognize your foul stench," Dane deadpanned.

"Star Wars quotes are my job," Bones said.

Dane stared at the spot where he heard Bones' voice. He thought about what Avery had said. Carnwennan *cloaked* its bearer in shadow. He wondered...

"Bones, do me a favor and move side-to-side a little."

"You mean like line dancing? You know I hate anything redneckish."

"Just do it."

"Fine, I'll do the Casper Slide. Ready? To the left!" Bones began chanting lyrics and, presumably, dancing.

Dane followed the sound and, sure enough, he saw movement.

"Avery, Corey, can you see it?" He drew them to his side and pointed. "If you really focus, you can tell a difference between the space where Bones is and the wall behind it."

Avery narrowed her eyes and, a few seconds later, smiled.

"It's like an imperfect piece of glass. You can see through it, but something's just a little bit off."

Bones stopped chanting and, an instant later, reappeared.

"I don' think a woman's ever called me imperfect and a little bit off in one breath."

"No one's ever made the mistake of thinking you were only a *little bit* off." Dane relieved his friend of the dagger and held it out so everyone could see it. "Look at the pattern on the blade and think about what this dagger does."

"It's a cloaking device!" Bones said, following Dane's line of thought almost immediately. "This isn't some magic weapon. It's seriously advanced technology."

"Scientist are in the early stages of developing technology that bends light rays, making a particular spot invisible," Dane said, noticing Avery's confused expression. "Nobody's achieved anything like this, though."

"But this has clearly been down there for centuries. And if it's really Carnwennan, how did they get their hands on such technology?"

"I don't know," Dane said, though he was turning over a myriad of ideas in his mind. "But know we know why someone would kill in order to get their hands on it."

CHAPTER 18

Angel sat perfectly still, her eyes on the widening band of gray light where someone was opening the door to her small room. She was locked in what looked like a basement storage room, but she didn't know where. A dark figure loomed in shadow, and then a light clicked on. In the instant before she closed her eyes against the sudden glare, she caught a glimpse of a blocky man with red hair.

"Glad to see you're awake." He smiled. "We need to talk."

Angel's only reply was to suggest he use an orifice other than his mouth when speaking. She usually liked a guy with a British accent, but not under these circumstances.

"That won't do." Still smiling, he shook his head, his eyes roving up and down her body. "I'll explain." He pulled up a stool and sat down next to her. "We want information, and we will have it. If you talk to me, things will go easier for you. If you talk to Locke..." He let the words hang there, and gave her a look that told her Locke was the last person she wanted to deal with.

"Where am I?"

"We're in the museum. Now, tell us what we need to know and we can have you back with your friends in a thrice."

"Right." She didn't believe a word of it. "Explain to

me why I should believe anything a kidnapper tells me."

"I didn't kidnap you, love. I'm merely gathering information." He winked, making her stomach twist. Even if he wasn't her captor he'd be creepy. That big, moon face and massive body reminded her of the inbred killers that hacked their way through so many horror flicks. "I'm not one of the bad ones."

"So, you'll take these off of me," she indicated her handcuffed wrists, "and let me go."

"Sure."

The reply surprised Angel. She searched his eyes for signs of deception.

"I'll take the cuffs off right now to show you I'm a reasonable man and, after you answer my questions, you can walk. Hell, I'll even give you a lift to the airport."

No way in hell was she getting in a car with this creep, not that she believed for a second that he intended to release her, but she played along. If he was willing to uncuff her, that meant he didn't expect a girl of her size to pose any kind of threat. At a good two hundred-fifty pounds, she imagined few women, or men for that matter, were a threat. She'd have to be fast and would need a bit of luck on her side, but what did she have to lose? They were going to kill her anyway.

"Fair enough." She held up her hands, and watched as he fished a key out of his pocket and unlocked one side of the cuffs. The moment he turned his attention to the other cuff, she struck.

She drove her fist into his Adam's Apple, and he reeled back, gasping and clutching at his throat. Angel sprang to her feet and whipped her left hand around. Still locked onto her left wrist, the handcuffs cracked across the bridge of his nose, sending up a spray of blood that spattered across the wall. She attacked with fury, knowing the blows she had struck were far from incapacitating. She poured all her strength into an overhand right that caught the taller man squarely on the chin, followed it up with a knee to the groin, and pounded away with rapid flurry of punches to the chin, face, and temple. It was like chopping down a tree. He was too stunned by surprise and the force of her blows to do more than throw up his beefy hands in a weak attempt to fend off her attack.

It did no good. Angel was a well-conditioned professional athlete and this was nothing more than a training exercise to her. She threw in a few hard kicks to the side of the knee and, slowly, the man slid down to the floor, Angel delivering kicks and elbow strikes as he went down. When he finally fell into a sitting position, his eyes were glassy and his face a mask of blood. She drove her knee into his forehead for good measure, smashing the back of his head against the wall. His eyes rolled back in his head and he was out.

She made a hasty search of the floor, found the handcuff key, and freed her wrist, then searched his pockets for a weapon or anything else that might be of use, but all she found was a key ring. She took it just in case and crept to the door, tried the handle, and found it unlocked. Holding her breath, she opened it an inch and peered out.

She was looking at a narrow corridor lit by a row of bare bulbs. At the far end, a staircase led up into the darkness. Her pounding heart was the only sound she heard, so she slipped through the door and closed it behind her. She tried three keys on the ring before finding the proper one, and locked the thug in.

Smiling, she trotted down the corridor, almost

wishing someone would try to stop her. She was ready to take somebody else down. She wasn't *that* stupid, though, so she proceeded up the stairs with caution.

At the top, she found herself in the middle of a long hallway lined with doors on one side. None were marked.

"How the hell am I supposed to choose?" she whispered. Figuring one was as good as the other, she tried the closest door. It wasn't locked. She peeked through and found herself staring at a dark figure holding an upraised sword. She gasped and almost slammed the door shut, but just as quickly had to suppress a laugh.

It was a wax figure, a pirate armed with a realistic-looking sword. He loomed over another wax figure posed as a cowering woman. She had discovered the access door to one of the museum's exhibits. She inferred from the dim lights and empty museum that it was early morning and the place was not yet open. Good!

Only a low rail separated the exhibit from the museum's viewing area and, across the way, a window beckoned to her. She crept into the exhibit area and closed the door behind her when heavy footsteps sounded in the quiet room only feet from her. She lay down behind the woman on the floor and tried to cram herself into the tiny space behind it. She watched, heart in her throat, as an armed man walked past. He wasn't a uniformed security guard, and that frightened her even more. She'd take a rent-a-cop over a dude who looked like he could handle himself any day of the week.

He was a tall, muscular man with a shaved head. He wore a pistol on one hip and a knife on the other. He moved with detached ease, as if nothing could harm him, but his eyes were alert. As a fighter, she was always the aggressor, taking the battle to her opponent without fear. That same drive urged her to jump the guy, but common sense prevailed. This guy wasn't a careless idiot like the dolt she'd taken out downstairs. She'd need more than her bare hands to deal with this fellow.

She held her breath, convinced he could hear the pounding of her heart, and prayed for him to pass her by without seeing her.

After three eternal seconds he did just that, continuing on through the museum. She didn't permit herself to breathe until his footsteps faded in the distance. When she was certain he was gone, she counted to three before rising and peering around the side of the exhibit. He was gone. What was more, the lobby was only fifty feet or so to her right. As she watched, a woman in a cleaning uniform appeared from somewhere near the lobby, unlocked the front door, and left. She did not lock it behind her.

Angel didn't hesitate. She sprang to her feet, knocking the pirate to the floor, vaulted the rail, and made a dash for the door. Outside, the cleaning lady was climbing into a van. Maybe Angel could catch a ride.

She hit the lobby at full steam and was just reaching out to push the door open when her world dissolved into ice and pain. She slammed face-down on the tile floor, her arms and legs suddenly useless. The wind was knocked out of her and she tasted warm, salty blood in her mouth.

"Was my little dove trying to fly the coop?" Locke loomed over her, holding a taser and smiling. "I must say, I do enjoy shattering dreams at the very moment they are to be realized."

"She almost made it." The big guy she'd seen patrolling moments before stood behind Locke, looking equally pleased. "I wonder what she did to Charles?"

"Yes, I wonder that as well." Locke dropped to a knee and leaned in close. "Charles was a test. He's a great fool, and I'd have been disappointed had you not escaped him. Just know that you can't escape me." He reached into his pocket and withdrew a syringe. "By the time we get you back to your cell, you should be most tractable."

Angel watched in horror as the needle descended toward her limp arm. She heard someone screaming, then realized it was her.

Tamsin stared across her desk at the surprise guest who had just interrupted her day. He was a pale man his blond hair nearly white. She'd have mistaken him for an albino, but his eyes were alarmingly blue. He grinned, his perfect white teeth blending in to his pale face. Ordinarily, she'd never have granted an audience to a perfect stranger, but his cryptic explanation of his business had been enough to get her attention. He knew something about Kidd, or so he claimed.

He smiled at her, his manner easy as if this were his office and she the visitor. Was he ever going to speak?

"Who are you and what do you want?" She immediately chastised herself for speaking first. Patience had never been her strong suit. "Tell me now or I'll have you tossed out." It was a feeble attempt at regaining the upper hand, but it was all she could think of. For a moment it seemed as if she would be forced to make good on her threat, because the man continued to smile. But, just as she was reaching for her intercom, he spoke one word.

"Herrschaft."

She held on to her calm exterior with the greatest of effort. Inside, she was a mess. Why would anyone from Heilig Herrschaft, that vile branch of the Dominion dedicated to restoring the Nazis to power in Germany, using the church, of all things, as its vehicle, dare come anywhere near her or any Sister? Was he an assassin? Surely not.

"Please, Fraulein." He spoke with only the mildest German accent. "Be at ease. I know who you are."

"Then you are a fool for coming here today." She ought to have him taken into custody immediately, but something stayed her hand.

"Perhaps, but a brave fool, no?" Each time he smiled, he seemed ever more wolflike. "There is enmity between our organizations, that is true, but I believe we can find common ground."

"Morgan would never hear of it."

"Not with Morgan and not with the Sisterhood. With you."

"What could we possibly have in common?"

"A common enemy. Your sister." He held up a finger, silencing her protest. "How much has Morgan told you about Oak Island?"

Tamsin's stomach lurched. The honest answer was 'nothing,' but she didn't care to admit it.

"Yes, I see," he said, correctly interpreting her hesitation. He leaned forward and adopted a conspiratorial tone. "Morgan has found something on Oak Island."

"Impossible. The island has been searched countless times, and nothing has ever been found. The Money Pit is well named, for too much money has been wasted looking for treasure that is not there."

"You know it is not treasure we seek." He paused. "A Kidd chest has been found."

This time she could not keep the surprise from her face. "How do you know?"

"Of course I cannot tell you that. It is enough that we know, and now, you know."

Tamsin stared at the man without seeing him. It was no surprise that Morgan was keeping secrets, but it galled her none the less. And this was one secret that belonged to all three Sisters. It was what they had been working for.

"How do I know you are telling the truth?"

"You do not, but you can find out. Put the question to your sister. Look into her eyes and see the lie. Or, perhaps, she will tell you the truth." He shrugged, as if the whole issue was of no import to him.

"Assuming you *are* telling the truth, and Morgan has found... something." She could not bring herself to say what, exactly. "What is it you want from me?"

"We want you to take control away from Morgan, with our help if you like. In turn, when you find what you seek, we ask only to be permitted to make use of it one time. Nothing more."

"You believe the stories?" she scoffed. "They are symbols, and only to Britons at that. To the rest of the world, they are mere curiosities." Her words rang false, and she knew it. She'd had enough glimpses in her lifetime of powers not understood by the modern world to know better.

"We believe," he said simply. "If you think they are, as you say, curiosities, then surely there is no harm in permitting us to try."

"Suppose it will do what legend says. How will you use it?"

"That is our affair." He sat up straight. "You should not so easily cede control to Morgan. What power does she truly wield, save the court of public opinion and the allegiance of a few politicians? You have authority."

"I am Chief Constable of the transport police. That is a far cry from powerful."

"You underestimate yourself, and we both know you have forged many alliances behind Morgan's back. Let us help one another. In fact, I have some information that might be of interest to you. Someone in America is making quite an effort to find Kidd's chests. I can provide you with specifics, should you choose to work with us."

"What benefit is there to helping Heilig Herrschaft? The last time your people controlled Germany, our nations tried to destroy each other."

"Yes, and now America has come to dominate the world. What if we had formed an alliance, instead? Where might both our nations be?"

She shook her head. Dealing with the Dominion? The very idea was mad. Then again, perhaps this was the opportunity she had long sought. She rose from her chair, turned, and gazed down at the slow-flowing waters of the Thames. On the opposite side, the London Eye stuck out like a festering boil on the landscape of her beloved city. Too few held on to the things that truly mattered any more. The ancient things rooted in history and tradition; things that held power to make modern inventions seem trite by comparison. If the Dominion could help her obtain them... Perhaps it was time to take a risk.

"Tell me more."

CHAPTER 19

"Jimmy has something for us!" Dane proclaimed, scrolling through the email he'd just received from Jimmy Letson, an old friend and accomplished hacker. "I gave him a list of everything in Dad's research to see if he could come up with any leads on Kidd's chests."

"And what did he find?" Bones lounged on the deck of *Sea Foam* with a steaming mug of coffee in his hands. "I'm already bored."

They'd met up with Charlie in a coastal town in Maine. He'd returned their belongings and informed them that Sheriff Meade wouldn't let him post bail for, or even visit, with Angel until Monday morning. The sheriff also declined to say what she was charged with. Incensed, Charlie vowed to bring all his resources to bear on the situation. He'd been disappointed to learn that his Oak Island project was at an end, but had been downright giddy to hear of what Dane and Bones had discovered and to see the pictures they'd taken.

Now they were cruising south somewhere off the coast of Massachusetts. Matt, who had come along with Charlie, had rejoined the crew and was piloting the ship.

"He's got a few possibilities," Dane said. "There's a museum on Gardiner's Island..."

"Already checked it," Avery said. She was seated next to Bones, drinking a cup of chai tea. "No joy."

"Okay. How about the Maritime Museum in Port Royal?" The thought of a trip to Jamaica definitely appealed to him.

"Been there. Done that." Avery frowned. "No offense, but I don't think your friend has much chance of finding the Kidd chests. It's not like I'm the first who's tried."

"Don't underestimate Jimmy," Dane said. "He's talented and has access to some really obscure stuff."

"Not necessarily legally," Bones added.

Dane ran through Jimmy's list, growing more discouraged as Avery eliminated each possibility. Finally, he was down to the final two items.

"Trinity Church, on Wall Street," he began.

"Nope. Nothing belonging to Kidd in their archives. I've been there several times, and so had Dad."

"But they just added the journal of a William Vesey."

Avery sat up straight, her eyes boring into Dane with raptor-like intensity.

"I take it that's somebody important?" Bones asked over his coffee mug.

"He was the first rector of Trinity Church," Avery said. "He served there while Kidd was a member."

"Jimmy read an email from the donor to an archivist at the church which says it includes an account of Kidd's confession to Vesey and," he paused for dramatic effect, "Vesey alludes to a treasure map."

"How did he get access to their... oh, never mind." Avery took a sip of her tea and pondered this new information. "No mention of a chest?"

"Not in the email. Jimmy would have mentioned it. But maybe in the journal?"

"It's possible," she mused. "I've researched Vesey and there's no indication that he ever possessed a sea chest, but maybe Kidd told him where one or more could be found. It's worth following up on. Anything else on the list?"

"It's not specifically a sea chest, but there's a chest connected with the Poe Museum. It once belonged to Edgar Allan Poe."

"No connection to Kidd?" Bones asked.

"No. I guess he made the connection because I included *The Gold Bug* in the list of Dad's research items."

"Poe was a Kidd aficionado," Avery said. "But I've been to the Poe Museum and there were no chests there that fit the bill."

"So, cross Baltimore off the list," Dane said.

"You mean Richmond," Avery corrected.

"No, the Poe House and Museum in Baltimore."

"What? That place is tiny. There's almost nothing there, and definitely no sea chest." Avery stood and began pacing.

"She's definitely got that Maddock intensity," Bones observed before breaking into laughter as Dane and Avery shot dirty looks his way.

"He's added a link here, let me check it out." Dane tapped on the hyperlink Jimmy provided and it opened to an article from the Baltimore Sun, in which an director at the Baltimore Maritime Museum bemoaned the city's refusal to continue funding the Poe House. Dane read it over twice and saw no mention of a sea chest. "I don't see anything here."

Avery snatched his phone away and read the article. Frown lines appeared in her brow and disappeared almost immediately.

"It's in the picture!" She tapped on the image that accompanied the article. "You missed it because it's so tiny on the screen, but check it." She held up the phone for both to see and, sure enough, a wooden chest sat on a shelf in the background over the director's shoulder. "You've never seen it, but this is an exact match for the Kidd chest that Dad discovered!"

"Do you think this director guy found this chest at the Poe House and helped himself to it?"

"Could be. Even if this is a Kidd chest, unless you know what's inside, it doesn't have much value. I can see how someone who admires Poe and also loves maritime history could give in to temptation."

"That would explain why it's never been identified as a Kidd chest. As far as anyone knew, it was just another wooden chest that Poe stored his crap in," Bones interjected. "Who knows, it might have been gathering dust in an attic somewhere until this guy found it."

"I think they're both worth checking out. Which one do we follow up on first?"Avery asked.

"New York's on the way to Baltimore," Bones said.

Dane nodded.

"Wall Street here we come."

"Questioning her will not get us anywhere." Locke shook his head and closed the door behind him. He had hoped Bonebrake's sister would be a reliable source of information, but it was not to be.

"Are you certain? I could use some more... intense techniques." Shears ran his hand over his shaved scalp. He wasn't prone to the excesses that made Fisher so erratic, but efforts were not needed.

"No. She told me everything she knew, which is not much."

"With all due respect, where's the harm in making certain?" Shears didn't quite meet his eye as he spoke.

Clearly, he had more on his mind than gathering information.

"Torture only motivates the victim to tell you whatever they think you want to hear." Locke kept his tone patient, though frustration was wearing on him. He dreaded his next call to Morgan. He needed a breakthrough. "Besides, if we keep her largely intact, we might possibly make use of her."

"How do you mean?" Shears asked.

"Never mind. Just keep an eye on her and let me know when she's fully awake. She and I are going to make a telephone call." He left Shears to guard the cell. Dane Maddock had stolen the prize out from under his nose, but now Locke had a bargaining chip.

Returning to his office, he logged onto his computer and performed a search on Angelica Bonebrake. He had not expected to find much, perhaps a social networking page from which he could glean a few bits of useful information, but the pages of hits that filled his screen took him aback. The girl was a professional fighter and a minor celebrity.

He stroked his chin and smiled. He did not yet have a treasure to give to Morgan, but this girl's unique set of skills would make her a perfect plaything for Morgan's little games.

CHAPTER 20

"This is most unexpected, Sisters." Morgan ushered Tamsin and Rhiannon into her private study. "Our next meeting is not for two days."

"We felt it was necessary for us to come early," Tamsin said. "We are certain you were eager to share your news with us."

"Of course."

Three chairs formed a triangle in the center of the room. They met in the middle, joined hands, and spoke the ritual words. As the ancient speech rolled across her tongue, Morgan felt a strong kinship to their forbears. She could almost feel the power coursing through her veins. How satisfying it would be when the three were made one again, and she wielded a power long forgotten by the world.

When the ritual ended, they took their seats and Morgan began her explanation.

"It's nothing really," Morgan said. "I have received yet another request to run for Parliament along with a hint that I would make for a fine Prime Minister."

"That is not what I'm talking about." Tamsin glowered at her. "What have you found at the island?"

It was the question Morgan had anticipated the moment they had appeared at her doorstep, and she was prepared.

"I have news, though it is not all I had hoped it

would be." She described in great detail the Templar church that had been discovered beneath Oak Island, omitting the smaller chamber where the lost item, whichever one it was, had been kept. She showed them the photographs researchers had taken, apologizing that she had not assembled them into a proper presentation.

"So you see," she finished, "the discovery confirms that the Templars did, in fact, reach Oak Island, but we have not recovered any of the items we seek." She gave a false sigh. "If the news had been better, I would have summoned you immediately but, considering the limited success of our search, I was not eager to give you my report." There. That should settle them.

"Do we have any leads on the artifact that was stolen from the church, or on the man who took it?"

Morgan froze in the act of shutting off her computer. How had Tamsin come by this information? She knew all of her Sister's key operatives and their activities and whereabouts. None of them could have possibly known. And Rhiannon's base of power lay in the church, so she could not be the source. It was a conundrum that would require her attention, but not right now. Now was the time to stand firm.

"Locke is working on it," she said simply. Maintaining her calm exterior, she returned to her seat, sat with her hands folded in her lap, and smiled at Tamsin. Ordinarily, Morgan would not waste time sitting in silence, but she knew Tamsin put great store in such trifles as not being the first to speak, thinking it somehow gave her power. Let her believe that. Right now, Morgan could use it to her own advantage. She watched as Tamsin's cheeks reddened and she began to chew on her lip and fidget slightly until finally she could take no more.

"What is this plan?" Her voice was hot with anger.

"We have taken into custody a young woman who is close to the culprit. When he has finished questioning her, Locke will arrange an exchange. The girl for what was taken."

"Details, please." These were the first words Rhiannon had spoken, and her velvety voice betrayed no emotion. Of the two, she posed the greater potential threat to Morgan. Tamsin had no guile, while Rhiannon was cool and calculating. Tamsin had authority, but lacked the ability to capture the hearts and minds of the people. Rhiannon was beloved as a spiritual leader, though if the world knew her true religion, she would be cast down. Fortunately, Rhiannon had never given any indication that her position, a step below Morgan, chafed at all.

Morgan could see no use in prevaricating. She outlined Locke's plan, assuring them that the long sought-after treasure would be in their hands in a matter of days.

"Do we know which of the three it is?" Rhiannon maintained her calm, courteous manner.

"No." Morgan had her suspicions, based on accounts of the thieves' escape, but she would not share them.

"Very well," Tamsin sighed. "I need not remind you that the plan..."

"I know, Sister."

"Then you understand our concern," Rhiannon said smoothly. "The window of opportunity is a small one. If our quest confounds us again, we will be forced to wait."

"Need I remind you that, a few days ago, we were utterly without hope?" Morgan met their stares each in turn. "Now that hope is rekindled, and I am doing everything in my power to see to it that we do not miss this opportunity. But do not forget, Sisters, the mere possession of any of these artifacts is no small thing. We can use them to cement our power and entrench ourselves in the imaginations of the people. We will be queens!"

"*You* will be Queen," Rhiannon corrected. "Your bloodline is more direct than ours."

Morgan smiled at the thought. Prime Minister was well within her reach, but her aim was higher. She longed for the day they could finally set the plan in motion. A wave of change was about to sweep the world, and she would ride its crest.

"Sister, do we know the thief's name?" Tamsin seemed, if not cowed, at least placated.

"Maddock," Morgan said. "Dane Maddock."

Chapter 21

Trinity Church stood at the corner of Wall Street and Broadway. Its ornate spire, nearly three hundred feet high, stood in stark contrast to the modern buildings all around. A wrought iron fence ringed the property, as if to stave off the intrusion of city life. Dane found it disorienting to look upon the centuries-old brown stone church, the gothic architecture, and the historical cemetery, with its weathered gravestones, crypts, and monuments, then turn his head to see congested streets choked with taxi cabs and sidewalks where pedestrians navigated an obstacle course of vendors' carts and gawking sightseers. He, Bones, and Avery paused in front of it, taking a moment to admire the famed landmark.

"So this was Kidd's church, huh?" Bones asked.

"It was." Avery quickly donned the mantle of lecturing professor. "Not this building, of course. This is actually the third Trinity Church. The original structure was built in 1698. During its construction, Kidd even lent the runner and tackle from his ship to help them move the stones."

"That's pretty old, for white Americans, that is." Bones gave her an evil grin and Dane chuckled. "The cemetery looks pretty cool. Maybe we'll have time to check it out."

"There are a lot of famous people buried here and

in Trinity's other two cemeteries. Alexander Hamilton, Horacio Gates, Robert Fulton, John Jacob Astor..."

"Wait, the Jingleheimer Schmidt guy is buried here?" Before Avery could reply, Bones laughed and gave her arm a squeeze.

"Good thing Angel isn't here. She'd have punched you for that one." Dane felt a pang of regret and realized how quickly he'd grown accustomed to Angel's presence. He missed her easy laugh, her self-confidence, and the way she rode herd on Bones.

"Yeah. Don't you know she's climbing the walls in that rinky dink jail?"

"You don't seem too concerned that your sister is sitting in a jail cell," Avery said. "Are you two not close?"

"She's fine." Bones waved her concern away like a wisp of smoke. "This isn't Angel's first rodeo. She wasn't as bad as me when we were kids, but she had her moments. I just feel sorry for her jailer. You think I can get under someone's skin, you ought to see her in action."

Dane smiled at the thought, but couldn't escape a feeling of guilt that they hadn't found a way to get her out of her predicament.

They spent a moment longer admiring the church and the grounds, soaking in the history.

"Doesn't it seem like we go to a lot of these places?" Bones asked.

"Yeah, but no complaints here." Dane examined the architecture, its blend of sturdy lines and artistic trappings. He loved these pockets of history that stood against the disposable construction of recent generations "At least, not too many complaints."

"You guys keep dropping these little comments about places you've gone and things you've done,"

Avery said, "but you won't dish. It's starting to tick me off." She gave them each the evil eye and stalked into the church.

Dane grimaced and looked at Bones, who chuckled.

"She's a spitfire." He started to say something, then hesitated. It was a strange thing for Dane to witness. Bones was never uncertain about anything. At least, he never let it show. "Say, Maddock, I've been meaning to ask you something."

"All right. Shoot." As eager as he was to go inside and begin the search, he was, at the moment, even more curious about what Bones wanted to talk about.

"It's kind of weird for a guy to have a thing for his best friend's sister, don't you think?"

Dane felt his face grow hot. All his conflicted feelings about Angel rose anew. Had he been that obvious? How long had bones known?

"Bones, I don't know what to say."

"Look, if you want me to stay away from her, I will. She's your sister and I don't want to mess up our friendship, but I wouldn't mind hanging out with her. She's cool." He looked at Dane then looked away.

It took Dane a moment to realize what Bones was talking about, and then he laughed.

"Oh! You mean Avery." Relief flooded through him.

"Yeah. Wait, who did you think I meant?" Bones cocked his head and looked quizzically at him.

"Nobody." He quickened his pace and didn't meet Bones's eye. "Yeah, that's cool. I could tell you have a thing for her, and she's only been my sister for a couple of days."

"Dude, you suck at math. She's been your sister all her life."

"You know what I mean. It might be different if we'd grown up together."

"Yeah, that might be a little different." Bones sounded thoughtful.

"We'd better get going." He strode through the gate, headed toward the entrance, relieved Bones didn't press the issue.

By the time they caught up with Avery, she had used her credentials and charm to gain a look at the journal. She sat at at table under the close scrutiny of an archivist, a stocky man with light brown hair, blue eyes, and a youthful face. He gave Bones a funny look before returning his attention to Avery, who was carefully turning the pages with gloved fingers. Dane and Bones sat down on either side of her and watched her work.

The journal was thin, its pages yellow, and the script faded. Avery worked her way through the book at a steady pace, her blue eyes moving back and forth across the page as she devoured the text, putting Dane to mind of a typewriter carriage. When she finally reached the end, she frowned.

"What is it?" Dane asked.

Avery held up her hand, cutting off further questions, and slowly leafed back through the journal. After a few pages, she paused and leaned closer.

"Careful," the archivist cautioned. "No sneezing or drooling allowed." He smiled, but his comment was not entirely meant to be humorous.

"Pages have been torn out." Avery slid the book across the table so the archivist could take a closer look. The ragged edges were just visible.

"Are you sure?" The man took a closer look. "Holy crap." He dragged it out into a good four syllables, and Dane thought he detected a trace of a southern accent, so out of place in the heart of New York City. "I'm sorry. I'm going to have to take this back." He donned a pair of gloves and gingerly reclaimed the journal from Avery.

"Do you know if the page was there when it came into your collection?" Dane asked.

"I assume so, but I haven't read the entire thing. The donor is meticulous and I think she would have mentioned if it was incomplete."

"Who else has looked at the journal since it came into your collection?" Avery sounded like a prosecuting attorney interrogating a witness, and her manner seemed to take the man aback.

"Only the..." He reddened and shook his head. "Only the donor." He averted his eyes, but Dane could see the lie there.

The guy was obviously protecting someone, but who, and for what reason? Instinct told Dane that the archivist was not a bad sort. Dane decided to take a chance.

"The part of the journal you read, was there any mention of Captain Kidd?"

"There was." The man's face brightened. "It was interesting and a little weird. Kidd was in trouble with the crown and he knew it, so he came to Vesey because he said he had a secret he wanted to confess. Vesey doesn't go into detail, but Kidd says a secret was entrusted to him that he didn't want to let die. He gave Vesey what he called a 'treasured possession,' but Vesey inspected it later and couldn't see that it had any value."

"Did he say what it was?" Avery had stripped off her gloves and now clutched the edge of the table.

The man shook his head.

"We're interested in Vesey," Dane began. "Are any of his personal effects on display at the church, or anywhere else? Maybe a wooden chest?"

"There is an old chest that's bounced around the church since Vesey's time, though I don't know if it belonged to him. It's nothing fancy, and has been ill used, I'm afraid. It was passed around and used for storage until someone finally realized its age and thought it was worth preserving. At the moment it's in St. Paul's Chapel."

Avery smiled and nodded at Dane. The pieces were falling into place. They thanked the man and left the chapel in a hurry. When they reached the street, Avery didn't pause, but turned left and took off down the sidewalk at a fast walk that bordered on a jog.

"So where is St. Paul's?" Bones asked, his long legs allowing him to easily keep stride with her.

"Just a few blocks down the street," she said. "It's a part of Trinity Church. I know where it is, but I've never been there. It's even at the corner of Broadway and Vesey Street. I'm so stupid."

"You're just like Maddock. Don't be so hard on yourself," Bones began, but clammed up at one look from Avery..

St. Paul's was a Georgian-style church, boxy and surmounted by an octagonal tower on a square base. From the Broadway side, a portico sheltered a statue of Saint Paul, which was flanked by double-doors on either side. To the left of the entrance, in a fenced, grassy area, stood an obelisk, on which was carved an eagle and a man's profile. Dane wondered if this Masonic symbol could have any connection to the Templars who built the church beneath Oak Island.

The interior of the chapel was elegant, but was not awe-inspiring like Trinity Church. Cut glass chandeliers cast slivers of light across the ceiling and the rows of white pews. All around them, banners memorializing the tragic events of the terrorist attack on the World Trade center a decade before hung as stark reminders of the disaster that St. Paul's had, according to Avery, miraculously avoided.

They fell in with the other tourists and made their way around the church. The history of the place was interesting. It had withstood not only the 2001 attack, but also the Great New York City Fire of 1776. Both George Washington and Lord Cornwallis had worshiped here at different times, as well as other figures of historical significance. Though he found it all interesting, Dane was growing impatient. Where was the chest?

And then he saw it.

A simple, wooden chest sat atop a plain table in the back corner. It was afforded no special place. In fact, it was being used to hold brochures. Dane took that as a good sign. No one who knew anything about the Kidd legend or the potential connection between this chest and the legendary pirate would ever put it to such a pedestrian use. If this was the chest they sought, there was a good chance its secret remained undiscovered.

He nudged Avery and inclined his head toward the chest. Her eyes lit up.

"That's it. It's identical to the one Dad found." She took a hasty step in toward the back corner, but Bones grabbed her by the arm.

"Slowly," he said. "Don't draw undue attention to yourself."

They moved casually in the direction of the chest, still looking around as if no single thing held their interest. When they reached the corner, Dane turned to Bones.

"Turn around and look scary."

"Can do, boss." Bones pretended to answer his phone, twisted his face into an agitated scowl, and began speaking in a harsh whisper. Dane had to admit Bones was a pretty good actor when he put his mind to it.

"Let's see if it opens the same way as the other chest." Avery pressed her finger against a raised wooden square and moved it side to side, then up and down in the shape of a cross. The square came free, revealing a hidden compartment.

Smiling, Avery reached in and removed a brass cylinder, uncapped the end, and plucked out a roll of aged paper, much like the Oak Island map. She handed the cylinder to Dane and was about to unroll the paper when someone called out.

"What's this now? Give me that."

A big man with a shaved head approached them from near the doorway. If his British accent didn't set off warning bells, his hand resting on the pistol at his hip did. The man took a step closer and held out his free hand.

"That's right, hand it over now."

Dane tossed the cylinder at the man's face and, as the fellow reached up to grab it, drove his fist into the man's chin. The big man's knees turned to rubber and he went down in a heap, his eyes glassy. Dane grabbed Avery by the arm and steered her toward the door. All around them, people were talking and pointing. A few had taken out cell phones and were probably calling the police.

"He was a Red Sox fan," Bones explained before following Dane and Avery out the door.

Beneath the portico, Dane looked out at the street and saw a dark-haired man leaning against the fence that ran along the sidewalk. Their eyes met and the man stood ramrod straight and reached behind his back.

"Gun!" Dane shouted. Still holding Avery by the arm, he made a hard right and ran around the corner of the church and onto the churchyard. They sprinted past the obelisk just as a bullet deflected off its surface.

"Looks like it's time to call in the cavalry!" Bones shouted, punching up a number on his phone while running at full speed. "Church Street at Fulton," he barked, then tucked the phone back inside his leather jacket.

They dashed through the cemetery, navigating the tombs, hurdling low gravestones, and ducking in and out of the trees that shaded the yard. They reached the end of the church and veered to the right just as another muffled pop sounded and a bullet buzzed past his ear. The streets were busy, but the guy didn't seem to care who he might hit.

"Get Avery to the street."

Bones nodded and pulled her along, ignoring her protests.

Dane leaned against the wall and waited. He heard the sound of footfalls and someone breathing hard. As their pursuer came around the corner, eyes on the receding figures of Bones and Angel, and his pistol leveled, Dane lashed out with a vicious roundhouse kick, catching the man across the shins and sweeping his legs out from under him. He landed face down on the stone path with a sickening thud, his breath leaving him in a rush.

Dane hastily relieved him of his weapon, as well as a radio and cell phone. He rolled the man over. His nose was broken, his forehead split, and his face thick with blood and mucous. He gasped for breath, staring up at Dane with hate-filled eyes.

"I know you're Locke's man," Dane snarled. "You tell him to back off. I might not be so nice to the next man who takes a shot at me. Got it?"

"You..." the man panted... "don't give orders... to Locke. He has... something you want."

"What do you mean?" Had Locke found the other chest?

The man clammed up.

"Maddock! Get over here!" Bones called from the street.

Dane left the man lying there and ran toward the sound of his friend's voice, dashing through the gate and arriving on the sidewalk by the entrance to the Church Street Subway station just as a motorcycle screeched to a halt in front of them, scattering pedestrians who shouted and cursed. Willis raised the face shield and smiled broadly at them. He loved bikes.

"Matt and Corey are on the way." He said.

"Get Avery out of here." Dane told him.

This time, Avery didn't argue, but leapt onto the back of the bike, pulled on the spare helmet, and wrapped her arms around Willis as he rocketed out into traffic.

"Look out!" Bones shouted, pushing Dane to the ground as a bullet whistled over their heads and the few people who hadn't been driven away by Willis's bike ran for the subway or the churchyard. The big man from inside the church had recovered his wits, circled around the outside of the churchyard, and was now coming at them head-on.

Dane reached for his Walther but, before he could draw it, a beat-up van flashed past them, and bounded up onto the sidewalk. As it drew even with the approaching man, the passenger stuck out his arm, encased in a hard cast, and clotheslined their attacker under the chin, linebacker style. The surprised man flew backward and tumbled down the stairs to the subway.

"Holy crap, that hurt!" Matt groaned as Dane and Bones clambered into the van and Corey hit the gas. Sirens sounded in the distance but Dane wasn't worried. They'd be long gone before the police arrived. Besides, it had been the other guys shooting at them, and in front of witnesses at that, and neither was in any condition to get up and run.

"Why did you hit him with your cast?" Dane asked as Corey wove the van through traffic.

"I don't know, it seemed like something Bones would do," Matt groaned, holding his arm to his chest.

"Amen to that, my brother." Bones high-fived Matt's good hand. "Nice rescue, by the way."

"Did you find it?" Corey asked, eyes locked on the street. "Because if I get points on my license, I want it to be for a good cause."

"We did, and as soon as we catch up with Willis and Avery, we'll see where it leads."

C<small>HAPTER</small> 22

"Let's see what we've got here." Avery took out the paper they'd recovered from the chest and laid it on the table in their hotel room. She carefully unrolled it, revealing another map. Unlike the Oak Island map, however, there was no code to break. Instead, someone had added on to the original map. The older, more faded ink, showed a river and a stretch of shoreline. A dotted line led inland to a spot marked with a cross. Distances were lined out to specific landmarks: a tree, a boulder, and a bend in a stream. In the bottom right corner, the creator of the map had drawn three of the cross-in-circle symbols they'd seen on Oak Island arranged in a triangle around another familiar symbol— two Knights on a horse. Over the top of this map, someone had inked in a street, a building, and an "x."

"That's the cross symbol we saw at Oak Island," Dane said, pointing to the corner of the map.

"I don't believe it," Avery said. "This is Trinity Church."

Dane hadn't even noticed the labels. Sure enough, the street was labeled "Wall" and the building "Trinity."

"Kidd, or one of his contemporaries, must have added these details," he said. "The land had probably changed so much that the landmarks on the original map were useless."

"So, once more into the breach?" Bones asked, drawing an amused look from Avery. Dane had long ago grown accustomed to Bones' occasional lapses in which he let his intelligence show, but people who didn't know him well were sometimes taken unaware.

"We'd have to be crazy to go back," Corey said. "They know we're here and they know what three of us look like. Surely they'll be watching for us."

"Maybe not," Dane mused. "They know we found the map, but they have no idea where it leads. They probably figure we're already on the way out of town, headed for wherever this map leads."

Just then, Bones' phone rang. He answered it, listened for a minute, then uttered a stream of curses. The conversation didn't last much longer, and when he hung up, he cursed again and slammed his fist into the wall.

"Locke's got Angel."

Dane felt like he'd been dropped into freezing water. He sat there, unable to speak, or even move.

"Charlie went back to see Meade. I don't know what he said, but the sheriff broke down and admitted they don't have her. The deputies tried to bring her to Meade on the island, and Locke's people basically intimidated them into turning her over."

The icy shock was melting quickly, warmed by Dane's kindled fury. He pictured Angel in Locke's power and suddenly felt a blood rage he'd only experienced in the heat of battle in the service.

"Locke said he'd give her back." Bones' tone of voice made it clear what he thought of that promise.

"Oh my God." Avery looked like she was about to faint. "This is crazy."

"We're going back to the island," Dane said. "Screw

the treasure hunt. I'll kill every one of those..."

"They're gone." Bones cut him off. "He left some researchers behind, and that's it."

"Damn!" Dane stood and began to pace the room. "Does Meade have any idea where they've taken her?"

"He gave us two clues: the museum, and somebody named Morgan."

"The Bailyn Museum?" Avery asked. "That's where Locke supposedly works, and it's right here in New York."

"Let's go." Dane headed to the door, his thoughts bent on mayhem."

"Hold on there, bro. We need a plan." Bones motioned to the chair Dane had vacated. "Sit down and let's think this through."

Bones acting the calm, rational part was such a departure that it brought Dane up short. He turned back to face the others, but didn't sit down.

"I want to hurt somebody too," Bones said, "but if we just go storming in there, we could get Angel killed, assuming she's even there. We need to do this right, and we need you at your best."

"You're right." Dane squeezed his eyes shut and turned the problem over in his mind. "They know me, you, and Avery by sight, but they don't know the rest of the crew. Corey, if we get you close enough, could you hack into their network?"

"Jimmy would be the better choice, but it's possible," Corey said. "It depends on what kind of security measures they have in place."

"It's worth a try. We don't need access to everything, just their security camera footage."

"I'll call Jimmy right now. Maybe he can give me some pointers." He excused himself and stepped out onto the balcony to make his call.

Dane turned to Willis.

"Would you be willing to go inside, take a look around?"

"Hell yes. Let me put on my nerd clothes and I'll be ready to roll." His smile, normally so open and friendly, was hungry and dangerous. "Nobody messes with our girl."

"What about me?" Matt raised his broken arm. "I'm ready to bash some more bad guys with my cast."

"I have a job for you too. We," he indicated Bones, Matt, and Avery, "are going wherever this map leads."

CHAPTER 23

Corey parked the van in the parking lot of the Bailyn Museum as close to the building as possible, cut the engine, and moved to the back, out of sight of passers by. He quickly located the Bailyn's wireless network, clicked to access it, and activated a program Jimmy had given him. He nervously drummed out the beat to "Apache" as the program began trying security codes at a dizzying rate. He worried that the Bailyn would have systems in place to detect intruders, but Jimmy had assured him this program was as good as invisible.

In a matter of minutes, he was in. Jimmy had programmed an Elvis icon that gave a thumbs-up and said, "Thank you very much," upon a successful hack. Corey chuckled at the image and moved on.

A few keystrokes and a list of directories scrolled down the screen. He selected /security and Jimmy's program began its work. Two minutes later he was looking at a list of sub-folders containing video from various parts of the building. Where to begin? Angel had been taken less than twenty-four hours earlier, so he chose a likely time frame and began his search.

He sighed, wondering how long this was going to take. He hoped Willis was having better luck.

Willis, clad in khaki pants, a baggy polo shirt, and

glasses, and wearing a camera around his neck, made his way through the museum. It wasn't the greatest disguise in the world. He was more than six feet tall, so he stood out in any crowd, but at least he was dressed appropriately for the setting.

He regularly consulted the map in his brochure, but it wasn't the exhibits he was interested in. He was marking off the rooms he had inspected, searching for access to offices, storage, or mechanical rooms. So far he'd met with no success. The few doors he had seen were locked and required electronic clearance to enter.

The only room he had not yet checked stood adjacent to the entryway. If he struck out here, he wasn't sure what he'd try next. Maybe go outside and look for a service entrance. The exhibits here were devoted to pirates. He took that as a good sign. A replica of a Seventeenth Century pirate ship hung suspended from the ceiling, with a second-floor viewing area up above. Tall windows lined the wall to his left and a series of exhibits filled the wall to his right.

He passed wax figures of Blackbeard, Captain Kidd, and Black Caesar. A heavy tarp was draped across the next exhibit and a sign taped to the rail indicated it was "closed for repair." That didn't necessarily mean anything, but he had a feeling about it, and his instincts had kept him alive through a youth spent in one of the worst neighborhoods in Detroit, and then through service in the Navy.

He checked to make sure no one was looking, then peered behind the plastic. A wax figure lay on the floor, one arm broken. Nothing too weird about that. And then he spotted something very out of place— the tip of a sneaker print. Even that might not have seemed unusual if it weren't for the fact that he'd seen enough bloody prints in his life to know one when he saw it. Whoever had come through here had stepped in blood. He leaned farther in and spotted a doorknob on the back wall.

"Can I help you?" A big man with a shaved head and battered face stood behind him. The man wore a museum ID badge that named him A. Shears, a radio on one hip, and a pistol on the other.

Willis immediately recognized him by the description Dane had given. This was the man who had accosted Dane and Bones in the chapel earlier in the day and whom Matt had taken out. He suppressed a grin, wishing he'd seen what Bones had described as an "epic takedown." He had to hand it to Shears, though. The guy bounced back quickly.

"Just wondering what this display was. First time I've been here, you know."

Shears looked him up and down before answering.

"Nothing special, just a diorama of a pirate raid. The bloke got himself a broken arm."

"All right. Cool." He continued down the line of exhibits, feeling Shears' gaze boring into him. He checked his watch. Forty minutes until closing time. If Shears didn't move along soon, he'd have to find a place to hide.

Thirty minutes later, he stood alone on the second floor balcony that afforded visitors a view of the pirate ship. Shears still stalked the ground floor, ushering the last visitors out of the museum. As the last group of people left, Shears mounted the steps, heading up to the second floor.

Willis was cornered. The stairs were the only way down and, with Shears already suspicious of him, he had no way to explain his presence here. He looked for a way out. He had less than ten seconds before Shears reached the top of the stairs, turned, and spotted him. He looked around, seeking a way out, and his eyes fell on the pirate ship.

It would be a bit of a leap, but he could do it. His mind made up, he clambered up onto the rail, not looking down at the floor below. Hoping this wasn't the day his impulsiveness finally came back to bite him, he jumped.

His stomach fluttered on the edge of nausea as he flew through open space. Next thing he knew, his arms and legs were wrapped around the stout cable that supported one corner of the stern. He slid down its length, his hands burning as the rough steel scoured his palms, and dropped with scarcely a sound into the ship.

He hit the deck and reached for the Beretta M9 he wore concealed underneath his shirt. If Shears spotted the gentle rocking of the ship, he might investigate, and Willis was through playing around. He waited, wondering if he'd be spotted and, if not, how he was going to get down.

"It's somewhere around here, I think." Avery let out and exasperated sigh and stamped her foot. "This is so frustrating. We need more to go on."

They stood in the Trinity Churchyard, looking at the rows of gravestones, many of which had eroded over the centuries until the engraving on them was nearly illegible.

"If we're looking for another Templar church, we have to assume it was built long before Trinity Church or this graveyard were here," Dane said.

"Thanks for that ray of sunshine," Bones replied. "If we don't find something soon, I'm going to get all weepy and emo like that Keep America Beautiful Indian."

"Iron Eyes Cody?" Avery said. "Did you know he wasn't even an Indian? He was Italian."

"Shut it! No freaking way."

"Yes, way." Avery laughed.

"Focus." Dane knew Bones was trying not to think about Angel. Dane too was having a hard time keeping his mind on the task at hand. "The map has three of the cross-in-circle symbols set in a triangle. Why don't we see if we can find that same pattern on any of the gravestones?"

They spread out, moving quickly because evening was rapidly approaching and the light growing dim. Dane soon found what he was looking for on the gravestone of William Bradford. The three crosses formed a triangle around a cherub face. Hope rose, but fell as he realized it was only a simple headstone and could not be the entrance to anything.

"Got one!" Bones called. "Three crosses around an angel dude. Just a headstone, though."

"Same here." Avery sounded disheartened.

"Wall, that was a fail," Bones said. "What now?"

Dane considered the situation. Like the crosses, the headstones formed an equilateral triangle, and at the center of that triangle stood...

"Alexander Hamilton's tomb," Dane whispered.

The tomb of Alexander Hamilton was perhaps the most impressive of all the structures in the churchyard. Square at the bottom, with columns at each corner surmounted by urns, the tomb was topped by a weathered obelisk.

Dane knelt down behind Bradford's headstone and followed the cherub's line of sight. Sure enough, it pointed directly at the obelisk. He instructed Bones and Avery to do the same with the headstones they had found and, moments later, they confirmed his theory.

Dane made his way over to the tomb and circled it, looking for any indication that this was what they were looking for. An epitaph to the famed patriot was engraved on one side, but he saw no Templar symbols. He let his eyes drift upward to the top of the obelisk where he thought he saw the faint outline of a circle engraved on the weathered top.

"You two, keep a lookout," he said to Bones and Avery, and climbed onto the tomb. The obelisk was short enough that he could easily see the four sides of the capstone.

"They're here!" he exclaimed. "A templar cross on three sides of the point. This is it."

"But Hamilton wasn't a Freemason. Why would that symbol be carved onto his tomb?" Avery looked puzzled.

"It *shouldn't* be here. Someone put that mark here for a reason." Dane had no doubt he was on the right track.

"What do we do now? Say *open sesame*?" Bones asked.

Dane looked down at the symbols and two details immediately caught his attention: a groove ran around the capstone, as if it were a separate piece; and on the fourth side, instead of a cross, a small arrow was carved. It was so tiny he almost missed it, but it was there.

"What's that thing you're always saying, Bones? Righty tightie, lefty loosie?" With that, he took hold of the capstone and gave it a deft twist. It didn't budge.

"Impressive." Avery smirked, then turned and gave Bones a wink.

"Thanks for the support." Dane got a better grip

this time and poured all of his strength into the effort. Slowly, inch by inch, the capstone began to rotate, and rose as it turned. After a quarter turn, Dane heard a loud thunk and the capstone froze. "Anything?"

"Nothing," Avery said.

"There are three crosses," Bones said. "How about three turns?"

"Or maybe three quarter-turns," Avery added.

"You're already correcting me, woman?" Bones asked. "We hardly know each other."

Dane tuned them out and gave the capstone another twist. He felt the strain in every muscle of his shoulders, arms, and back as he turned the stone another quarter-turn, and then another. When he'd completed the third turn, the tomb vibrated beneath his feet and a hollow, grating sound rose up from down below.

"Yahtzee!" Bones exclaimed.

"You did it, Maddock," Avery whispered.

Dane leapt down and looked down at the base of the tomb on the side facing away from the street. The entire side of the tomb had sunk into the ground, revealing an empty space below. They had found it!

CHAPTER 24

Corey sighed and opened the last sub-folder. His search had been utterly fruitless, and now it was closing time. He wondered if Willis had fared any better. Considering how long he'd spent in the museum, he'd better have found something. If Willis had been browsing museum displays while Corey worked his butt off, they would have a talk later.

This folder contained footage from the security camera in the delivery area. He quickly scrolled through the clips, as the museum apparently didn't get many deliveries. One clip after another, all showing an empty loading bay, rolled by. He was ready to give up, but figured he might as well keep going, at least until Willis showed up, which ought to be any minute now.

The most recent clip was from this afternoon, and ended shortly before they'd arrived. For no particular reason, he skipped down to it and double-clicked. This clip began the same as the others, footage of an empty room, but it soon grew interesting.

On the screen, a heavy-set man with a pistol on his hip opened the bay door and a black sedan with tinted windows rolled in. Another man, short and dark, also armed, stepped out. The two spoke for a minute, then moved off screen. Two minutes later, they returned, supporting a figure in jeans and a t-shirt.

It was Angel.

She could barely stand, as if she was under the influence of some sort of drug. She also might have been injured, and unable to walk on her own, but he didn't want to consider that. Her hands were cuffed in front of her and ankles shackled. They weren't taking any chances with her.

They put her into the back seat and the big guy got in after her, while the dark-skinned man took the wheel. A minute later, a lean, tawny-haired man climbed into the passenger seat and they drove away. Corey scrolled through the rest of the clip, but the car did not return.

Angel was gone. They had missed her by a matter of minutes.

Corey reached for his cell phone, then thought the better of it. They had agreed Corey would not call Willis, in case his phone should ring at an inopportune time, but Willis would call Corey if he needed help.

When they weren't certain anything was amiss at the museum, he hadn't been too concerned about Willis, but now things had changed. What if the guys he'd seen leaving in the car weren't the only armed, dangerous men on the premises? Willis should know that Angel was gone and there was nothing more he could do in there, but how could Corey let him know? He supposed he could go in after him, but the very thought made his stomach threaten to heave up. He was a computer guy, not a soldier. Besides, what if he walked into a trap and they both wound up...

He dismissed the line of thought with a shake of his head. Willis had been in worse situations than this plenty of times. He'd be okay.

Willis checked his watch. Thirty minutes since he'd

heard so much as a footstep down below. Hoping Shears and the rest of the museum staff had gone, he crawled to the bow of the pirate ship and peered over the edge.

Down below him, the museum was empty. He watched for another five minutes before deciding it was safe to come out. But how to get down? He scanned the deck and his eyes fell on a coil of rope in the stern. Unlike most of the ship, which was constructed from new materials, this appeared to be an authentic rope from an old sailing ship. It looked dry and brittle, but he had no choice.

He lashed the rope to the stern and tossed it over the edge. It was too short, ending about ten feet above the floor, but it would have to do. Not willing to waste time fretting over something beyond his control, he took hold of the rope, climbed over the rail, and shimmied down.

The coarse rope scoured his already scraped hands, but he worked his way down in a controlled slide.

Halfway to the floor, he heard a snap and the rope gave an inch.

"Oh hell." He dared a look down. Twenty feet was too far to fall.

Another snap as strands of the aged rope began to break under the strain of his weight. And another.

He slid a little faster, bracing himself for the fall that now seemed inevitable as, far above him, the rope frayed and, fiber by fiber, fell apart. He was twelve feet up when it finally gave way.

He hit the ground hard, landing skydiver style, but the impact on the hard floor jolted him all the way up his spine. He grimaced as pain lanced through his knees, and he wondered if he'd torn something. It didn't matter, though. He had a job to do.

One positive was that he didn't have to leave a length of rope dangling from the stern of the ship where it could draw unwanted attention. He coiled up the fallen rope and carried it with him to the closed exhibit where he hid it beneath the fallen pirate figure. He paused to listen in case anyone was still here and had heard his fall, but the museum was silent as a tomb. Figuring it was time to move on, he took a deep breath and stepped through the door at the back of the exhibit.

He found himself in a spartan hallway that ran along the back of the exhibit hall. Doors on either side provided access to the various exhibits. In front of him, a stairwell led down to a lower level, and he spotted another smudged, bloody footprint a few steps down. Hand resting on his Beretta, he made his way down into the darkness.

He found himself in a poorly-lit basement area. He spotted more footprints and followed them past doors labeled according to what was stored inside them, to a small room, perhaps a large janitor's closet. Inside, he found a folding chair and a stainless steel table.

And a great deal of blood.

A dark spatter slashed across the wall to his right, and more spots trailed down to the floor, where more dark, dry patches spotted the gray surface. Trembling with rage, he gave the room a once-over, in case he'd missed an important detail. A small wastebasket was shoved into the corner on his left. At first, he thought it was empty, but then he spied a glint of silver. He knelt and fished it out. It was a broken necklace with a turquoise and silver Kokopelli pendant. He recognized it as Angel's. This definitive proof she had been here.

"I'm gonna kill somebody," he muttered, pocketing

the necklace.

"Not today, my friend," someone said from behind him. Damn! He'd let his anger distract him, and someone had crept up behind him. "Very slowly take that gun out of the holster."

"Hey man, I was just looking for the john. Is it anywhere around here?"

"If you don't want a hole in your head, do what I say, and do it now."

He did as instructed, slipping his Beretta out of the holster with two fingers, making it clear he was not reaching for the trigger, and setting it on the ground.

"Good. Now turn around slowly."

Still squatting down, Willis turned to see Shears pointing a gun at him. The man smiled, clearly pleased with himself.

"Slide the gun over to me."

Willis did as he was told. He gave the Beretta a shove, sliding it toward Shears' gun hand with enough force that it slid past him.

Shears took his eyes off of Willis for only a split second, but that was all Willis needed. He whipped his Recon knife from his belt, hurled it at Shears, and dove into a forward roll as a bullet pinged off the ceiling. He came to his feet ready to wrestle the gun from Shears, but there was no need. Willis' aim had been true, and the hilt of his knife protruded from Shears' chest. He'd gotten him in the heart.

Willis retrieved his knife and his Beretta, and dragged Shears' lifeless body into the room where Angel had been held. He regretted taking the man's life, not because he placed any particular value on it, but because he would have liked to question him. As it was, he had no clue as to Angel's whereabouts. He only knew she had been here. He guessed that would have to be enough.

The space beneath Hamilton's tomb was a tight box, but deep enough that even Bones could stand up straight. A round seal was carved in the center of each wall: the Templar cross, an Eagle clutching a spear in its talons, and the familiar temple seal and two knights seal.

Dane moved immediately to the two knights on horseback, as it was the one drawn in the corner of the map. He ran the beam of his flashlight back and forth across the carving. It didn't take long to realize what made this seal different from the traditional rendering. In most versions of the seal, each knight carried a lance. In this carving, the two lances were carved as one thick lance with a prominent point. Closer scrutiny revealed a fine seam running around the top half of the lance. Dane blew the dust away from the edges.

"This looks like a button," Avery said. "May I?"

"Sure." Dane stepped back and watched as she gingerly pressed on the top half of the lance. It sank into the stone with a hushed click, and the seal slowly rolled to the side, vanishing into the wall and revealing a dark shaft with handholds in the side leading deeper into the ground.

"Maybe you should stay here." Dane looked at Avery. "I don't know how far down we'll have to climb. It could be dangerous."

"Are you stupid?" Avery looked scandalized. "This is Dad's quest and we're going to finish it together. Besides, despite what our first meeting might have indicated, I can climb a little." With that, she clambered through the hole, ignoring Dane's urges for her to exercise caution, and began her descent.

"Sisters," Bones said. "You gotta' love 'em." He grinned. "I'll make sure she doesn't get into trouble." He followed Avery into the shaft, and Dane went last.

At the bottom of the shaft, a doorway opened onto a dark chamber, with steps leading down into the bottom. Dane and Bones played their lights around the room. It was another Templar church. Like the church beneath Oak Island, the walls were adorned with ornate carvings but, instead of scenes showing knights in combat, the images told the story of the crucifixion. Directly in front of them, behind a simple stone altar, the image of the centurion piercing Jesus' side looked down upon them. The agony on Jesus' face was almost palpable.

"This is amazing!" Avery took out a camera and began snapping pictures. "A Templar church beneath New York City. Hard to believe." She paused, lowering the camera. "Wait a minute. This had to be here long before the Hamilton tomb was constructed. So that means..."

"Someone was in on the secret and built the tomb specifically as a cover-up," Bones finished.

"The Freemasons?" Avery asked.

"I think it was Elvis and The Colonel, but that's just me."

"You're useless." Avery looked around, and her eyes suddenly widened. "But if someone or some group knew about this place, what if they took whatever was hidden here? I don't see anything."

"If it's like the church under Oak Island, and I think it is, this place hasn't revealed all its secrets." Dane pointed to a spot high on the wall and the symbol of six crosses in a circle, identical to that in the Oak Island church. "If my guess is right, the map to this temple didn't include everything someone would need to know. Bones, a boost?"

Bones chuckled and hunched down against the wall below the crosses and served as a ladder for Dane to climb. Bones stood up straight, then took Dane by his feet and lifted him up until Dane reached a ledge beneath the crosses.

"Maddock, you have got to lay off the bacon cheeseburgers," Bones grunted. "You're too fat for me to keep doing this."

"Quit whining." Dane hoisted himself up onto the ledge and cautiously climbed to his feet. The ledge was narrow and the drop was far enough that he didn't want to risk a fall.

"Careful," Avery warned.

He smiled down at her, then reached up to the topmost cross, took hold, and turned it in the same way Bones had turned its counterpart in the Oak Island church. It didn't budge at first, but then, slowly, it moved. Gradually, he rolled the circle back into the wall, and climbed through.

The space here was much like the one beneath Oak Island— a domed, turret-like chamber with the same double-line of symbols spiraling from ceiling to floor and the same wedge-shaped pattern in the ceiling's center, and a stone altar off to one side. In this chamber, however, there was no wooden casket atop the altar, but a long wooden cylinder. He took a minute to make a photographic record of the chamber before moving to the altar.

He was tempted to crack open the cylinder right then and there and see what was inside, but common sense won out. He hefted the cylinder and carried it back to the entrance.

"Hey Bones, can you catch this?" he called.

"Only if you don't throw like a girl."

Dane chuckled and tossed it down to Bones, who managed to snag it in both arms before it hit the ground.

"What's inside?" He turned it over, giving it a close look.

"Don't know. We'll see when we open it."

CHAPTER 25

"What do you think it is?" Matt asked. "It's really long."

"That's what she said," Bones jibed. He elbowed Avery, who gave an exasperated sigh and shook her head.

They were back on board *Sea Foam,* docked, and waiting for Corey and Willis to return. There was no word from them, and he didn't know how to interpret that, though he kept his hopes up.

"Let's find out." The cylinder was a good five feet long, and capped on each end. The caps were held in place by resin. Dane needed only a few minutes to work one end free. He twisted the cap off and pulled out a handful of coconut fibers.

"I see it," Avery whispered.

A brass circle gleamed beneath the stark light. Dane took hold of it and drew forth a spear. The shaft featured the same spiral band he had seen on the walls of the two chambers. The oversized spearhead was made of the same mottled metal as Carnwennan and, like the dagger, a deep channel ran down one side of the blade. The head was held in place by a band of the now familiar white stone. As he held the spear out for the others to inspect, lights began to swirl deep in the stone.

"It's Rhongomnyiad. King Arthur's spear. It's got to be," Avery said. "It's clearly a mate to the dagger."

"Is it a cloaking device too?" Bones asked.

"There's no legend of invisibility surrounding the spear. In fact, there aren't many legends about it at all." Avery looked thoughtful. "The only one I can think of says it could take a life with a single touch. But the same story claimed that it carries life within it."

"So, who wants to be the one to touch the big, scary spear?" Bones asked. No one volunteered. "Let me see that thing." Bones took the spear from Dane and looked it up and down. "Do you think the butt turns it on, sort of like the dagger?" Before anyone cold object, he pressed on the bronze butt and the spearhead flickered. "Sweet. I wonder..."

"Bones, don't..."

Before Dane could finish the sentence, Bones prodded a metal folding chair with the spear. Avery screamed and everyone covered their faces as, with a loud crack, the spear sent up a shower of blue sparks and the chair flew across the cabin and clattered to the floor. Bones hurried over and picked it up so everyone could see the smoking hole the spear had burned through it.

"Well, now we know what it does." He grinned. "Who's next?"

"Bones, give me the spear before you sink us." Dane took the spear back and held it loosely by his side. He turned to share a pained smile with Avery, and was surprised to see her gaping at him.

"Maddock," Bones said, "your butt is glowing."

Dane looked down and saw that the dagger, which he had tucked into his belt, and the stone band around the spear, had begun to shine. The closer together he held them the brighter they shone.

"This is crazy." Avery said. "How can you guys be so calm about this?"

"Like we said before, we've seen this phenomenon a couple of times." Dane drew Carnwennan and held it next to Rhongomnyiad. The white stones glowed like small suns, though they produced no heat. Strangely, he felt a tingling down his arms, and decided he shouldn't toy with forces he did not understand.

"Stones like this are unheard of." Avery took the spear from Dane for a closer look. "So, what are they? Did you study them?"

"We've never actually been able to do that. We sort of keep losing them."

Just then, Dane's phone vibrated, sparing him of further questions. The number was unfamiliar.

"Hello?"

"We each have something the other wants."

He'd only heard the voice once before, but he recognized it instantly. It could only be one person.

"Locke." He couldn't keep the growl from his voice. Silence fell in the cabin as everyone stared.

"One and the same. Now, time is short, so I shall keep this simple. I want what you found on the island..."

"I don't know what you're talking about."

"Mister Maddock, I assure you I have no attachment to this girl. In fact, I find her crass and tiresome. The only value she has to me is as an object for trade. If you do not have what I want, rather, if you insist on pretending so, she will no longer be of use to me, and I shall dispose of her. Now, shall we begin again?" He took Dane's silence as assent, and continued. *"I want what you found on the island, and I want the map you recovered from Saint Paul's."*

Dane's mind worked furiously. As he'd predicted, Locke knew about the map, but assumed it led to somewhere else entirely. That was good.

"What do you want with the map? It was right here

in New York all this time, right under your nose. Why didn't you take it?"

"Yes, disappointing, that. You beat my men there, literally and figuratively, by minutes."

"We have a bad habit of doing both those things."

Locke ignored him.

"For your convenience, we will make the exchange in Baltimore. I believe you are already headed in that direction. Don't bother with the Poe House. My people will be there before you."

Dane's heart pounded and thoughts hummed through his mind at a lightning pace. Locke had caught him off guard with that detail.

"I'm not making any kind of deal with you until I talk to Angel." Just saying her name felt like a vice clamping down on his chest. He could hardly breathe, so powerful was his rage.

"How cliche," Locke sighed. *"Very well, if it will make you feel you have some semblance of control, you may speak to her. But first, I want something in return."*

"What?"

"Tell me which one you have. My man got a good enough look that I know it is not the spear."

"The dagger." Dane saw no point in lying.

"Excellent. Very well, here's your bird."

There was two seconds of agonizing silence, and then he heard Angel's voice.

"Maddock?" For a moment, she sounded fearful, almost childlike, and then her resolve hardened. *"Are you there?"*

"Yeah, are you all right?" He wondered if the look on his face or the tone of his voice revealed anything to the others in the cabin, who still looked on in rapt silence.

"Doesn't matter. Don't you give this poncey asshat

anything." Now she sounded like her old self. *"I'll kick your ass if you do. You hear me?"*

"Sorry, Angel. You know I don't follow orders very well. You just hang tight, okay?" He almost smiled at the stream of profanity she hurled at him.

"Very well." Locke was back on the line. *"Tomorrow at one o'clock in the afternoon. You will receive specific instructions at noon. If I, or any of my people, have so much as a hint you've notified the authorities, she dies, and then I will hunt you down and kill you too. Do we understand each other."*

"Yes to the first part. As to the second, you're welcome to try your luck any time." At that moment, Dane would have liked nothing more than a shot at Locke, but he had Angel to think about.

"How I do love bravado." Locke chuckled. *"By the way, don't believe her when she says she doesn't want you to come for her. She made some very interesting admissions under sedation."*

Dane was about to tell Locke exactly where he could stick his advice, but heavy footsteps on deck distracted him momentarily, and he looked around to see Willis and Corey hurry in.

"Maddock," Willis began, "Angel was at the museum, but she's gone."

Dane nodded and turned away.

"Just make sure you've got her there tomorrow."

"It's a date, then," Locke said. *"Be sure to dress smart."*

The call ended and Dane stared at his phone for a moment before tucking it in his pocket.

"They'll trade Angel for the map and the dagger. They don't know we've already found the spear."

"A trade's not good enough." Bones took a deep breath, holding in his anger. "I want to hurt somebody, and I really don't want to give them the dagger."

"We might not have to," Dane said. "I've got a plan."

CHAPTER 26

Avery looked out at Baltimore's Inner Harbor, drinking in the sunshine and watching the boats zip across the gray waters of the harbor. She looked to the southeast to see if she could catch a glimpse of Fort McHenry, but the distance was too great. All around her, tourists swarmed like insects, visiting the various attractions, including historic ships and the National Aquarium. Despite the pungent air that carried a hint of rotting fish beneath the damp salt smell, it was a pleasant enough place. She looked across the harbor to the west, where she could just make out the shape of the *U.S.S. Constellation,* and wondered how Maddock fared.

"Miss Halsey? I'm Director Sweeney." A dark haired man with a thick circle beard approached, smiling, and shook Avery's hand.

"Thank you so much for meeting me on short notice." Avery put on her most coquettish smile. "I know how busy you must be, and here you are giving us a private tour."

"Not a problem. We don't get many college professors here, and none from Canada that I can remember. Certainly none as attractive as you." He leaned in just a little too close. Oh well, flirting was part of her strategy, so she couldn't blame the guy for responding.

"Aren't you sweet?" She reached out and gave his arm the gentlest touch. "I'd like you to meet Corey, he's my graduate assistant."

Sweeney's smile, which had faltered when he saw Corey, returned immediately.

"Good to meet you." He shook Corey's hand and turned back to Avery. "I thought for a minute he might be your husband. I was afraid I was going to have to get jealous."

"Nope. Single as they come." Avery wriggled the fingers on her left hand, calling attention to her bare ring finger. She hated this girly-girl crap, and the guy probably deserved better than to be manipulated, but this was too important to let feelings get in the way.

"Well, if you're ready to see the lighthouse, we'll go on in."

Seven Foot Knoll was like no lighthouse she'd ever seen. The squat, round metal building, painted barn red, was supported by a stilt-like metal framework and topped by a short beacon.

"It looks like some Wisconsin dairy farmers tried to build a UFO," Corey observed.

Sweeney flashed him an annoyed look, but quickly forced a smile.

"It's called a screw pile lighthouse. The supports, or piles, are screwed into the sea bottom or river bottom and the lighthouse is built atop them. It's not the design most people think of, but it's not uncommon. This is the oldest screw pile in Maryland."

Avery could tell by the look in Corey's eyes that he was about to make a really bad pun, and shook her head. She had no doubt this was Bones' influence.

"I guess these have the advantage of not having to waterproof them against the rising tides?" Avery asked, feigning interest.

"Very astute," Sweeney said, leading them up a staircase to the deck that encircled the lighthouse. "Of course, the primary advantages were their relative cheapness and ease of construction. Here we are." He opened the door and ushered them inside.

The interior was well-lit by the sunlight streaming through windows all around. Avery gushed over the various displays, asking detailed questions about the model ships and other exhibits, while Corey wandered around pretending to take notes.

Their plan was simple. Avery would keep Sweeney distracted while Corey found the chest and removed the map. She'd told him how to open the compartment, and hoped he wouldn't be too clumsy about it.

"Is that the Mayflower?" She pointed to a model high on a shelf.

"Good eye. She doesn't really belong in a Maryland museum, but she's a personal favorite of mine." He shrugged and gave her an embarrassed smile.

"I thought I detected a touch of Massachusetts in your accent."

"Wow. Nothing gets past you. You ought to be a federal agent." Sweeney winked.

Out of the corner of her eye, she saw that Corey had found the chest, and her pulse quickened. Now was the moment. Cursing herself for what she was about to do, she pulled Sweeney's head down and kissed him, at the same time turning him around so his back was to Corey. He tensed, then relaxed and put his arms around her and kissed her back. It wasn't the worst kiss in the world, but she'd never been one to use her sexuality to manipulate a guy, which made this all the more uncomfortable. That, and she sort of had a thing for Bones, and hoped Corey wouldn't say anything to him about this.

Hurry up Corey.

The kiss stretched beyond all natural and

comfortable limits, and Sweeney started to pull away. Avery tangled her fingers in his hair and held on.

"Ahem!"

Avery broke the kiss and saw Corey standing beside them, an amused smile on his face.

"Sorry to interrupt, but we have a plane to catch." He tapped his watch. "We need to head out."

"Oh." Sweeney was clearly disappointed. "Do you need a ride to the airport?"

"That's good of you, but we're flying out of Dulles, and we're in a rental car." She gave his arm a squeeze. "Thank you so much for showing us the museum. I'll text you next time I'm in town."

"Sounds good." He still seemed a bit dazed. "I'll email you. You know, so we can keep in touch."

They left as quickly as they could without rousing suspicion. It wasn't until they were crossing the Harbor Bridge Walk that she felt comfortable asking the question that was foremost on her mind.

"Did you get it?"

"Yep." He unzipped his jacket, pulled out a brass cylinder, and handed it to her.

The smooth metal was cool to the touch and she held it in trembling fingers, excited by the thrill of discovery. She couldn't wait to take a look. She removed the end cap and withdrew the paper inside. Passing the cylinder back to Corey, she unrolled the paper, revealing another map. She wanted to take time to examine it, but suddenly felt a keen sense of vulnerability. She was standing in a very public place, and Locke's men could be anywhere.

"Hold this, and don't you dare drop it!" She handed Corey the map, took out her phone, snapped a few pictures of it, then uploaded them to a private album. "Better safe than sorry," she explained. Before she could return it to the cylinder, Corey frowned and looked over her shoulder.

"That guy keeps staring at us."

Avery glanced over her shoulder and gasped. It was one of the men who had chased them at St. Paul's church. She looked away, but not before their eyes met. She saw recognition in his face, and he began walking toward them.

"Get out of here!" Corey gave her a push in the back to get her moving, and then followed along behind her.

"What do we do?"

"He sees I've got the cylinder. When we get to the next bridge, I'll lead him away. You blend in with the crowd and make your way back to the street and meet up with Matt. You and the map need to stay out of their hands."

"But, you..."

"There's the bridge. Go!"

Before she could protest, Corey took off in the opposite direction. Avery hated to leave him to the mercy of Locke's men, but what could she do? Cursing him under her breath, she weaved through a crowd of college kids who were poking along, taking in the sights. When she reached the end of the second bridge, she stole a glance behind her.

Corey's ruse had not worked. The man was after her.

Dane stood on the deck of the *U.S.S. Constellation,* a nineteenth-century sloop-of-war. The last remaining intact Civil War ship and one of the last sailing warships built by the United States Navy, she had also seen action in both World Wars prior to her final decommissioning in 1955. She was now a National

Historical Landmark and served as a floating museum and attraction.

"Right on time, I see." Locke seemed to materialize out of the crowd. The man was good. He stopped a few feet from Dane. "Do you have them?" His tone was relaxed, as if they were two friends engaged in a casual conversation.

"Where's Angel?" Dane hated feeling he was at Locke's mercy. Hopefully, their plan would turn the tables.

By way of answer, Locke pointed toward the harbor, where a speedboat floated fifty feet from *Constellation's* stern. A man stood guard over the hunched figure of a dark-skinned young woman. She was gagged, her hands were bound, and her face was a mask of bruises. Anger surged through him.

"You bastard. I'll kill you for that."

"Not today, unless you want your girl to meet the same fate. Now, give it here and don't try anything foolish." He held out his hand.

It was only by supreme force of will that Dane did not knock the man's teeth down his throat. He looked again at the speedboat, and spotted an odd disturbance in the water by its stern. Good!

"Fine. But I want Angel released now." He slid the backpack he'd been wearing over one shoulder, and handed it to Locke.

"Of course." The lie was evident in his eyes. Locke opened it just enough to expose the dagger's white hilt. He fished deeper into the backpack and withdrew a clear plastic bag that held the map. "Very good. Now..."

He cut off in mid-sentence as two men, so pale they looked almost like albinos, converged on him. Somewhere in the crowd of tourists, someone yelled, "Stop right there!"

And then it all went to hell.

Bones hauled himself over the speedboat's stern, careful not to make a sound. At his hip, the dagger gently vibrated, concealing him from sight. He wondered, absently if someone who looked in his direction would see water dripping from... nothing. He wasn't about to waste time finding out.

There were two men in the boat: one at the helm and the other standing behind Angel. He wore a pistol at his hip, but his arms hung loosely at his side. Both were staring up at *Constellation,* where Maddock and Locke should be making the exchange right about now.

Bones crept up behind the guard and, fast as lightning, slipped the gun from its holster, clamped his free hand over the man's mouth and nose, and pressed the gun to his temple.

"Don't move and don't make a sound," he whispered, quiet enough not to be heard by the man in the helm over the sound of the idling engine. The man froze. If the barrel of a gun against his temple wasn't enough to guarantee his cooperation, the shock of being held by an invisible enemy did it. "Down on your knees."

The man complied instantly. Bones clubbed him across the back of the head with the pistol and he crumpled to the ground.

Angel still sat slumped forward, and hadn't seen him. Even though she was gagged, if he frightened her, she might cry out and alert the man at the helm, so he reached down and pressed the dagger, turning off the cloak.

"Angel, it's me." He kept his voice soft. "I'm getting you out of here."

Angel sat up fast and jerked her head around.

It wasn't Angel.

"Who are you?" Bones whispered, forgetting for a moment the danger and that the girl couldn't speak. "Never mind. Let's go." He helped her to her feet, removed her gag, and led her to the stern.

"What's happening?" she whispered, her voice trembling.

Just then, chaos erupted on the *Constellation*. An instant later, the boat lurched forward as the man at the helm made a beeline for the sailing ship's stern.

The woman was thrown off balance and tumbled into the water. For a split second, Bones considered letting her swim for it. If he waited on the boat, maybe he could ambush Locke, but the woman had sank out of sight and showed no sign of surfacing.

His decision was made for him when a bullet zipped past his head. Someone on shore had spotted him. Cursing his luck, he dove into the dark water.

Avery hurried on, looking back on occasion, only to see the guy gaining on her. Every time she thought she'd lost him in a crowd, he turned up again— sometimes ahead of her, sometimes behind her, but always closer. She looked around for a police officer, security guard, anyone who might offer some help, but there was no one.

As desperate panic welled inside her, her eyes fell on an oblong, modern building of gray metal and glass. The National Aquarium. Surely they'd have a security staff there. She made a beeline for the front door. Let them bust her for gate crashing. She'd be safer in custody than out here pursued by Locke's man. She circled around an arguing young couple and there he was again. He stood twenty feet away barring her way to the entrance, smiling.

"No more of this foolish chase. Give it to me and you can be on your way."

She didn't even think. She just ran. Behind her, she heard him call out, more in annoyance than surprise, and then she heard his feet pounding the concrete, hot on her tail.

She rounded the building and saw a man in a work uniform unlocking a side door.

"Hold on!" she cried, adding a burst of speed she hadn't thought she had at her disposal. The man gaped as she sprinted past him, crashed through a set of double doors, and clambered up a staircase to her left.

She had only a moment to consider where she might be. It definitely wasn't any sort of public area. At the top of the stairs, she brushed past a girl in a polo shirt and khaki shorts, causing the girl to spill her bucket of chum or something equally stinky.

"Hey! You can't go that way! That's..."

Whatever it was, Avery didn't know because her pursuer chose that moment to take a shot at her. Avery and the girl both screamed as the roar of the gunshot filled the stairwell and the bullet tore through the ceiling. The door in front of her was propped open and Avery dashed through.

Big mistake.

She had only a split second to realize her mistake and then she was flying through the air. She flailed her arms and legs as if she could take wing, and then she splashed down into deep water. As momentum and the weight of her sodden clothes dragged her down, she kicked and paddled, trying to arrest her descent. When she finally got herself headed back up to the surface, she opened her eyes. Another mistake.

The cold salt water stung but that wasn't the worst

part. A dark gray shape swam into view, bearing down on her. A shark! She had run right into one of the tanks. She opened her mouth to scream as the creature came closer, and choked on a mouthful of salt water. If the shark didn't get her, she'd likely drown.

She watched in horror as distance between her and the fierce aquatic predator shrank. Ten feet. Five feet.

And then the shark veered to the side at the last instant, its rough hide brushing her bare arm. And then it was gone. For a moment she hung there, shocked into immobility by her close call. Looking down, she saw the ghostlike shapes of aquarium visitors watching her through the glass. She wondered if they thought they were seeing a performance, or if they realized what was really happening.

And then she looked directly beneath her. There wasn't one shark in the tank, there were a half dozen, and they were circling. All thoughts fell away except the need to get the hell out of that tank and fast. The map, the man with the gun, Maddock and Bones' attempt to save Angel, all forgotten. She fought for the surface with everything she had, but no matter how hard she swam, it seemed to come no closer. She felt as if an invisible hand were holding her underwater, inches from precious air and a chance at safety.

Suddenly, she broke the surface, gasping for air. Half blinded by the salt water, she swam for the edge, wondering when the feeding frenzy would begin. Her vision cleared as she reached the side and found herself staring at a pair of shiny, black shoes. She looked up into the barrel of a gun.

"Dead end," the man said. "Now, give me the map."

The map! What had she done with it? She remembered tucking it into her bra when Corey first hurried her away from their pursuer.

"It's right here." She reached her numb fingers into her shirt and pulled out a sodden wad of brown paper. "It got a little wet." She held it up to the man, wondering if she might be able to pull him down into the water when he reached for the map, but he stood stock-still.

"You carried it into the water?" He trembled, either from shock or rage, and his finger twitched on the trigger.

"I didn't exactly plan to jump into a shark tank. It might not be ruined. Take it."

"You've bloody well ruined it, I'm sure." He chewed on his lip, thinking for a moment, and then his eyes lit up. "But you got a look at it."

"No," Avery said immediately. "I didn't have a chance before you came after us."

"We'll soon find out. We have people who are very good at getting answers. Now come on."

She heard a sick thud, and the man's eyes rolled back in his head. His knees buckled and he tumbled into the tank. Jimmy stood there, smiling, holding the lid of a toilet tank.

"I passed a bathroom on the way up. It was the only heavy thing I could grab."

"I'm glad you did. Here, pull me up." She was surprised at the strength with which he hoisted her up. He'd never seemed very physical. "Thank you." She gave him a quick hug. "Now, let's get out of here."

"I'm afraid you *will* be leaving," said a voice behind Jimmy. Two police officers stood, weapons drawn. "But it's going to be with us."

Chapter 27

As the two men converged on him, Locke whirled about and made a dash for the stern rail. Surprised by the sudden chaos, Dane was an instant late with his attempt at tackling the fleeing man. Three strides and Locke vanished over the edge. Dane regained his feet in time to see Locke swimming for the speedboat, which was on its way to pick him up. Angel was no longer aboard, and he soon spotted Bones helping her swim to shore.

Relieved, he turned around just as shots rang out. One of the attackers was firing wildly into the crowd, which broke apart as everyone fled for safety. His partner had gone over the rail after Locke, but he wasn't a strong swimmer and was losing ground with every stroke.

Dane didn't know who these guys were, and what he really wanted was to get the hell out of there, but he couldn't let this madman kill an innocent person. He sprang onto the gunman, pinning the man's arm to his side as he wrestled him to the ground. He wound up on top of the man, one hand pinning his gun hand to the ground, the other at his throat.

"Who are you?"

The man's blue eyes, so pale as to almost be white, shone with icy contempt. He worked his lips and then spat on Dane. Dane raised his fist, intending to turn the guy's nose into a waffle, but a sharp voice rang out.

"Hold it right there! CIA!"

Dane froze as three men, weapons trained on him, came running up.

"Put your hands in the air," one of them barked.

"I will as soon as you relieve this guy of his weapon." He wasn't about to give the albino a chance to take a shot at him or anyone else.

In an instant, the government agents, all clad in plain clothes, had him and the other man cuffed. They were patting him down when a familiar voice rang out.

"Oh no! Oh *hell* no!"

As he turned his head to face the music, he couldn't help but smile.

Tam Broderick was an attractive woman, with a solid, athletic build, dark skin, and big eyes. At least, she was pretty enough when she didn't look like she was about to waterboard someone. They'd met under unusual circumstances and forged a temporary alliance. Since then, they'd spoken a couple of times, but only to discuss a situation he and Bones had stepped into the previous winter. She marched up to Dane, her hand resting on the Makarov he knew she carried, and stopped, her face inches from his.

"Dane Maddock." She spoke his name like a curse. "Every time I get a lead on the Dominion, you stick your big, ugly nose in and jack it all up."

"My nose is not big," he said. "I know for a fact that you like my nose."

"Save the wise comments or I will cut you." She was still angry, livid in fact, but there was now a flicker of amusement behind her glower. "Now tell me, why does the Dominion keep following you around?"

Her words hadn't registered the first time, but now they brought him up short.

"Wait. Locke is with the Dominion?" The Dominion was a shadowy organization about which little was known, yet Dane and Bones had a knack for running afoul of them. Had it happened again?

"Who is Locke?" She threw her hands up in the air.

"The guy who went over the side. The first guy, that is. He kidnapped Bones' sister and we were getting her back." He looked around, wondering where Bones had gone.

"And you didn't think to notify the authorities? Never mind, don't bother." Tam sighed. "Let him go, but take mister pale and pasty into custody, and see if you can fish his partner out of the harbor." She turned and looked down into the water. "Don't hurry. Looks like he's a floater." Tam put her hands on her hips and fixed Dane with a disapproving stare while her man uncuffed him. "Give him his weapon back," she said. The agent gave her a quizzical look, but followed orders.

"Where are the rest of your boys?"

"Matt's waiting in the getaway vehicle. Willis is down below, incognito, as it were, and Bones and Angel ought to be climbing out of the water by now."

"Let me get this straight." Tam pressed her fingertips to her temples. "You boys tried to stage your own rescue operation in the middle of the Inner Harbor, where who knows how many innocent people could have gotten killed?"

"We didn't choose the location," Dane said. "And yes, we rescued Angel."

"No we didn't." Bones and Willis, both in handcuffs, were being ushered to Tam by a pair of agents.

"What do you mean?" Dane felt cold all over. "I saw you with her."

Bones shook his head.

"It wasn't her. They found a girl her size and coloring, then beat her beyond recognition." Bones glared out at the water, as if he could take flight and chase down Locke and his men.

"Where do you think she is?" Dane couldn't remember feeling more helpless.

"Enough!" Tam shouted. "I want to know who the hell this Locke is and why you almost got a whole mess of civilians killed out here."

"Calm down, girl," Willis said. He and Tam had fought side-by-side in the Amazon, and were on friendly terms. "Nobody likes an angry black woman."

"I am not an angry woman, I just have a low tolerance for stupidity." She glared at Willis until the smug grin melted from his face. "I suppose you can take the cuffs off of these two dummies too, and give them their weapons back. You boys won't try to run, will you?"

Bones and Willis shook their heads, both looking like chastened schoolboys.

"Even the dagger?" the agent standing behind Bones asked, holding up Carnwennan.

Tam's eyes narrowed as she looked at the odd weapon.

"What kind of knife is that?" She took it from the agent and held up for a closer look. "You boys have a whole mess of explaining to do."

"I know," Dane said. "But not until we go somewhere private, and the sooner the better. We've got to find out what Locke's done with Angel."

"Fine," Tam sighed. "I commandeered an office downstairs. We'll go there."

"Do you want us to go with you, Ma'am?" The agent who had handed her the dagger looked at Dane and the others like they were about to sprout fangs.

"No. Just take the lead here. You know what to do." When the agent looked uncertain, she raised her voice. "Agent Paul, as hard as it might be to believe, I owe my life to these three stooges. I'll take one man to guard the door, but that's it. I'll be safe with them. Besides, they just might be able to help us." She turned back to Dane. "Come on. This sounds like it's going to be a long story."

On the way downstairs, Dane remembered something.

"So, when did you become CIA? Last I knew, you were FBI."

"Oh, right about the time somebody stirred up a branch of the Dominion in Germany." Her glare left no doubt whom she meant. "All of a sudden our little domestic problem became international."

"Hey, I filled you in on that right away," Dane protested.

"Yes you did." She sounded neither pleased nor upset. "Funny how you keep butting heads with the Dominion, but you don't want to join in the fight against them."

Dane didn't bother to argue. They'd had this conversation before. The previous summer, Tam had asked him and his crew to join her in her work rooting out the Dominion.

When they settled into the small office in the museum section of the *Constellation*, he wasted no time bringing her up to speed.

"So, we've got the dagger and the spear, but Locke still has Angel," he finished.

Tam looked down at the dagger lying across her lap.

"You're telling me this thing is..."

"Carnwennan. King Arthur's dagger. We also have

his spear."

"Oh, holy Lord Jesus." She rested her head in her hands. "Would it kill you to have an ordinary life?" She sighed for what felt like the twentieth time, and handed him the dagger. "You really expect me to believe not only was King Arthur real, but that thing belonged to him? It doesn't exactly look ancient."

"Think about what we found in the Amazon," Bones said. "Then ask yourself if this seems any more unlikely."

"I don't suppose it does, at that, but it's hard to get used to." She stood and moved to the window that looked out on the harbor. "You've got the spear and the dagger. Aren't you missing something important?"

Dane, Bones, and Willis exchanged glances. They'd discussed this very subject. The way they saw it, the final map could only lead to one thing.

"We have a lead on one more map," Dane said. "My sister is looking into it."

"Avery Halsey?" Tam turned around and grinned at him. "You finally found her?"

"Yeah, she's... Wait a minute! You knew about her?" Dane trusted Tam, but to find out she'd been keeping a secret like this hidden from him? It was hard to swallow.

"Not until recently. I've done my homework on you and your whole posse. By the way," she turned to Willis, "there's a stripper in Detroit who said to tell you the baby is yours."

"What?" Willis gaped at her.

"Don't worry about it. I checked. The boy's daddy is a five foot nothing Latino." She smirked.

Willis sagged, visibly relieved.

"How do you know all this stuff?" Bones asked.

"I'm with the government, sweetie. We've got

resources you've never dreamed of."

"Any other long lost relatives I should know about?" Dane asked, only half-jokingly.

"Oh no. You don't get access to privileged information." She paused. "Unless you're ready to take me up on my offer."

Dane grimaced. Arguing with Tam was pointless. She was one of the most focused people he'd ever met.

"You never told us how you wound up here," Bones said. "What's the Dominion's connection to all this?"

"I don't know how they're connected. For months I've mostly combed through the phone and financial records of suspected leaders in the Dominion, but I haven't gotten anything solid. Just suspects from every walk of Christendom. And then, after not hearing a peep from them since your Christmas vacation..."

"Shitter was full!" Bones said in his best Cousin Eddie voice.

Tam went on as if he hadn't spoken.

"...we finally got a hit on Heilig Herrschaft. You know, your German Dominion buddies. Two suspected members, twin brothers, were instructed to be here at one o'clock today and to intercept something the Dominion wanted. We were waiting for them to make their move, so we could get them and whatever it was they were after."

"And then Maddock screwed it up," Bones finished.

Dane ignored the jibe. His thoughts drifted back to something Tam had said moments before. She had tremendous resources at her disposal. But would she agree to help them?

"Tam, look, I'm sorry we interfered. You do know we had no way of knowing the Dominion was involved?"

She sat down in an antique wooden chair and

drummed her red lacquered fingernails on the armrest.

"I'm sensing you've got more to say and, whatever it is, it's going to make me cuss. I don't even have my swear jar here."

"We need help finding Angel. The only clues we have are Locke and the museum. For all we know, they've taken her to England. We don't have a prayer of tracking her down, but you can." He took a deep breath. "Please?"

Despite her prediction, Tam didn't cuss. She stared at him for a full ten seconds. Bones and Willis looked on, afraid to break the silence. Finally, her features softened.

"You've got a thing for this girl, don't you?"

Dane couldn't stop his face from reddening, nor could he keep himself from looking at Bones. To his surprise, both Bones and Willis looked to be on the verge of laughter.

"The lady asked you a question, Maddock." Bones crossed his arms and smiled expectantly.

Dane couldn't find his voice.

"Wait a minute!" Willis laughed and slapped his thighs. "You'd take on a whole army with nothing but your bare hands and never flinch, but can't admit you like a girl?"

"He doesn't like her," Bones said. "He loves her. He can't hide something like that from me."

"I want to hear it from him," Tam said, clearly enjoying the moment. "Well?"

"Maybe," Dane said, watching as the others exchanged frustrated looks. How could he make them understand? After the way his wife had died, he felt... cursed. Like he'd bring misfortune onto the next woman he truly loved. He knew that wouldn't fly with any of them, though.

"Dane Maddock," Tam took on the lecturing tone of a middle school teacher scolding an underachieving student, "it's no wonder you won't join up with me. Willis is right. You're not afraid of dying. You're afraid of real commitment."

"No I'm not. I'm a decorated veteran in case you've forgotten."

"I know that. I also know when and why you quit the service." She looked like she wanted to say more, but a knock at the door interrupted her. A moment later, the agent standing guard ushered Matt into the room. He greeted Tam and then turned to Dane.

"When I saw the Feds had taken over here, and you guys hadn't shown, I figured my getaway driver services were no longer needed. Anyway, I just got a call from Corey. He and Avery have been arrested."

"You've got to be kidding me. Is it at least a real arrest? Locke doesn't have them too?"

"No. One of Locke's men chased them into the National Aquarium and Avery wound up jumping into the shark tank, or falling in, or something. Corey bashed the guy's skull pretty good. It's a mess."

Dane groaned and closed his eyes. When he opened them, he saw Tam grinning at him like a cat who had cornered a mouse.

"I guess I might need two favors."

"Join my team and I will. We can wait til all this is over to work out all the details. I've got a place for all four of you, plus the little nerd boy."

"Dude, are you seriously blackmailing us?" Bones anger was returning.

"Excuse me? You forget, I know *all* about you. If I wanted to blackmail you, I could have done it long ago. Defacing national historical sites?"

"That was Maddock." Bones pointed at Dane.

"The Fremont ruins?"

"Okay, that was sort of me." Bones said.

"Desecrating graves?"

"It was only one grave," Dane said, "and I didn't exactly..."

"Kidnapping a patient from a hospital in Utah."

"Me again." Bones raised his hand.

"Missing Italian nationals who, rumor has it, were sent after you."

"Good. I was feeling left out," Wills said to Bones.

"Bringing down half a mountain in Jordan. Lord only knows what you did in Utah. Breaking and entering all across Germany. And," she paused for effect, "we found the bodies in that well."

There was nothing Dane could say. Everything she mentioned had an explanation, a greater purpose, or was a case of self-defense, but they'd never be able to defend themselves in court. The cumulative weight of the charges against them was too great.

"But, as I said, if I wanted to blackmail you, I would have already done it. I've been in the field with you. I know what you can do. I trust you." She stood and offered her hand to Dane. "I'll get your friend and your sister out, and I'll help you get your girl. But you've got to help me."

Dane looked at Bones, Willis, and Matt. They exchanged glances, then all nodded solemnly.

"All right." Dane clasped Tam's hand. "You've got a deal."

CHAPTER 28

Dane sat aboard the jet Tam had secured for a flight to England, waiting for takeoff and for her to tell him what she had learned. He passed the time by scrolling through the pictures they'd taken of the two underground Templar churches they'd discovered. It wasn't long before something caught his attention.

"Hey guys, check this out," he said to Bones and Avery who were seated behind him. "You see how, right at the top of the ceiling in both of these places, there's this pie-shaped carving?" He clicked between the images to illustrate his point. "They aren't exactly the same, but don't they look like pieces of a map?"

"You might be on to something," Bones agreed.

"Each one is about one third of a circle. I'll bet, when we find the last chamber, we'll find the missing piece."

"And that will lead us, where?" Bones mused.

"I don't know. I'm going to message Jimmy and ask him to see if he can match it up to any known locations." Just then, Tam arrived.

"All right. Here's what I've got." She took the seat next to Dane. Bones and Avery listened in, as did the others, who were seated all around.. "Locke is former MI6. He was a rising star with an exemplary record, but he left unexpectedly to go to work for this woman." She held out a photograph of a blue-eyed blonde woman of early middle years.

"Smoking hot!" Bones said.

"Oh, is that what you like?" Avery snapped.

"I just like women." Bones smiled at Avery who made a face at him.

"Morgan Fain. She is the director of the British History Museum in Truro. The same museum that owns the Bailyn."

"Wait a minute." Avery cupped her chin, thinking. "One of the biggest treasure hunts on Oak Island was conducted by the Truro Syndicate back in the mid-1800's. Could there be a connection?"

"Hers is an old and powerful family, so maybe."

"Truro. That's kind of off the beaten path, isn't it?" Dane asked. He'd imagined any powerful players in England would be based out of London.

"It works for her." Tam said, returning the photograph to the folder and pulling out a sheet of paper. "She has political aspirations, and she's set herself up as an outsider. She's never held public office, but she writes editorials for the biggest newspapers in Britain, and makes guest appearances on news shows. Ninety percent of the time, she's talking politics, not history. When she does talk history, it's about England's past greatness."

"That doesn't sound so bad," Avery said.

"Her underlying message, and I'm paraphrasing here, is that the lowlifes and scum are dragging all of the United Kingdom down, and they've got to go. She wants all the resources that go to supporting the bottom feeders to go toward re-establishing their military strength and political influence. She even thinks Ireland should bend the knee and join the United Kingdom. I won't go so far as to say she sounds like Hitler, she's too smart to talk like that, but I don't think she'd be too disappointed if the people she thinks are not 'true Britons' vanished off the face of the earth."

"Plenty of American politicians talk that way," Dane observed.

"True, but there's more here than meets the eye. I don't know for sure how the pieces fit together, but here's what I've got. People have been begging her to run for Parliament for years, even talk about her being a shoo-in for Prime Minister, but she won't do it, even though it's obvious that's her long-term goal."

"It's like she's waiting for something," Dane said. "What else do we know about her?"

"She's also got people working hard to strengthen her royal bloodline. There's no question she has royal blood but, rumor has it, she thinks she has a better claim to the throne than the current monarch or her heirs."

"Who is she tracing her roots back to that she could make such a claim?" Avery looked puzzled.

"Arthur," Dane said, half to himself. "Think about it. If she can produce Arthur's weapons as proof that he was an actual, historical figure, and as evidence that she's his heir, wouldn't that capture the minds and hearts of the British people?"

"It's not enough," Avery said. "Even if she could convince people the weapons aren't fakes, that won't prove she's descended from Arthur."

"But if she finds his body, DNA testing certainly could," Bones said. "Hey, if he really lived, and it looks like he did, that means his body's got to be somewhere, doesn't it?"

"Even then, the Queen's not going to abdicate," Avery argued.

"Not voluntarily." Tam's tone was dark. "If half of

the rumors we've gathered are true, Morgan's reach is broad, and she's got people in all segments of society who are devoted to her. The Dominion agent we captured mentioned something called "The Sisterhood," but clammed up when I mentioned her name. He seemed scared. Anyway, she lives in a castle, a compound, really, outside of Truro, and her private staff is all ex-military or ex-intelligence. Guys like Locke. When I put this all together, it paints a grim picture."

"You think, once she's got her connection to Arthur established, she'll move into the political arena," Dane began, thinking it through as he spoke, "become Prime Minister, and then..."

"She uses her connections to make sure something terrible and permanent happens to the Queen," Bones continued.

"Not long afterward, it's revealed that the beloved Prime Minister is descended from the legendary King Arthur," Dane finished.

"I'm not convinced she's going to wait that long," Tam said. "She's hosting an event this weekend at her estate, and the Queen will be there."

"Only the Queen?" Dane asked. "What about the rest of the Royal Family."

"Morgan might act now and step into the gap later. She might figure if she cuts off the head, the monarchy will fall. Who can tell?" Tam shrugged.

"Have you notified the British authorities?" Dane asked.

"I've told our people what I suspect, but I did not tell them anything about King Arthur, which makes my suspicions pretty flimsy. What do I really have but a bunch of theories about a politically connected woman who doesn't seem very ambitious? On paper, she looks like an upstanding citizen, if maybe a bit too conservative for some people. She gives a lot of money to charity. She supports genetic research to fight all sorts of diseases. They even named the reptile house at the London Zoo for her because of all the money she gave them. She ain't bulletproof, but she's close."

"Queen and Prime Minister," Avery said. "And if she can find a way to harness the power of Arthur's weapons, replicate it, even, there's no telling what she could do."

Tam nodded thoughtfully.

"An army that can become truly invisible. Objects that can amplify rays of light into powerful energy weapons."

"You'd never have to reload," Willis said.

"And we haven't even found the final piece of the puzzle," Matt added.

"Okay, you've convinced us she's up to no good. But what have you found out about Angel?"

"We've got her arriving in England, alive, with Locke." Tam handed him a grainy printout of a frame of security footage. "We've got her being put in a van." She handed him another printout. "And a van like this one showed up at Morgan's headquarters an hour ago." She took a deep breath. "I can get you in and out of the country, and I can give you what you need to pull off this rescue, but I can't be directly involved and neither can my people. It's on you."

"I understand," Dane said. "Now, tell me all you know about this compound."

CHAPTER 29

"Who the hell are you?" Angel said to the man who opened the door. He was a solidly built black man with a shaved head. As he stepped into the room, she revised her opinion. He wasn't just solid, he was built like a rhinoceros.

"Jacob." His soft voice stood at stark odds with his build. He stopped in the center of the room and stared at her. There was no kindness in his eyes, nor was there cruelty. He was a blank slate.

"You don't look like a Jacob. You look more like a Rufus." Perhaps she shouldn't cop an attitude with these people, but she was resigned to the fact that they were going to kill her, so she really didn't care what they thought of her. If her needling made them kill her sooner, fine. She was tired of being held captive.

Jacob didn't answer. He hoisted her to her feet and walked her toward the door.

"You don't say much. Are you stupid or something?"

"No," he replied, just as softly as before. He steered her along a featureless hallway of gray stone that ended at a suit of armor.

"How the hell do you get lost in a freaking hallway? Remind me not to let you navigate next time. You probably don't even stop to ask directions, do you?"

This time she didn't even get a one-word answer

out of him. He pushed up the face guard on the helmet, revealing a number pad, punched in a code, and stepped back as the suit of armor swung forward, revealing an elevator.

"Where am I, some kind of Scooby Doo haunted castle?" She realized her chatter was covering for a rising fear she thought she'd worked past early in her captivity. Truth was, she wasn't eager to die, no matter what she told herself.

"You're at Modron, on Bodmin Moor near Truro," Jacob said as the elevator door closed and they began to descend.

"Okay, now I wish I'd paid attention in Geography class." She'd hoped that might have elicited a smile or a chuckle from Jacob. Any sign of emotion would be welcome at this point. "So, where are you taking me?"

"Morgan wants to see you."

"Captain Morgan? I could go for a drink right now." Still no emotion.

The elevator came to a stop and the door opened onto an octagonal room with blue carpet, a television, and a rack of nasty looking weapons. Angel stepped out onto the soft carpet and looked around.

"Cool dungeon, bro."

"It's merely my exercise room." She hadn't noticed the woman standing off to the side. She was about Angel's height, but fair and blonde. "This is where I hone myself to a fine edge."

"I take it you're Morgan."

"I am. And you are no longer of use to us." Morgan stared at her as if expecting a reply.

"Yeah, I don't play well with others, especially when they kidnap me."

"Fortunately for you, that time is at an end."

Angel's stomach lurched and she looked at the

weapons rack. Was this where she was to die? She swallowed hard.

"Cool. So I can go, right?"

"Yes. After you fight me." This time Morgan did smile, but there was neither laughter nor guile in her eyes. She was serious.

"That's stupid. If you're going to let me leave, just point me to the door and I'll be gone. No need for anybody to get hurt."

"That is my condition, the same one I give everyone who is of no use. Fight me. If you win, you leave by the front door. If I win, you leave by the back door. It's all very simple."

"Right. I win and your lackey shoots me in the back, I suppose."

"No. I meant what I said. Leave with honor or leave in disgrace, but you will not leave until you fight me. Locke thinks you might afford me a challenge."

"You're crazy. I guess you want to fight with those swords and spears and crap?" Angel hoped the answer was "no." Knife fighting she could handle. Maybe a spear, if it was anything like a bo staff. But a sword? No way. And she didn't even recognize some of the weapons, which looked medieval and more than a little sinister.

"If you wish. I prefer hand to hand fighting," Morgan said.

"Mano a mano, huh?" Angel stared into Morgan's eyes for a full five seconds, waiting for any indication that this was all a big joke. No dice. As she stared, she reminded herself that this woman was apparently the boss, which meant she was the one responsible for Angel's kidnapping. Now she stood there, the arrogant cow, wanting to fight her. Fine. If there was one thing Angel knew how to do, it was fight. "All right. Take these cuffs off of me and let's do this."

Jacob removed her cuffs and Angel took a moment to rub her wrists and work the kinks out of her shoulders. This wasn't an ideal situation. She'd been captive for a few days now, and her body wasn't at its best. There was nothing for it now. She took a deep breath, turned, and faced Morgan.

"Say when."

Morgan raised her fists and flowed gracefully into a fighting stance. Despite her beauty queen appearance, she looked like she knew what she was doing. They circled one another, eyes locked.

Angel snapped a quick jab which Morgan evaded with ease. She'd obviously done this before. Angel had better take her seriously.

Morgan whipped a roundhouse kick that Angel checked and answered with a kick of her own that just missed. If she was fit and warmed up, she'd have landed it. Morgan grabbed Angel's leg and tried to take her down, but Angel kept her balance and fought free. They traded kicks, to little effect, and Angel missed with a jab.

Now Morgan sprang forward with a flurry of punches. Angel blocked them, landed an elbow that split Morgan's cheek, and followed with a back fist that Morgan sprang back from. Angel pursued her backpedaling opponent, knocking her into the wall with a front kick, but Morgan danced away before Angel could close the gap.

It became a chess match. Morgan kept Angel at bay with kicks and jabs, always circling. She had correctly assessed that Angel was a brawler who hated this kind of fight, and thus refused to get in close. Angel's lip was bleeding, her eye was puffy from taking several solid punches, and she was wearing down. Her arms felt like they were made of lead.

Morgan feinted a jab and, when Angel raised her hand to block, drove a side kick into Angel's ribs, sending her sprawling to the carpet.

Knowing she was in serious trouble, Angel rolled to her feet before Morgan could pounce. *Okay, time to get to work.*

She stalked Morgan, watching the woman's footwork, the way she held her hands, the movements that indicated she was about to strike, looking for a pattern. Morgan pivoted her back foot, a sign that a roundhouse kick was on the way.

As Morgan's weight shifted to her front leg, Angel lashed out with a kick of her own that smacked into Morgan's kneecap. Morgan grunted in pain and tried to circle, but her leg betrayed her and she staggered.

Angel leapt into the air and drove a knee into Morgan's gut. Morgan absorbed the blow and caught Angel on the chin with a left hook, but there was no power behind it. Angel barely felt it as she grabbed Morgan by the back of the neck, held her head down, and punished her with a flurry of knees to the face and body.

Desperate, Morgan struck blindly, clawing at Angel's face, but scratches weren't going to stop her. And, if Morgan could fight like a girl, so could she. She grabbed a handful of blonde hair, slammed Morgan's hair into the wall, and followed with three hard punches to the side of the head that wobbled Morgan, followed by an uppercut that put her on the ground.

Morgan struggled to rise, made it to her knees, and fell again. She raised her battered and bloodied face, glared at Angel, and whispered two words.

"Kill her."

Chapter 30

"Here comes one." Bones stepped into the roadway and raised his hands. The delivery van slowed to a halt and the driver rolled down the window. Willis approached the vehicle, holding a clipboard.

"Is there a problem?" The driver sounded annoyed. "I'm already behind schedule."

"Modron security," he said in a lame British accent. "We need to inspect your vehicle."

"But Modron's another kilometer down the road. Why are you stopping us out here."

"Only following orders." Willis shrugged as if to say, What are you going to do? "We'll need to inspect the cab as well as the cargo bay. If you'll step out, we won't waste any more of your time than necessary."

The driver frowned, and Bones wondered if the man had picked up on Willis' fake accent. He looked Willis up and down, taking in his plain, black clothing and the radio clipped to his belt. Finally satisfied, he nodded, and he and his father climbed out of the cab.

Before the men knew what was happening, Bones and Willis had them stunned, bound, and hidden near the side of the road. Later, they'd make sure the authorities got an anonymous tip on the men's whereabouts, and they'd be sure to implicate Morgan's security staff. Matt and Corey, who had been hiding nearby, joined them.

Matt took the wheel, and Willis joined him in the cab, while Bones and Corey climbed inside the cargo area, which was packed almost to the ceiling with tents and folding chairs for the upcoming event, and rolled the door down behind them. As the truck lurched into motion, Corey fired up his laptop and prepared for his part of the job.

"This had better work," Bones muttered.

"Think positive." Corey's words rang hollow. He hated these types of situations, and much preferred to remain somewhere safe and make his contributions from a distance. Bones had to hand it to his crew mate. Corey had really stepped up the past couple of days. Perhaps his confidence would grow. "They don't have any reason to turn us away, or even inspect the truck closely. Matt and Willis have the driver's paperwork. That should be enough."

"But if they do turn us back, we're going to have to find a way past motion detectors, over an electrified fence, and past whatever other security measures they've put in place." Bones gripped his pistol and imagined how he might put it into use. Ever since Angel's abduction, he'd tried very hard to remain optimistic. Things always seemed to work out for him and Maddock, and he figured it would be the same for her. He'd even managed to block the worries from his mind, until now. He was angry and a little afraid— not for himself, but for his sister.

"Getting past those things is Maddock's job. Besides, when did you turn into a rain cloud?" Corey asked. "Usually he's the one talking about everything that could go wrong."

The truck made a sharp right, then came to a stop. They waited in tense silence, straining to hear the conversation outside, but all Bones could make out was the muffled sound of voices. His fingers itched, and he felt the sudden urge to jump out of the truck and start fighting. He stilled his rising ire and waited.

Finally, he heard the doors of the truck close and they began to move again. He and Corey exchanged relieved smiles that were quickly wiped off their faces when Willis' voice sounded in their earpieces.

"Bad news, boys. They bought the ruse, but they want their people to do the unloading. Left us standing outside the gate. Looks like you two are on your own for now. The guy at the gate is watching us close. If you need us to take him out, just call."

"Great." Bones turned to Corey. "Get as far back into the truck as you can. Make yourself a space behind the boxes. That'll buy you some time."

Even in the dim light that filtered in, he could see Corey swallow hard, color draining from his face, before clambering out of sight. Bones squeezed into a gap to one side, where he wouldn't be readily visible when the back doors opened. He waited, Glock in one hand and Recon knife in the other, but the doors did not open. A minute passed. Then another. Nothing.

"How are you coming on that hack, Corey?"

"The signal's weak, probably because we're inside a metal box, but it looks like the same system that was in place at the museum, at least the security part of it. I'll see what I can do with it." A minute later, he heard Corey's triumphant whisper. "I'm in. Are you ready?"

"Always." Bones sheathed his knife, but kept his Glock handy. Tension and exhilaration surged through him in equal measure as he raised the back door and climbed out. Now, to find Angel.

"This is a stupid idea, Maddock." Tam grimaced as she

looked him up and down. "Have you ever even used one of these things?"

"Sure. Bones talked me into it." It was the truth. He'd used a wingsuit exactly one time, though he'd found the experience exhilarating.

"From a helicopter?" Avery looked at him nervously. It was odd to once again have a family member worry about him, but it wasn't bad.

"No, but I can handle it. Trust me."

"Are you sure you don't want to use a regular parachute?" Avery asked.

"No. The wingsuit is the better choice because I can be cloaked all the way in. By the time I have to deploy my chute, I'll be well beyond their perimeter and into the forest."

"Be careful." Tam's expression was grave. "Remember, I can't come in after you. Once you jump, you're on your own until you find the girl and get off the property."

"I understand. Thanks for everything." They clasped hands briefly. "See you when I get back."

"Maddock?" Avery said, her voice tremulous.

"Yeah?"

The next thing Dane knew, she was crushing in a tight embrace. He hugged her back, a little awkwardly. When she let go, tears glistened in her eyes.

"Don't get yourself killed. We haven't finished Dad's quest yet."

Not trusting himself to answer, Dane gave her a wink, before fixing his goggles in place, taking out the dagger, and depressing the butt.

"That's seriously messed up," Tam said as he vanished.

Dane chuckled, turned, and dove out into open air.

The speed at which he descended was

breathtaking. He soared over the desolate moor, his eyes locked on the thick forest that covered several acres behind Modron and, not for the first time in his lfe, he envied the eagles and other great birds of prey. The sea was his first love, but flying was pretty sweet.

As he approached Modron, he could clearly see the high brick wall, topped with an electrified fence, that ringed the property. Outside the wall, a dry moat afforded another layer of security, and he knew from Tam's intelligence that the entire property was guarded by security cameras and motion detectors. He flew on, passing high above the perimeter wall and looked for his chosen landing place.

There it was! In the very center of the forest lay a small clearing and a pond, its waters glimmering in the sunlight. He angled toward it, waiting until the very last moment to release his parachute. This was the most dangerous part. The dagger would not cloak an area much larger than his body, so if someone looked his way at the wrong time, they might spot the parachute. Oh well, what was life without a little risk? He released it, and felt a hard jolt as it arrested his momentum. He held his breath, waiting for bullets to fly, until he floated down below the level of the treetops.

When he hit the ground, he hastily stripped off his wingsuit, stowed it in the trees, and then took a moment to get his bearings. The forest was unnervingly quiet, yet he sensed a presence there. Someone, or something, was watching him. Well, not for long. He moved into the shadow of an ancient oak tree, and activated the dagger.

Time to storm the castle.

CHAPTER 31

"Kill her." Morgan's eyes glazed over and she lapsed into unconsciousness.

Angel looked at Jacob. He was too far away for her to close the distance between them before he could draw his gun. Besides, she didn't know if she had enough left in the tank to take him on. Her eyes flitted to the weapons rack. If she had a knife, maybe she could... no. It was too far. She was at his mercy.

Jacob looked from her to Morgan's supine form, then back to Angel. For the first time, emotion registered on his face. Uncertainty.

"I won. That means you show me the front door, right?" She tried to sound confident, but fatigue gave her voice a breathless tenor that made her sound weak.

"I can't let you go." Jacob looked down at Morgan again, as if she would rise and tell him what to do.

"This is bullshit." She tried to keep the rising panic from her voice. "A deal is a deal."

Morgan groaned and began to stir, which spurred Jacob into action. He hurried over to her and grabbed her by the arm.

"You can leave by the back door, but we have to be quick about it."

She stumbled along beside him as he guided her through a dark corridor, stopping in front of another suit of armor.

"More secret doors?"

"Yes." He opened this door in the same manner as the last. Behind the suit of armor, a narrow corridor led to a wrought iron gate. Jacob hit another button and the gate began to rise. "Go straight ahead. Follow the path through the forest. You'll find a gate at the far end. Go!"

Angel didn't wait for him to change his mind. She ran and didn't look back.

Locke found Morgan lying on the floor in her workout room. He helped her to her feet and escorted her back to her study, reluctant to comment on her injuries.

"You were correct," she said. "The girl was a worthy opponent." She sat down behind her desk and looked up at him, her eyes their usual icy calm. "Report."

"The map that Maddock gave us was accurate. We located the Templar church beneath the graveyard at Trinity Church." He did not want to tell her the rest, but knew better than to make her ask. "There was nothing there. Maddock, or someone else, got there first."

For one of the few times since he'd begun working for her, Morgan looked weary. She closed her eyes and went through a series of calming exercises, breathing deeply and exhaling slowly. When she finally opened her eyes again, her face was a mask of serenity, though anger lurked beneath the surface.

"I had the dagger examined by experts at the museum. It is a fake."

Locke did not react to this bit of news. Dane Maddock had outwitted him, but the game was not over.

"Where is the girl?" he asked. "You did not let her go, did you?"

"Of course not. I told Jacob to kill her." She logged on to her computer and called up the security cameras that overlooked the grounds. "He should be burying her about now." She pursed her lips. "It looks as if he put her out the back door. I intended for him to kill her himself, not feed her to the children." Scowling, she turned the monitor around so Locke could see the young woman running through the forest.

"He must not have sent the signal yet. One of them is just watching her, see there?" He pointed to the upper branches of a leafy tree, where a scaly green and gold figure perched. "I'll go get her."

"No need," Morgan said. "I can send the signal from here. He tried to stop her, to tell her he had further use for the girl, but it was too late.

A high-pitched tone sounded all around her. It was there only for a moment and, when it faded, something rustled in the trees high above her. Angel kept running, looking up to see what was there, but she saw nothing. Her feet kept pounding the soft earth and she wished she knew if she was close to her goal, but the forest up ahead seemed to go on forever. Her body ached and her lungs burned, but she kept going.

It's just like training, she told herself. *Feel the burn. Embrace the pain. Fight through it. Keep chopping wood.* Every bullshit phrase a trainer had ever spoken ran through her mind, each more absurd than the one before. *I just want to get out of here.*

Up ahead, something moved among the trees. She quickened her pace and, as she hurdled a fallen log, something leapt out and snapped at her feet. She cried out in alarm as razor sharp teeth closed on empty air where her foot had been an instant before, hit the ground, and kept running.

Her eyes must be playing tricks on her, because what she'd seen wasn't possible. Behind her, the thing was in pursuit and it was gaining on her. Up ahead, a low hanging limb dangled over the path. She leapt up, grabbed hold, and swung herself up into the lower branches of the tree. Down below, she heard and angry hiss and the scraping of claws on the tree trunk. She began to climb, and didn't stop until she was a good fifteen feet off the ground.

She sagged against the tree trunk, gasping for breath. What the hell was that thing? She could still hear it down on the ground. Apparently, it couldn't climb, and that was fine with her. She didn't want to look, but she had to know what was after her. Clutching the tree so she didn't fall, she leaned over to peer through the foliage.

A vision from her darkest nightmares peered back at her. It was reptilian, and at least ten feet long from its snout to the tip of its powerful tail that lashed back and forth. Its body was dark green in color, its throat copper. Its toes ended in sharp, black claws that dug furrows in the ground and shredded the tree trunk as it struggled to get at her. Her first thought was of a komodo dragon that forgot to take its Ritalin. It had the size, general shape, and forked tongue of the giant lizard, but there were some significant differences. Aside from the coloring, the creature's hide was sleeker, and its movements more agile. The biggest difference, however, was the bright orange and gold frill that flared out behind its head.

"What the hell are you?" She muttered. Of course,

the real question was, how was she going to get away from it? Climbing from tree-to-tree was out of the question. The limb she sat on would not support her weight should she move more than a few feet out from the trunk. Outrunning it wouldn't work either. The thing would be on her as soon as she hit the ground. How could she have been so stupid as to let herself get treed?

As she contemplated her next move, panic welling inside her, she heard another hiss. She looked up to see another of the lizard-looking creatures high in a tree farther down the path. It had spotted her, and it flared its flame-colored frill and hissed angrily. And then it leaped out of the tree. She watched, mesmerized, as it it spread bright red wings and glided toward her.

"Holy crap," she whispered. "It can fly."

The man, a powerful-looking black man with a shaved head, stood staring at a suit of armor. That was weird. He was the first person Bones had seen since entering the castle, so Bones decided not to kill him... yet. Maybe the guy would lead him to Angel.

All of a sudden, the man shook his head, turned, and headed off down the corridor. His Glock at the ready, Bones crept after him. The man came to a door with an electronic keypad lock, entered in a code, and the door swung open. Bones moved in behind him, ready to shoot should the man go for his weapon, but he seemed unaware of his surroundings as he walked slowly across the blue carpeted room, picked up a remote, and turned on a flat screen monitor, which displayed what looked like security footage of the grounds. He pressed a few buttons, and four images appeared on the screen, each displaying a section of forest.

Bones was disappointed to see that no one else was in the room. He guessed it had been too much to hope that Angel would be in the first room he entered. So much for that. Time to see if he could squeeze any information out of this guy. Three silent steps, and he held the barrel of his Glock to the base of the man's skull. The man froze.

"I'm in a really bad mood, so I suggest you don't make any sudden moves." Bones poured every ounce of his hate and anger into his voice. "Put your hands out in front of you. Slowly." The man complied, and Bones relieved him of his weapon. "What's your name?"

"Jacob." His voice was dull, not so much unafraid as uncaring.

"All right, Jacob, where's my sister?" He figured he'd have to do some persuading, maybe with his knife, but Jacob answered right away.

"She's gone. I let her go."

Bones wanted to feel relieved, but he wasn't buying it.

"The hell you did. Tell me the truth, or I'll cut your eyes out and feed them to you for lunch."

Now Jacob didn't seem so uncaring.

"I swear. She's not here anymore. Morgan will probably kill me for it, but I let her go."

Bones didn't know why, but he sensed the man was telling the truth.

"Is she all right?" He bit his lip as he waited for the answer. If something had happened to Angel, he'd burn this place to the ground, that is, if Maddock didn't do it first.

"She was when she left here. A little banged up, but not by me."

Bones finally took a moment to look around the room. There was little to see, except a rack of weapons.

"What are the swords and crap for?" He had a few ideas the uses someone could find for such a sinister array of weapons, but he forced those thoughts from his mind.

"Morgan trains with them."

As he continued to look around, his eyes fell on a dark spot on the carpet. Blood. He turned to ask Jacob whose blood it was when he glanced at the monitor on the wall, and what he saw erased all other thoughts from his mind.

"What the hell is that?" The image of a winged creature with a long, scaly tail and a fiery frill filled the screen.

"A dragon," Jacob said.

"Don't mess with me." Bones dug the barrel of his pistol into Jacob's neck. "What is it, really?"

"That's what Morgan calls them. They're lizards, really. Her family began importing different varieties from around the world centuries ago: komodos, frilled dragons, flying dragons. They bred them and culled out the smallest and weakest. But when Morgan took over, she started messing with their DNA."

Bones remembered what Tam had told them about Morgan's philanthropic efforts. *She gives a lot of money to charity. She supports genetic research to fight all sorts of diseases. They even named the reptile house at the London Zoo for her because of all the money she gave them.*

"Is she crazy?"

"Maybe. But she's fascinated with dragons, it's sort of a legacy, and if she couldn't have the real thing, she was determined to create the next best thing."

"Don't tell me they breathe fire." Bones didn't

bother to keep the scorn from his voice.

"No, but they're deadly all the same. The one on the top left has the power and ferocity of the komodo, and the agility of the frilled lizard. The one on the bottom right is almost as big, just as vicious, and it can fly."

Bones' mouth was suddenly dry, and a sick feeling hung in his gut. Maddock was out there with these so-called dragons.

"Morgan has them trained to hunt at a signal," Jacob continued. "And the smartest one will even obey her commands." Just then, a high pitched note, almost like a whistle, rang out, and the dragons on the screen suddenly became alert.

"Oh no." Jacob wobbled and almost lost his balance. "Morgan must have seen her and sounded the call. I thought she could get away."

"You thought who could get away?" Bones asked, though he already knew the answer.

Jacob hesitated, and when he finally replied, his voice was cold.

"Your sister."

Chapter 32

Angel wanted to scream, but her voice was frozen in her throat. The beast glided toward her, growing ever closer and ever more frightening. She had nowhere to go, but she'd be damned if she would sit there. If she was going to die, she'd die trying to escape. She looked down, searching for a soft place to land. She was up on the balls of her feet, ready to make the leap, when a shot rang out and the creature in the air shrieked.

Two more shots rang out, one tearing a gash in one of the creature's winglike membranes and causing it to veer off into the woods. The second shot caught it in its belly, and it tumbled to the ground and thrashed about in pain.

The creature at the bottom of the tree cocked its head, sniffed the air, then tore off down the path toward the sound of the gunshots. As Angel watched, another shot came seemingly out of nowhere, pinging off its skull and tearing a ragged hole in its fril. It hissed and kept moving. The thing was tough.

Another shot rang out, the bullet striking the beast in the foreleg, and she thought she saw a muzzle flash in the middle of the pathway, but that couldn't be. There was nothing there, but somehow she knew who had come to her rescue.

"Maddock!" she shouted. Suddenly, all the fear and uncertainty of the past few days overwhelmed her, and she burst into tears. Crap! She didn't want Maddock to see her acting girly, but right now, she couldn't help herself.

The creature continued to charge, ignoring its wounded leg. Angel wanted to help, but what could she do without a weapon? As the tears welled in her eyes, the world became a kaleidoscope, where a myriad of crystallized lizard beasts attacked an invisible assailant.

Two more shots rang out. She didn't see where the first one struck, but the second one did the job, catching the beast in the eye and dropping it in its tracks. Ten feet down the path, the air rippled and Maddock appeared, holding a pistol in one hand and a weird-looking knife in the other.

Sobbing and laughing, Angel shimmied down the trunk of the tree and, by the time she hit the ground, he was there. She wanted to save face by saying something sarcastic but, before she could open her mouth, Maddock swept her up in his arms and kissed her. She kissed him back, the way she'd wanted to for years. He broke the kiss all too soon, and she was suddenly aware of the sounds of more of the lizard things approaching from all directions.

"I love you," she blurted.

"Yes you do." He winked and smiled, and she punched him in the chest.

"Ass." She kissed him again. "You were, like, invisible. How..."

"Not now. We need to get out of here." He took her hand and turned to lead her back in the direction from which he'd come, and froze. Two beasts barred the way. "The other way, I guess. Hop on my back."

"I can run," she protested.

"Just do it. I'll explain later."

She saw no point in arguing. She hopped up on his back and, as they headed along the path back toward the castle, something strange happened. The air shimmered around them and the world got weird for a second.

"What did you do?"

"The knife is a cloaking device." If he was feeling any strain from the added burden of her weight, he didn't let it show. He kept up a steady pace, though she could hear the beasts on their tail coming closer.

She was about to steal a look behind them when she saw one of the beasts leap from a tree up ahead and come soaring at them. She called out a warning, but Maddock had already leveled his pistol and fired two shots. Both of them caught it in the wing and sent it spinning into the trees. Now she looked back.

"Maddock, I think they can smell us, and probably hear us. They've almost caught up!"

He quickened his pace.

Angel held her breath as the castle appeared in the distance. Would they make it?

"Come on, come on," Corey urged as he waited for Jimmy's program to worm its way into the cracks of Modron's security system. It hadn't taken this much time at the museum. Surely it wouldn't be much longer. He wondered how Bones and Maddock were faring. If he couldn't break into the system, they might not be able to get out again. No, he couldn't think that way.

He looked down at the spinning icon that indicated the program was still at work and tried to hurry it along by tapping the screen. Waste of time, he knew, but he hated this impotent feeling.

Just then, he heard voices close by, and the cargo

area was suddenly bathed in sound and light as someone rolled up the back door. They were finally getting around to unloading the truck. Corey performed a few mental calculations. If it was only a couple of guys and they worked slowly, he might have ten minutes before they found him.

He was keenly aware of the weight of the pistol on his hip. He wasn't much of a shot. Heck, he didn't even know what kind of gun Tam had given him, but he would have surprise on his side. No way they'd be expecting and armed geek to be hiding here. Maybe he could get them first. He'd have to try.

Heart racing and palms sweating, he sat back and waited, hoping the computer, or Maddock and Bones, or both, would be hurry up.

"You sent my sister out there with those things?" Bones snapped. "You're dead."

"No! I was trying to help her escape," Jacob protested. "I couldn't take her out the front door, so her only chance was the security gate in the back. The dragons don't attack unless the signal is sounded. I thought she could make it."

"What security gate? This whole place is walled and fenced in."

"There's a hidden gate in the wall at the far end of the property. Morgan thought it would give people a sporting chance against her children, as she calls the dragons. The path leads directly to it. You can't see it from the outside."

"How many people have made it out?"

"The next one will be the first." Hands still outstretched, Jacob slowly turned to face Bones, who kept his Glock trained on the man's head. "I don't expect you to trust me, but you'll need me to get you past the security system if you want to go after her."

Bones knew Jacob was right.

"Fine, but consider this an audition for the rest of your life. You do anything else to piss me off, I'll kill you, and I just might shoot you in the gut first. You know, to make sure it hurts."

Jacob nodded and, hands on his head, led Bones back the way they had come.

"The suit of armor hides a passageway leading out," he explained, "and there's a security gate at the end. I have to put in a code to open them."

They turned a corner and Jacob stopped short, his hands falling limply to his sides. The suit of armor was swinging open of its own accord. Behind it, Bones saw a gate slowly raising, and daylight glimmered beyond. Jimmy had done it!

He clubbed Jacob in the temple with the butt of his Glock and dashed past him before the man hit the ground. Maybe he'd just been knocked unconscious, maybe Bones had scrambled the guy's brains. He didn't care about anything but finding Angel.

He dashed out of the tunnel onto a manicured lawn. The overcast afternoon gave everything a dull, gray overtone, matching his mood. He ran toward the distant forest and the path Angel had taken. He was a hundred yards away when three dragons burst forth from the forest, making a beeline for him. He dropped to one knee and took aim.

"Bones! Hold your fire! Hold your fire!" Maddock's voice came from somewhere in front of him, but where was he?

Then it clicked in Bones' mind. The dagger! Maddock was cloaked. Bones concentrated on the space between him and the charging dragons and, in an instant, he spotted it. A rippling outline, like heat rising in the desert, coming right at him. Now that he knew where Maddock was, he took aim again at the dragons, who were gaining ground fast.

"He said don't shoot, you assclown!" It was Angel. Maddock had found her.

"Relax. I got this," he shouted as relief spread through him.

"Go for the legs!" Maddock shouted.

Bones took careful aim and fired two shots at the closest dragon. One bullet found its mark and the dragon shrieked and stumbled, but got right back up again and continued its pursuit. The other two dragons quickly overtook their wounded counterpart, and Bones stepped up his rate of fire. Most of his shots deflected off their solid skulls or grazed their tough hides, but a few were on target, and soon all three were hobbling along, slowed, but still relentless in the pursuit of their prey.

Suddenly, Maddock appeared, carrying Angel on his back.

"Let's move!" he shouted. He slowed long enough for Angel to hop down, and the three of them headed for the open gate.

Corey took control of the security system," Bones said, "but who knows how long he can keep it?"

"Just lead the way." Maddock was clearly winded from the run, but he kept pace with Bones, as did Angel.

"Take the dagger," Maddock said to Angel. "Press the butt to activate the cloaking mechanism. Don't argue. Just stay close and, if it comes to a fight, don't get in our line of fire."

To Bones' surprise, Angel did as Dane said without a word of complaint. Moments later, she vanished.

Bones thought he'd never get used to that. It was too creepy.

As he ran, he ejected his Glock's magazine, which was nearly spent, and replaced it with a fresh one. He had a feeling he was going to need it.

"The cameras just shut off," Morgan said. She clicked the mouse a few times, but nothing happened.

Locke circled around behind her desk, grateful for the distraction. They had discussed his failures at length, and he had grown weary of the conversation. He knew he was still useful to Morgan, but she was very unhappy with right him now.

"It's probably your computer," he said. "Try shutting it down and restarting it."

The computer was in the process of rebooting when he realized they had greater problems than a frozen computer. A loud popping sound came from somewhere in the distance.

"Are those gunshots?" Morgan rose from her chair, a little slower than normal, and tapped a button on her phone. "Jacob, where are you?"

No reply.

"Jacob, can you hear me?"

Still no answer.

Locke heard another rapid burst of gunfire, and then all was eerily quiet. He hurried to the window and looked out. The forest was alive with dragons. They charged out of the woods or launched from the trees, all headed for the castle. What the hell was going on?

Then he spotted three dragons hobbling across the lawn. They had clearly been injured. But by whom? He knew immediately.

"We've been infiltrated by Dane Maddock."

Bones led them through a series of twists and turns, moving deeper into the heart of the castle. They made their way without encountering resistance but, when they reached the underground garage where Bones had left the truck, Morgan's men were ready.

A torrent of bullets zipped through the space where Dane's head had been only a moment before. He hit the ground, rolled, and came up firing. One man went down, but the other retreated into the truck's cargo bay, took up a defensive position, and continued firing. Dane cursed. It would take time to dig this guy out— time they didn't have.

He was about to tell Angel to give him the dagger when a single shot rang out. Seconds later, a stunned-looking Corey appeared at the back of the truck. He dangled a pistol loosely at his side. He looked at them in stunned amazement.

"I got him."

"Hell yeah!" Bones shouted as they dashed for the truck. "I'm driving." He ran to the left side of the cab and cursed when he remembered he wasn't in America.

Dane took the wheel and fired up the engine while Angel joined Corey in the back. Tires squealed as he stepped on the gas and the truck peeled out of the garage. In the rear-view mirror, he saw a body go tumbling out— the man Corey had shot. As they barreled down the long drive, Dane was pleased to see the security gate standing open. Corey's hack had done the trick.

He was not pleased, however, to see armed men barring the way, and others dashing across the moor in hot pursuit. Modron's grounds suddenly resembled an upset anthill. Shots rang out, and bullets pinged off the sides of the truck. Bones returned fire, sending the attackers diving for cover. Up ahead, the gate guards leveled their weapons at the oncoming vehicle...

...and went down in a heap.

Matt and Willis had entered the fight. They now turned their fire on the rest of Morgan's security force. Surprised by this new development, many of them retreated, while others went down, never to rise again. At the gate, Dane slowed down so Willis and Matt could climb inside.

They continued firing at the remaining security guards, keeping them at bay. For a moment, Dane thought they were home free, but then a new threat reared its head. A group of riders on motorcycles shot down the drive and fell in behind the truck. As they gained on the vehicle, they drew weapons and began to fire.

Dane yanked the wheel hard to the left, then back to the right, zigzagging across the road.

"You're making it kind of hard for us to shoot back!" Bones shouted. He leaned out the window and fired off a shot at the pursuing motorcycles.

Dane glanced back and had to laugh as folding tables came flying out of the back of the truck and tumbled across the road. Angel and Corey must be unloading the remainder of the cargo. The motorcycles scattered, one rider losing control and skidding off the road.

One biker managed to skirt the flying furniture and accelerate past Matt and Willis' line of fire and, as he drew even with Dane, he raised his weapon. Before he could pull the trigger, Dane kicked the driver's side door open, sending him tumbling off the road. Behind them, the tables kept flying, followed by chairs. Two more bikers crashed and another fell to gunfire. After that the pursuit melted away. Dane turned to Bones and managed a grin.

"We did it. Now, call Tam and tell her we're ready for a pickup."

Locke stopped his bike on the side of the road, dismounted, and went to check on his men. It galled him that Maddock had gotten away, but a squad of men on motorcycles stood little chance against men who could aim and fire from the back of a truck. He also had to admit that pitching the tables and chairs onto the roadway had been resourceful, and it had been the girl who had done it.

For a moment, he considered following them on his own, but the appearance of a helicopter landing atop a tor farther up the road told him he'd missed his chance.

He smiled, in spite of the grim circumstances. He hadn't lost them entirely. As long as the girl remained alive, he could track their every move.

Chapter 33

"Nice boat." Dane admired the sleek lines of the cabin cruiser Tam had secured for them. The helicopter pilot had dropped them at the coast, not far from Bodmin, where one of Tam's agents, a tall, dark haired man who introduced himself as Greg, had been waiting for them. They were now headed north along the coastline.

"Glad you like it. Your boy, Jimmy, came through for us about two minutes after you jumped. He's got a location for the map Avery found, and he's working on something else that I'll tell you about after you finish the next job." She tilted her head and looked thoughtfully up at the cloudy sky. "He's pretty good. You think he'd come to work with us?"

The word "us" gave Dane pause. He still wasn't accustomed to the idea that he and his crew would soon be working for Tam.

"Doubt it. He's not the type, but I think we could count on him for some freelance work here and there."

"You don't give classified information to a hired hand, Maddock," Tam sighed. "Lord have mercy, I've got so much to teach you."

Dane smiled, leaned against the bow rail, and gazed at the dark water up ahead, feeling the cool salt spray on his face and breathing deep of the sea air. He thought of Angel, down below, nursing her wounds, and Avery, who had narrowly avoided capture just the day before. Was it worth risking their safety just to track down a treasure?

"Do you think we should hand things over to the authorities?"

"You don't really mean that," Tam chided. "This is your family's quest. Your daddy passed it down to you and your sister. Besides, I know enough about you to know you never leave a job unfinished."

"But what about Angel and Avery?"

"Don't worry about them. I already offered to fly them both back home but they wouldn't hear of it."

"I figured as much. I just don't want them to pay the price for my hubris." He took a deep breath and let it out in a rush. "I lost my wife and my parents in a very short time..."

"And now you're in love, and you've got a family again, and you're afraid of losing them," Bones said, dropping to the deck alongside him.

"I didn't know you were there."

"No one expects the Cherokee Inquisition." Bones made a face, and then grew serious. "Listen to me, Maddock. Until this mystery is solved, none of our group are safe. They'd kidnap us like they did Angel in order to get information, or they'd kill us to shut us up. You know that. We've been in situations like this before."

Dane nodded. He'd had the same thoughts.

"Another thing. When I was growing up, my grandfather didn't spend a lot of time telling me what I should and shouldn't do. He taught me what it meant to be a Bonebrake. He said every family has something they stand for, and a set of values they live by. That's what holds them together. And that doesn't just go for blood relatives."

Dane thought he knew what Bones was getting at.

Their crew was a family, and their dedication, their courage, and their commitment to one another was what gave them their identity.

"And don't forget the Dominion," Tam said. "Even if Morgan was out of the picture, they're still out there. And if they want to get their hands on whatever we're going to find, it's important enough for us to get there first."

"Understood. So, are you going to tell us where we're headed next?"

"Tintagel Castle."

Dane frowned. The ruins of Tintagel Castle stood atop high cliffs on the peninsula of Tintagel Island in Cornwall. Legend held it to be the birthplace of King Arthur, and a nearby coastal cave was known as Merlin's Cave.

"That can't be right. It's a popular tourist destination and it's been thoroughly excavated. Plus, it's in Morgan's backyard. She has to have already searched it."

"Oh, it's not in the castle, it's under it. Way under it. Now, you boys go down below and get your speedos on. We'll be there in a few minutes and you've got work to do."

Twenty minutes later, he and Bones were suited up in full diving gear, and standing on deck in the shadow of Tintagel Island. They were anchored in a sheltered area between the island and another peninsula to the east. He had to hand it to Tam. She worked fast.

"All right," Tam said. "The entrance should be underwater between those two rocks." She pointed to two huge rock formations poking out of the water. "It's got to be well below the low tide mark, or else someone would have found it by now."

Dane and Bones exchanged glances, both thinking

the same thing. What if someone *had* already found it?

"Don't you make that face," Tam scolded. "The map shows a channel that runs straight west. The only clue we have is, *Walk in the Way of Sorrows.*"

"Great," Bones said. "We're looking for an emo treasure."

Tam checked her watch.

"We've got plenty of daylight, but don't dally. Once you're in the water, we're going to head up the coast. We don't want to draw undue attention. Call us when you're out, and be careful."

Angel and Avery hugged Dane and Bones in turn, and Willis complained about the lack of a third set of diving gear. Matt, who had taken over the helm, guided them as close as he dared to the stones shown on the map, and Dane and Bones dived in.

"Report," Morgan snapped as Locke entered the room. She seemed to have recovered her faculties and energy, though the cuts and bruises on her face bore testimony to the damage she'd taken.

Jacob had not bounced back so quickly. He'd sustained a severe blow to the head when Maddock, or one of his men, had crept up on him from behind just as he was about to set the dragons on the Bonebrake girl. He still attended Morgan, as always, but he seemed detached. Probably a mild concussion.

"I planted a tracking device on the girl while she was sedated. I sent two men to follow them."

"Only two?" Neither her tone nor her expression betrayed her feelings, but he knew she disapproved.

"We've been decimated here. Worse than decimated, in fact. They only killed a few of our men, but too many have sustained serious injuries." He stopped there. Morgan knew what she had to do, and she wouldn't thank him for telling her how to respond to present circumstances.

"Of the losses we've sustained, how many are essential to our plans for the Queen's *visit*?" She raised her eyebrows as she said the last word.

"Only a few. SO14 is the critical piece, and our people have been in place there for years." SO14 was the branch of Special Operations that provided protection for the Royal Family, and several of its members were loyal to Morgan and the Sisters.

"Very well. Are you tracking Maddock right now?"

"Of course. They appear to be headed to Tintagel Castle."

Morgan threw back her head and laughed. It was a rare display of amusement from the stolid woman.

"Tintagel? They must not have the third map, or else they would not be wasting their time. The castle has been thoroughly excavated."

Locke nodded, though he lacked Morgan's confidence. Maddock had already surprised him too many times for Locke to underestimate him.

"In any case, our men will keep us apprised of the situation."

Locke nodded again. With so many of his men out of commission, he'd been forced to send two of his younger, more enthusiastic charges. He'd given them clear instructions, but worried they'd overextend themselves by trying to be heroes.

"Most of our remaining men will need to remain here to clean up the damage and prepare for the event. How large is Maddock's party?"

"Seven, that we know of, including the women. At least, as far as we know. Four of them ex-military."

"Seven. A number of power, but fitting somehow.

Even better, it is a number we can easily overcome, with help." Morgan struck the desk once with her open palms and rose to her feet. She turned toward the wall where "Le Morte D'Arthur" hung, and gazed almost lovingly at the image. "The time has come. Summon the Sisters, and tell them each to bring their seven best men. We will follow Maddock, and be prepared to strike at any moment."

"Seven of our own men as well?"

"In addition to you and Jacob, I want four reliable men." She turned to face him, the ghost of a smile on her face. "And bring Mordred."

The water was cool and the dull sunlight shone gray-green beams into the depths. As Dane swam deeper, the two stones converged, leaving a space between them not much wider than a chimney. He followed it to the bottom, which was not as deep as he'd expected, and found nothing. Undeterred, he began digging in the loose sand, and soon exposed a portion of the rock face that was unnaturally smooth and even.

Bones lent a hand and, within minutes, they found what they were looking for— a stone circle carved with a Templar cross. Working together, they turned it until it gave way. The stone rolled out of sight, exposing a dark tunnel. Dane turned on his dive light and swam inside.

The passageway dropped straight down for twenty feet, then made a sharp right angle and, as Tam had said, led west, back toward Tintagel Island. They swam through the featureless tunnel until it turned upward and then, thirty feet up, they broke the surface and emerged in an underground cave, facing two stone doors.

Each had a circle and cross stone where a doorknob should be, and each depicted a scene from Jesus' life. The door on the left showed a Nativity scene. The door on the right showed Jesus struggling to carry the cross to his crucifixion.

"I know which one looks like sorrow," Bones said.

Dane contemplated the doors. What was it about the Way of Sorrows that rang a bell? He had it!

"*The Way of Sorrows* is another name for the stations of the cross. We're looking for scenes of Jesus on his way to the crucifixion. It's the one on the right."

He spun the Templar cross and the door opened on a passage that led up and curved to the left. He shone his light inside, looking for signs of danger, but finding none. Holding his breath, he led moved into the passageway and followed it up into the heart of the island.

They continued on until they'd passed through six sets of doors, each juxtaposing a triumphant event of Jesus' life with one of his road to Calvary, and every subsequent passage winding higher and higher. He wondered what lay behind the other doors, but didn't really want to find out.

At the seventh set of doors, they faced their first real conundrum. The doors were identical. Each showed the entombment of Jesus, with seven people, four male and three female, carrying him toward the tomb, which lay in the background on the left. In the background, on the right side of the picture, stood Calvary, with its empty crosses looking down on the scene.

"Any ideas?" Bones was looking at the doors like they'd insulted his mom.

"Take a closer look," Dane said. "See if anything's different."

"Man, that's too much like those stupid puzzles in the newspaper. I vote for the door on the right."

"Fine. You can go first." Dane grinned and pushed his friend aside as he moved in for a closer look. They spent five frustrating minutes gazing at the two doors. The images seemed to meld together until he couldn't separate them in his mind. Finally, he rubbed his eyes in frustration and backed up to look at it from a distance.

And then he saw it.

"Bones, come back here and take a look." When Bones joined him, he pointed to the crosses atop Calvary. "What do you see?"

Bones stared blankly at the doors, and then his eyes widened. "The crosses on the right are Templar crosses. How did we miss it?" He moved forward a few steps. "You have to be in just the right place to see the subtle differences. I wonder..." He walked up to stand between the doors and rubbed an identical spot on each with the tips of his index and middle fingers.

"Bones, those aren't boobs."

"Check out the stone that blocks the tomb. It's too small to see, but I can feel a cross carved in the one on the right."

"Just like the stones that have gotten us into the treasure chambers." Dane nodded approvingly. "You want to do the honors?"

Bones grinned and opened the door on the right. It slid back to reveal another chamber. In its center stood a three foot tall block of stone, and protruding from its center...

"Holy crap!" Bones exclaimed.

Even though it had been what he'd expected to find, the sight of a sword embedded in a stone took Dane's breath away. He entered the room, feeling like he was in a dream, and stopped in front of the sword.

"Excalibur." He spoke the word reverentially. From the moment Avery told them they'd found Arthur's dagger, he'd known they were on a path that would lead to the legendary sword, but the reality was still more than he could comprehend. Arthur had lived, had borne this sword, and, apparently, had drawn it from a stone.

Much of the sword was buried in a three foot-high block of stone, but he could see enough of the blade to know it was made of the same metal as the spear and dagger, while the hilt was made of the same white stone that gave them their power.

"Well, who's worthy to draw the sword?" Bones asked with a sly smile.

"You first."

Bones reached out, took hold of the handle, and pulled. It didn't give an inch.

"Fine," Bones sighed. "Your turn."

Dane gave him a knowing look and aimed the beam of his flashlight onto the white stone hilt. Lights immediately began to swirl in its depths, reminding Dane of a line from Tennyson's "Morte d'Arthur."

"And sparkled keen with frost against the hilt, for all the haft twinkled with diamond sparks." The stone pulsed faster and faster until it finally shone with a steady light.

"Here goes nothing." Dane pressed the stone, and flickers of light began to dance along the flat of the blade and run up and down the fuller. The edge shone a bright blue, and the light seemed to run up one side and down the other.

He took Excalibur in his hand and pulled. The blade slid free easily. He knew he should shut it down right then and head back to the boat, but the little boy inside of him, the one that, in his youth, had daydreamed of being a Knight of the Round Table, wouldn't let him.

"Stand back," he told Bones. "I want to try something." He took aim, raised the sword, and brought it down at an angle. Excalibur sheared the corner off of the stone like the proverbial hot knife through melted butter.

"Sweet! My turn." Bones looked like a kid on Christmas morning as he sliced two more corners off the stone. Then his expression grew sober and he shut pressed the pommel. As the lights in the blade faded and died, he handed the sword back to Dane. "This is serious stuff, you know."

"I know." Dane had pondered the implications of their discoveries many times. The weapons might be ancient, but they represented an advanced, maybe even unearthly, technology.

"A cloaking device. A weapon that turns a little bit of light into a powerful electrical weapon. Now a sword that can cut through stone." Bones shook his head.

"And none of them require a power supply," Dane added. "Just solar energy, or even a little bit of artificial light. If scientist can unlock the technology, they could do incredible things."

"Or incredibly terrible things." Bones rubbed his chin and stared down at the ground. "Tam's going to want to turn them over to the government, you know."

Dane nodded. "Better that than the Dominion getting its hands on them."

"I guess. Let's take some pictures and get out of here."

While Bones made a photographic record of the chamber, Dane finally took the time to look around. It did not differ in any significant way from those chambers on the other side of the Atlantic: circular with Templar symbols carved in the walls, the double-band of code winding down the walls, and a wedge-shaped image up above.

Dane took a last look at the stone where Excalibur had been embedded minutes before, still amazed and intrigued by what they'd found. He stowed the sword in a bag Tam had provided, slung it over his shoulder, and began the trek back to the outside world.

Back on the surface, he radioed Tam to pick them up.

"Three down," Bones said. "I wonder what Jimmy has come up with. This kind of feels like it should be the end of the line, you know? Arthur only had three legendary weapons."

Before Dane could answer, their cruiser appeared around the tip of the peninsula, and shots rang out from up above. He turned and saw that two men had taken up positions on the cliffs below Tintagel and were firing on their cruiser. Nearby, a sleek-looking boat bobbed in the surface. He and Bones had been so dizzy with success that they'd ignored what was right in front of their faces.

"Tam, get out of there now!" he barked into the radio.

"We're coming to get you!" came her reply.

"I've got a plan. Just get out range and fast!" He breathed a sigh of relief as, moments later, the cruiser turned and headed back around the peninsula.

"Are we swimming for it?" Bones asked.

"We'd never outrun them. Give me a minute." Before Bones could ask what he had planned, he submerged and swam to the boat. He surfaced on the side opposite the gunmen, who were clambering down from the rocks. He didn't have long.

He drew Excalibur from his pack, gave it a few

seconds to absorb the sunlight, then activated the blade. He could almost feel the energy coursing through him as the edges shone with blue light. He checked to make sure the men still had their backs to him before he took his first swing. The sword sliced through the hull with ease and, moments later, he'd cut a gaping hole near the stern, just above the waterline. He covered the hole with a life jacket, knowing the ruse wouldn't last for long, but maybe it would be enough.

He met up with Bones just as the men got into their boat and fired up their engine. The boat shot past them and, moments later, it slowed and began to sink. The men cursed in surprise and anger, the chase abandoned as they tried to plug the leaks with whatever they had on hand.

Dane smiled as he and Bones hit the water, keeping well below the surface and passing unseen beneath the foundering boat. Now, to finish the job.

CHAPTER 34

"That place is crazy-looking," Bones said.

"Inishtooskert," Tam replied. "They call it the Sleeping Giant, or The Dead Man."

"How many skirts was that?" Bones asked.

Tam shook her head and Angel punched him.

Dane had been correct about the wedge-shaped images on the ceilings of the three chambers. When put together, they formed a map to this, the northernmost of the Blasket Islands off Ireland's southwest coast. The lonely island had been uninhabited for years, and was home to many ancient ruins. And, as its nickname suggested, when seen from the east, the island did, indeed, look like a man lying on his back. Blanketed by silver moonlight, it put Dane to mind of a corpse lying on a funeral bier.

"What do you think we're going to find there?" Dane asked no one in particular.

Everyone exchanged glances, unwilling or unable to hazard a guess. Finally, Avery spoke up.

"Avalon. Legend holds it was somewhere across the water. They could have crossed the Irish sea and rounded the coast until they found the perfect place. What better place to lay a king to rest than an island that looks like a giant crypt?"

No one disagreed.

"You think King Arthur is somewhere inside that

island?" Willis asked.

"Why not? If our theory is correct, Morgan believes she's his descendant and would need his remains in order to conduct a DNA test. She's a museum director, so the public wouldn't look at the find with the same suspicion they would if some random person claimed he'd found Arthur's final resting place."

"I guess we'll find out soon enough," Dane said, "So, who's going and who's staying?"

Everyone spoke at once. None of them wanted to remain behind. Not even Corey.

"We can't all go. Somebody's got to stay with the boat." He looked pointedly at Matt's broken arm. "And we need a lookout and someone to be our communications man."

"That's me, as always," Corey grumbled.

It was agreed that Greg, Tam's agent, would go ashore and find high ground from which he could serve as lookout. As the the rest of the group made their preparations, Dane pulled Angel aside.

"I really think you should stay behind. You've dealt with too much already."

"Forget it. After what I've been through, I deserve to see this to the end as much as anyone, if not more. Besides, you can't tell me what to do." She grinned, gave him a quick kiss, and left him standing alone belowdecks.

She was right. He couldn't tell her what to do, though he wished he could. He vowed to keep her close and not let anything happen to her.

"There you are." Avery poked her head in the door. "You *are* coming aren't you? I mean, we can handle it without you, if you'd rather stay here." She reached out, took his hand, and pretended to haul him up the stairs. He played along, feigning reluctance. When they reach the deck, she laughed and gave him a hug.

"We're going to do it, Maddock! After all these years, Dad's quest is at an end."

"Do you think he had any idea where it would lead us? This is a far cry from a pirate's treasure."

"I doubt it, but I think he'd have loved every minute of it." She stopped, blinked a few times, and cleared her throat. "I wish he was here."

Dane looked out across the moonlit water, and fought down a sudden wave of sadness. He put his arm around Avery's shoulders and gave her a squeeze.

"Me too."

It was a steep climb up the side of the Dead Man, and they were all exhausted from the ordeal of the past few days but, buoyed by enthusiasm, they made the climb in good time. Reaching the top, they paused to look out across the water at the chain of islands to the south. It was a beautiful sight, and he found himself wishing he and Angel were here alone, with no thoughts of Morgan or the Dominion to distract them. He looked down at her and could tell by the look in her eyes she was thinking the same thing.

"All right, Maddock," Tam said, "take charge of your troops or I'm going to do it for you." She handed him a flashlight and a sheet of paper.

Jimmy had made a major breakthrough. He'd broken the bands of code carved on the chamber walls. The resulting message, they hoped, marked out the path they were to follow.

"Okay, the first line reads, *Beneath the eye of the giant lies the door to eternity.*"

"I hate poetry," Bones mumbled.

"The head is that way." Avery pointed to the east.

They picked their way across the rough terrain, navigating the old ruins, then faced an even more challenging climb up to the jagged rocks that formed the giant's head. Avery shone her light aross the rocks and cried out in triumph. Where the right eye should be, a round boulder four feet across sat in the center of a circular depression.

"The eyes have it," Bones proclaimed. He, Dane, and Willis rolled the boulder out of the way, revealing a shaft carved into the rock. Handholds ran down to the floor twenty feet below. Dane insisted on going first, in case there was a trap. The ladies exchanged wearied looks, but didn't argue. He reached the bottom without incident, and looked around.

He stood in a cave. Evidence of occasional human presence in the distant past lay all about in the form of fire rings, the charred bones of small animals, smoke-stained walls, and carvings. What he did not see was any sort of door, trapdoor, or portal, and certainly no Templar cross. The others reached the bottom and joined him in examining the cave.

"What's the next line?" Bones asked.

"The three come together and show the way to the Dead Man's heart."

"The three what? Wise men? Amigos? Blind mice?"

"The three weapons, genius." Angel said, pointing to Rhongomnyiad, which Bones wore strapped across his back.

"Definitely," Dane said, pretending he'd known all along. He suspected he wasn't fooling anyone, but that was all right. "Everybody spread out and look for carvings that resemble the sword, spear, or dagger.

It wasn't long before Willis found what they were looking for. A triangular shape formed by carvings that exactly matched the three weapons.

"So what do we do now?" Avery asked.

"I think the weapons are the key." Dane drew Excalibur and pressed it into the carved outline. As if some magnetic force were pulling it, it clicked into place and light danced in the stone haft. Next, he set Carnwennan, then Rhongomnyiad. For a moment, the three blades burned like a blue sun and, when the light winked out, they found themselves staring at an open doorway. The weapons no longer glowed, but hung in the stone doorway. Gingerly, Dane touched Excalibur. When it didn't zap him into oblivion, he removed it and the other weapons, and they moved on.

The passageway opened onto a sheer cliff. Dane shone his light down into the yawing abyss, to the rock-strewn bottom a hundred feet down.

"Did I mention I don't like heights?" Avery asked, moving back from the edge.

"It's not the height that scares me," Angel said. "It's falling from heights."

"Hey, I'm the one who's supposed to make the bad jokes," Bones protested.

Dane shone his light up ahead. Two stone bridges spanned the gap, each only wide enough for one person to cross at a time. He consulted their list of clues.

"*The hand of God will carry you across.* That's got to be the bridge on the right. In Biblical times, the left hand was unclean."

"You'd better be sure," Tam said. "That's a long way to fall."

"One way to find out." Bones turned and strode out onto the bridge. He reached the center, stopped, and turned back. "Seems pretty solid, and I'm heavier than any of you, so I think we're good." He hopped up and down to illustrate his point and, with a crack, a chunk of the bridge rail broke off and fell down into the abyss. "Sorry."

"Holy crap, Bones." Dane shook his head. "I still think this is the only way to cross. Anyone who wants to hang back, that's fine." They all shook their heads in unison. "All right. One at a time. Heaviest first." Tam, Angel, and Avery all exchanged appraising looks. "Fine. Willis first, then the ladies in any order you like." He watched with bated breath as, one by one, his companions crossed over, and then he followed. On the other side, they followed a steep passageway and disappeared down into the darkness.

"I've lost the signal." Locke pocketed his tracking device. "They must have gone underground."

Tamsin looked at her Sisters. Rhiannon, flanked by her men, was her usual, calm, detached self. The ocean breeze whipped her red hair about like a fiery halo. She didn't meet Tamsin's eye, but stared at Morgan, waiting.

Morgan's implacable stare had been replaced by a manic gleam once they arrived at their destination. She didn't bat an eye at Locke's news.

"It is of no matter. Mordred will track her."

Mordred was Morgan's prized pet. Bottle green with a bronze chest and red streaked frill and wings, he was the the most successful product of her genetics experiments. At sixteen feet long and standing nearly four feet at the shoulder, he was the largest of Morgan's children, as she called them. He was also vicious, but that was not what bothered Tamsin about the beast. Mordred was intelligent... too intelligent. He was well-trained, responding to Morgan's every command, much like a loyal dog, but one look in his eyes suggested there was a limit to his restraint. She only hoped she was not there when he finally broke free of his mistress's control.

Morgan took a scrap of bloody blue carpet from her pocket and held it out in front of Mordred. The dragon flicked its forked tongue several times, even licking it it once, then looked up at her, indicating his readiness.

Tamsin shivered at the sight.

"Hunt."

At Morgan's single word, the dragon dropped his head close to the ground and began flicking his tongue in earnest. Back and forth he went until he hit on something. He stopped, turned his head to look at Morgan, and hissed.

"He has the trail," Morgan said. "Come." She moved to walk alongside her pet, while her men kept a safe distance behind. Rhiannon and her men followed.

Tamsin hesitated, stealing a glance at the horizon, before following. She had kept her word to the Dominion, secretly apprising them of the Sisters' departure and notifying them as soon as she knew their destination. Now she waited for them to fulfill their end of the bargain. They had assured her they had resources embedded in England, ready to move at her call. If they did not arrive soon, all would be lost.

Mordred led them to a passageway at the eastern end of the island amongst the rocky crags. He paused only long enough to make sure the others were coming, then disappeared into the hole. Only one person could climb down at a time, so Tamsin again held back, hoping for some sign of her new allies. Finally, as she was about to descend, she caught sight of a light in the distance, growing larger as it approached. A helicopter! They had not abandoned her after all. Smiling, she began the descent toward her destiny.

"Maddock, can you hear me? Tam! Come in!" Corey cursed and pounded the console. All of his attempts to reach Maddock had been unsuccessful. Wherever Dane and the others had gone, they were well out of radio contact.

"I didn't get a good look," Matt said, dropping a pair of binoculars in a chair, "but I think it was Morgan and her men. I caught sight of them at the top of a ridge."

"How many?" Corey asked. They were anchored in a sheltered cove, well out of sight, but still he worried about being discovered before Maddock and the others returned.

"A lot. Close to twenty." Matt drummed his fingers on his pistol grip and worked his jaw. "I thought about following them, but it would take me forever to climb up there. They'd be gone."

Just then, they heard the drone of an engine. Matt hurried out of the cabin, returning minutes later, his face ashen.

"That was an AS532 Cougar."

"One more time, in English," Corey said.

"A German transport helicopter. It just dropped a dozen armed men up on the slope."

Shots rang out in the distance.

"I hope that wasn't Greg."

"I'm going to find out. You keep trying to reach Maddock, and be ready to get the hell out of here at the drop of a hat."

"Matt! You can't do that! You'll be killed!"

But Matt was gone. Corey punched the console again and returned to the radio. It was all he could do.

CHAPTER 35

They entered a cavern honeycombed with side passages, large and small. The floor was cracked and wisps of steam rose all around.

"I don't like this." Tam looked down at the ground, as if expecting it to give way at any moment.

They shone their lights all around, the beams slicing through the mist and revealing carvings of mythical creatures above the various passageways. The room was a veritable menagerie: a griffin to the left, a manticore to right, and various others all around. All of them looked fierce... and hungry.

"How about we move along?" Bones asked, looking nervously around.

"The directions say we're supposed to feed ourselves to the dragon," Dane said. "Look around for it, and watch your step."

They scattered and, moment later, gunfire and shouting erupted from the passageway by which they'd entered. Everyone looked around in alarm, those who were armed drawing their weapons.

"Find the dragon and let's move!" Dane shouted, moving as quickly as he dared across the precarious ground and shining his light above every passage.

No sooner had he spoken than a group of armed men burst into the cavern. Though the mist limited visibility, the ambient glow of a dozen flashlights playing off damp stone was sufficient to see the gleam of weapons in their hands. The newcomers froze for an instant at the sight of a cavern full of people, then opened fire.

The chamber thundered with the sound of gunfire. Dane hit the ground turned off his flashlight, and returned fire, as did the others in his party. The mist, moving lights, and confusion made him feel as if he were in a madhouse. Bullets ricocheted all around, adding to the danger. More men poured into the chamber, and Dane knew they were outgunned.

"Maddock! The dragon's over here!" Angel shouted from behind him.

"This way!" he called, keeping low as he ran toward her voice. "Let's get out of here."

Avery was nearby, and vanished into the tunnel along with Angel. Dane looked around for the rest of his group, but they had all killed their lights. He could tell by the occasional gunshot from the cavern's perimeter, however, they were scattered all around and cut off from him.

"Just go!" Tam shouted. "We'll catch up with you."

"No way." Dane dropped to the ground as someone fired off a shot in his direction.

"Maddock, you get out of here or I'll shoot you myself!" Bones' voice came through the fog. "Finish it!"

Indecision kept Dane frozen in place long enough to realize the sounds of gunfire on the perimeter were growing fainter. His friends were retreating into the side passages, drawing the attackers away from him. Cursing and blessing them in the same breath, he turned and dashed down the passageway.

Tamsin stumbled through the darkness. Her face was

bloody and her body bruised from tripping over unseen obstacles and banging into walls. Her men had abandoned her the moment the fighting started and the Dominion operatives didn't seem to care who they killed. They had surprised the Sisterhood's forces and started shooting. They were supposed to have made contact with her and joined forces. How had it gone so wrong?

She grimaced at the question. It had gone wrong because she had placed her trust in Heilig Herrschaft, the most sinister sect of the Dominion and had been betrayed. Now she and her Sisters were paying the price. Morgan had lost all her men except Locke and Jacob. Rhiannon's force had fared better, taking up defensive positions and holding the attacking force at bay, though who knew how long they could keep it up? If Tamsin's own men had stood their ground, they might have turned the tide, but the cowards had shown their true colors and now she was alone.

As she reeled forward, she sensed that the space around her had opened up. She had lost her flashlight when the fighting started, and was now, for all practical purposes, blind. She slowed her pace and felt all around her. She was definitely in a large chamber of some kind. She felt around for a wall to guide her and stepped out into open space.

She fell, screaming and grabbing for a handhold. Her fingernails tore as she clutched at rough stone, still falling. And then she hit the ground hard. For one irrational moment, she thought she had fallen to her death. Then she laughed. Feeling around, she realized she'd landed on a ledge. Of course, she didn't know how she was going to get out of this predicament, but at least she was alive. If only she could call for help, but there was no way her phone would get a signal so far underground.

Her phone!

She cursed herself in three languages as she dug her phone from her pocket and turned it on, using its faint glow to light the space around her. She saw immediately that she had not fallen far, and the rocky face above her was ripe for climbing. Relief flooded through her, renewing her energy.

She had raised her head and shoulders over the top of ledge when she heard a faint sound coming toward her. It wasn't exactly footsteps, but more of a scraping sound. She froze, hoping it would pass her by, but it came right toward her and, as it approached, she knew what it was.

Mordred.

She knew she should climb back down and wait for the dragon to go away, but fear kept her frozen in place, and she was trembling so hard she was afraid she would lose her grip and, this time, miss the ledge. Mordred had always terrified her, but this was far beyond any fear she had ever felt.

Far down the passageway behind Mordred, she saw a flicker of light. Someone was coming. She tried to cry out, but managed only a whimper. As the light grew stronger, she could finally see the dragon. Its snout was inches from her face.

She shook her head, furtively praying that the beast would go away, but it hissed, and opened its mouth wide.

She found her voice in time to manage a shrill scream that cut off when razor sharp teeth closed around her throat.

CHAPTER 36

"Oh my God," Angel whispered as they emerged into a vast cavern. Like one from which they'd just come, tunnels branched out from it on all sides, but that was where the similarities ended. Its walls were sprinkled with crystals that twinkled like tiny stars, the source of their light not readily apparent. In the center of the room, a pit, twenty feet across, plunged down into the earth. Deep in its depths, a vortex swirled, sending up wisps of steam.

All around them, carvings depicted events from King Arthur's life, but they weren't exactly what he'd expected. One showed Arthur climbing out of a deep pool, clutching his three weapons— no lady in a lake to be seen. Another image showed him standing before a glowing man. At least, he thought it was a man, but there was something different about him. He looked... alien.

"Bones would love that one," Angel said.

"Do you see what's written below it?" Avery's voice was filled with wonder. "Merlin."

Not for the first time in the past few days, Dane felt overwhelmed by the magnitude of their discoveries. His mind was abuzz, wondering if what they saw here connected with other, similar finds he and Bones had made in the past.

"Do you want to see him?" Avery's voice drew him

from his thoughts. "Arthur," she whispered, as if they were attending a viewing in a funeral home. "Come on."

Two stone footpaths formed a cross above the chasm, supporting a central platform. Upon it, a casket of blue-tinted crystal lay on a bier in the center. As they drew closer, Avery gasped.

"He looks like he just died yesterday."

Indeed, Arthur's had to be the most remarkably well-preserved corpse he had ever seen. He was a handsome man of early middle years. His wavy brown hair and thick beard were streaked with silver. He wasn't as tall or broad of shoulder as Dane had imagined, but had probably been a big man for his day. He had been put to rest in simple garments— no armor or chain mail like Dane had always imagined. His expression in death was serene, as if he were enjoying a pleasant dream.

"What is he holding?" Angel asked, pointing to a simple, stone bowl Arthur held upon his chest. It was carved of chalky white stone, but sparkled throughout with the same substance found on his weapons. It was deeper than an ordinary bowl, and three holes, evenly spaced, were bored just below the rim.

"I think it's the Holy Grail." Avery's face was as pale as the stone from which the bowl was carved.

"Doesn't look like a chalice to me," Angel said.

Dane considered what he knew about Grail lore.

"There are a lot of different ideas about the Grail. Some said it was a chalice, a bowl, even a dish. One legend said it was a stone that fell from the heavens, and later fell into the hands of the Templars."

"Lapis Exillis," Avery whispered. "Though some people call it Lapis Elixir."

"The Philosopher's Stone," Dane finished. "I see

how it could be both. It's a bowl that could be used to catch blood, but it also looks like a chalky stone someone could scrape a bit off of and use it for an elixir."

"Yeah," Angel said. "It's sort of got that Alka Seltzer look to it."

"It's not quite that simple."

They whirled about to see Morgan enter the chamber, flanked by Locke and another man on one side, and a huge dragon on the other. She and her men aimed their pistols at Dane.

"Hello, Jacob," Angel said to the man standing between Morgan and Locke. "Thanks for letting me go, but you forgot to tell me about your boss's reptile fetish."

Jacob looked uncomfortable, but Morgan ignored Angel.

"I must commend you on your resourcefulness," she began. "I did not anticipate the challenge you and your people would pose, but we beat you in the end. Now, I want the three of you to lay down your weapons. You should know, Mister Maddock, that if you try anything, we will shoot the ladies first."

Dane gritted his teeth. He didn't see a way out of this one. He wasn't fast enough to kill all three before they could take a shot, and even if he could take hold of Carnwennan, which he had sheathed on his hip, its cloaking power would not help Angel or Avery. Slowly, he drew his Walther and laid it on the ground. On either side of him, the ladies did the same.

"Very good. Now, back away from them."

They did as they were told, moving to either side of Arthur's casket.

"Arthur," Morgan breathed, her expression enraptured. "After all this time, I shall finally fulfill my destiny." She looked up at the glowing walls. "And tonight is a full moon. How fitting. It only remains to be decided who will provide the sacrifice."

An icy certainty crept over Dane. If Morgan was going to sacrifice someone, it wouldn't be him. Morgan would delight in his agony as he watched the woman he loved, or his sister, die. He couldn't let that happen.

Morgan took two steps closer, then froze. "Where is it?" She hissed. "Mordred will drink your blood for this."

Dane just stared at her. What was she talking about?

"Where?" she shrieked. "Where is Rhongomnyiad?"

"It's right here, you crazy witch." Bones stepped out of a side passage and hurled Rhongomnyiad at Morgan. She dived out of the way and the spear embedded in the far wall in a flash of blue light. The crystals all around the cavern shone white hot and showered the chamber with sparks.

Dane made a move for his Walther, but Mordred was almost upon him. He sprang back, drawing Excalibur. He hit the pommel and its blade burned.

"Get out here!" He called over his shoulder to Angel and Avery, who turned and ran. He only had a moment to register that people were pouring like angry bees from a hive out of the warren of passageways and into the chamber. He heard someone bark orders in German, and he caught a glimpse of Tam and Willis enter the room, guns blazing, and then Mordred was on him.

He thrust the glowing sword at the oncoming dragon, but it sprang back with incredible agility. Dane drew back, and the creature stalked him. The chaos all around him seemed to fall away, like turning down a television set. It was him and the dragon. And then it struck him that, as a child, he'd often pretended he was a knight doing battle with a dragon. He almost laughed.

Mordred sprang forward again and he thrust. The blade opened a smoking gash in the dragon's hide, but it kept coming. Dane continued to backpedal around the crystal casket, keeping the dragon at bay, but not dealing it enough damage to incapacitate it.

The dragon charged again, and he took a mighty swing, hoping to split its head in two, but Mordred sprang to the side and Excalibur sheared off a chunk of its frill. The creature hissed and slashed at Dane's leg with its razor sharp claws. Dane wasn't quick enough, and the dragon opened a gash in his leg. Dane stumbled, and Mordred lashed out with his powerful tail. Dane leaped just high enough to avoid a broken leg, but the strike knocked him off his feet.

Mordred tensed to strike, but a torrent of bullets stopped him in his tracks. Avery had circled around and retrieved both her pistol and Dane's. Most of her shots missed, but enough struck home to put the dragon on the defensive.

As she emptied the magazines and her weapons fell silent, Dane regained his feet, raised Excalibur, and brought it down with all his might, cleaving the dragon's head from its body. Still snapping, the head rolled off the platform and down into the pit.

Dane leapt back from the dragon's tail that, even in death, lashed about with deadly force, and ran back across the footbridge onto solid ground.

"Avery, you've got to get away," he ordered, and pushed her toward the nearest tunnel. He looked up just in time to see Locke standing before him, clutching Rhongomnyiad.

"Say good night, Maddock." Locke thrust the spear at him and Dane parried, sending up a shower of sparks, and struck back. Locke blocked his stroke, and the blades flashed as they met.

They circled one another, locked in a dance of death. Dane's injured leg slowed his movement, and he found himself increasingly on the defensive. Each of Locke's slashes and thrusts came ever closer to striking home. Step by step, he drove Dane out onto the foot bridge, forcing Dane to give way until Locke had him backed up to Arthur's casket.

Dane glanced behind him and saw his chance. As he fended off another vicious slash, he pretended that his injured leg had given way, and reeled backward. As a gleeful Locke leapt in for the kill, Dane threw himself over Mordred's still-thrashing body.

Locke, whose attention had been focused entirely on Dane, sprang right into the path of the dragon's powerful tail, which struck him square in the side of the knee. Locke went down, screaming agony. The tail caught him again, this time in the side of the head, and Rhongomnyiad fell from his limp fingers and rolled to the edge of the platform.

Dane dashed around the far side of the casket and scooped it up before it could go over the edge. He stood over Locke, who looked up at him with bleary, hate-filled eyes.

"I know how you think, Maddock. You won't kill an unarmed man. You're too noble for that."

"Maybe." Dane reversed Rhongomnyiad and held the tip just above Locke's heart. "But I'll kill any man who lays a hand on my girlfriend." Fear flashed through Locke's eyes in the moment before Dane drove the spear home. Blue light danced across Locke's body and smoke poured from his mouth, nose and ears. Dane grimaced as the sickly sweet odor of burnt flesh filled his nostrils. He watched as Locke's body burned down to a blackened husk and crumbled to dust.

And then a voice sounded above the din, cold and clear.

"Drop the spear or the girl dies!"

CHAPTER 37

Dane heard Morgan clearly over the waning sounds of the battle. It sounded to him as if a lot of people had run out of ammunition, been killed, or both. He wanted to look around for Angel and his friends, but he could not tear his gaze away from Morgan who held a pistol trained on Avery. Dane's sister stood with her hands upraised, quaking with terror. Why hadn't she run?

The room fell silent. All around them, the fighting stopped. Willis and Tam were on their knees, hands behind their heads, guarded by three white-clad men, as was another man he didn't recognize. Bones, knife in hand, faced off with another man in white, who aimed a pistol at him, but seemed reluctant to use it. Behind Morgan, Jacob had Angel in a headlock, though she was still fighting to free herself.

"I will not be denied." Morgan spoke the words like an oath. "Especially not by you."

"That is enough, Sister. It is over."

A beautiful woman with red hair and green eyes entered the chamber.

"What are you talking about, Rhiannon? Have you forgotten who I am?" Morgan quaked with rage, but she held her gun steady.

"I know exactly who you are, and it is time I put a stop to your plan." She snapped her fingers and the men who guarded Willis and Bones now trained their weapons on Morgan. "Jacob, stop choking that girl," she ordered. "And you," she said to Bones, "may stand down. We mean your people no harm."

Dane nodded at at Bones, who reluctantly lowered his knife.

Morgan's beautiful face was cold with fury. For a moment, it looked as if she would turn her weapon on Rhiannon, but instead she lowered it a few inches.

"A wise choice," Rhiannon said, walking toward Morgan.

"You mean to take my place."

"I mean to stop your foul plan, and to prevent this," her gesture took in the entire chamber, "from ever being revealed to the world."

"Why?"

"Show him, Adam." One of Rhiannon's men pulled down the neck of his shirt, revealing a brand on his chest. A Templar cross!

"No," Morgan whispered. "The Templars are dead."

"We are very much alive, Sister, and we find your pagan rites foul in the sight of God."

"God." Morgan laughed. "After what we know about these weapons, you still believe in your God?"

"Perhaps His creation is greater than our imaginations, but He is still the author of it all."

Morgan began to laugh. It was a crazed, mad sound that chilled Dane to the bone. But her laughter cut off when her eyes fell on Mordred's body. The dragon's death throes had nearly subsided, and he now twitched weakly.

"You killed him!" She cried in a voice that was beyond pain, beyond sanity. "Very well." Her entire body quaked. "You kill my family, I kill yours."

"No!" Jacob dove at Morgan, wrapping her in his bearlike arms and bearing her to the ground just as she pulled the trigger. Morgan cursed and fought him with all her might, struggling to free her gun hand, but Jacob held her down. "Don't do this," he pleaded. "I believed in you. Believed in your vision for Britain, but I don't believe in this."

Morgan spat in his face and fought to break free. In the midst of her struggles, Dane heard a loud pop. Morgan gasped, her eyes wide with shock. Jacob took the gun from her limp fingers and rolled off of her, revealing a gaping wound in her side. She raised her trembling, bloody fingers in front of her face.

"Damn you all," she gasped.

Dane barely heard her. He rushed to where Avery lay on the ground, blood seeping between her fingers as she held them pressed to her stomach.

"We've got to get you out of here," he said. "Somebody give me something I can bandage this with." His voice rang hollow. She wasn't going to make it. It was Melissa and Mom and Dad and too many good friends all over again.

"Shut up, Maddock." Avery managed a smile. "I hate it when you treat me like a child. Big brothers are all alike."

"I don't want you to die," he choked.

Tears spilled down Avery's cheeks as she reached out and took his hand. Suddenly, Dane was aware of someone shaking him hard. It was Rhiannon.

"I said, it's not too late to save her. Give me the dagger."

Dumbly, Dane handed Carnwennan to her.

"Bring me the Grail," she snapped as she collected Excalibur and Rhongomnyiad.

Bones and Willis hurried to the casket and raised the crystal lid while Dane reached inside and withdrew the Grail.

Up close, it looked even more ordinary than it had before. The outside still sparkled in the light, but he noticed the was stained a dark reddish brown. He sat the Grail down next to Rhiannon and returned to Avery's side. She lay with her head in Angel's lap, looking up at the ceiling.

"It's beautiful here," she whispered. "I think Dad would have liked it."

"He would," Dane said. "Now just hang on a little longer."

Rhiannon knelt down beside Morgan, who stared balefully at her.

"We need a sacrifice, Sister. Will you give it?"

"No," Morgan hissed. "Sacrifice her and save me instead."

"I will not. I am giving you this chance to make your final act in this world one of redemption. Perhaps you can atone for the evil you have done."

"I'll do it." Jacob said, dropping to a knee beside Morgan. "For all the wrong I've done in her service."

Morgan looked at him in bewilderment, and then, to Dane's utter amazement, began to cry. She took Jacob's hand and kissed it.

"No, Jacob," she whispered, "I will do it if you will hold me up. I want to face death on my feet."

Jacob lifted Morgan like a baby and stood her up, wrapping his arms around her to keep her from falling.

Rhiannon lay the three weapons in a triangular pattern as they had seen on the doorway to this place. They all watched the weapons shone brighter and brighter, each seeming to draw energy from the other. When they shone so brightly that Dane could not stand to look at them, she reached down and picked up the dagger. The glow subsided, but each weapon pulsed with palpable energy.

"Hold the Grail for me," she said to Dane. "It must be family." Dane picked up the stone bowl and, together, they turned to face Morgan.

"Are you ready?" Rhiannon asked.

Morgan nodded.

Rhiannon sliced open the front of Morgan's shirt, turned the knife flat side up, held it above her heart, and slowly pushed it into her Sister's body. Morgan gasped as the blade entered her, but she maintained her mask of serenity.

Rhiannon did not push the knife in deeply, only far enough to draw blood. She waited until the fuller, the groove in the center of the blade, filled with blood, and then she turned and poured it into the Grail. She repeated the process with the spear, and then she hefted Excalibur.

As she pressed the sword to Morgan's chest, their eyes met.

"Goodbye, Sister," she whispered.

"May the gods forgive me," Morgan replied, closing her eyes.

With a powerful thrust, Rhiannon drove the sword deep into Morgan's heart. Morgan made not a sound as her lifesblood flowed onto the blade. When Rhiannon withdrew the sword, Jacob laid her gently on the floor.

When Rhiannon poured this last measure of blood into the Grail, it began to glow. Flecks of light swirled, and the blood inside bubbled and steamed.

"She must drink it now."

Dane knelt in front of Avery and tipped the cup into her mouth. She choked and gagged, but was too weak to resist. In a few moments, she had gulped down the contents of the cup and, with a sigh, fell back onto Angel's lap.

She lay there for only a few seconds before her

eyes jerked open. Her breath came in gulps and her legs twitched. She clutched her wounded stomach and cried out in pain.

And then, she was calm.

She looked up at Dane in disbelief. Rhiannon knelt and raised Avery's shirt high enough to reveal that the wound was healed.

"It worked." Dane shook his head. Another thing he couldn't believe.

"Is she, like, immortal?" Bones asked, looking at Avery in wonder.

"No. All Morgan's remaining years now belong to her. Morgan was a healthy woman, so she should have a long life ahead of her."

Now that he knew Avery was going to be all right, Dane had questions.

"So, you're a Templar?"

"We are what remains of them," she said.

"Did you know about this place?"

"We knew of its existence, but its location was lost over three hundred years ago, along with the hiding places of the three weapons." She sighed. "The knowledge was believed to be lost forever, until 1701, when William Kidd, imprisoned in Newgate for piracy, offered three lost Templar maps in exchange for his freedom."

"But how did he get the maps in the first place?" Dane asked.

"Through one of his acts of piracy. The captain of the ship he took was a Templar. He had recovered the maps and was taking them to England when he was mortally wounded in Kidd's attack. Kidd promised to deliver them, but he betrayed the captain. He tried to recover what he assumed was a treasure from Oak Island. When he failed, he left a false trail in the form of a stone inscribed with runes. By this time, accusations of piracy were catching up to him, so he tried a new tactic. He hid each map in a sea chest and secured them in various locations for safe keeping until he could see his way free."

"But it didn't happen," Bones said.

"No. He attempted to negotiate his release, but no one in authority believed he had anything real to offer, and Kidd refused to provide proof until he was set free. Finally, on the eve of his execution, he made his confession to a priest, though he refused to tell to whom he had entrusted the chests. We began our search immediately, but failed to locate them, and the secret faded into legend."

She picked up Excalibur in one hand and Carnwennan in the other.

"Now we can finally complete our task." With a look of regret, she stepped to the edge of the pit and tossed them in.

"Wait! What the hell?" Bones, Avery, and Angel shouted over one another.

"Why did you do that? Those are irreplaceable treasures. The technology..." By the look on Tam's face, it was a good thing she no longer had a loaded gun.

"They're too powerful," Dane said. "Imagine if one nation harnessed that technology, or a terrorist group got hold of it."

"It is more than that," Rhiannon said, picking up the spear and the Grail. "People need faith, and these," she held them up for emphasis, "have the power to destroy that faith."

"Why, because they might be alien artifacts, or leftovers from an undiscovered, advanced civilization?" Bones asked. "Hell, I've believed in that stuff for years."

"No. It is because of what they are. What they were

used for."

Understanding began to trickle through Dane.

"That's the Holy Lance!" he exclaimed.

"Precisely. But it never pierced Jesus' side. And the Grail did not catch his blood. Quite the opposite, actually."

"Wait a minute." Avery, who was now back on her feet, held up her hands as if trying to slow Rhiannon down. "What are you saying?"

"Just as Morgan's blood saved you, the blood of another restored Jesus to life after his ordeal on the cross."

"Whose?" Avery looked stunned.

"Who among those closest to him died shortly after the crucifixion?"

"Judas," Dane said. "Are you saying he wasn't a traitor? He didn't kill himself out of remorse?"

"The betrayal was planned, as was his sacrifice for his lord."

"I don't buy it," Willis said in a scornful tone. "That might be the story you all have passed down, but that don't mean that's the way it happened."

"Perhaps not," Rhiannon mused, "but, in any case, we cannot risk that story getting out. You can see the damage it could do."

One by one, they all nodded, except for Tam, who was doubtless thinking of the uses to which the government could put these items.

With a sad smile, Rhiannon dropped the Holy Grail and the Holy Lance into the pit. Dane watched them fall, wondering if they'd made a mistake, but knowing deep down they had not.

"So, what happens now?"

Rhiannon's sad expression melted into a look of determination.

"I am the last remaining Sister, so I shall assume leadership. Morgan's body will be found on the grounds of Modron, a victim of her misguided attempt to tamper with nature. I shall also put a stop to her plot against the Royal Family."

"What about this place?" Avery asked.

"We will move Arthur's remains to a secret location, and then this chamber, and the passageways leading to it, must be destroyed. I suggest you leave as soon as possible."

"If you're leaving, we scored a sweet helicopter." Matt entered the chamber, followed by Greg, Tam's agent. "It belonged to the Dominion, so we figured it was okay."

"How did you find us?" Willis asked.

"Just followed the dead bodies. You guys really make a mess."

"That's another thing," Dane said to Rhiannon. "How did the Dominion get involved in all this?"

"I suspect my Sister, Tamsin, betrayed us, but I cannot be sure. We will know more after we question our prisoner." She reached out and shook Dane's hand. "You should go now. Good luck."

"I don't know how to thank you for saving my sister's life."

"Keep our confidence, and continue the fight against the Dominion."

The moon was low on the horizon when they returned to the surface. Dane put his arms around Angel, holding her close and feeling more alive than he had in... he didn't know how long. There was no need to talk. He could tell she felt it too.

"You two going to stand there all night?" Bones

asked.

"I guess we'd better get going," Dane agreed. "We've got a long trip home."

"So, who's riding in my awesome helicopter?" Matt asked.

"I could go for a ride," Tam said. "Who else is coming?" Willis and Greg volunteered. "How about you, Maddock?"

Dane looked from Angel to Avery to Bones.

"I don't think so," he said. "I think we'll go for the relaxing cruise. You know, have a little family time."

Tam smiled.

"Enjoy your night, then. Because, tomorrow, you start working for me."

THE END

About The Author

David Wood is the author of the *Dane Maddock Adventures* series and several stand-alone works, as well as *The Absent Gods* fantasy series under his David Debord pseudonym. He enjoys history, archaeology, mythology, and cryptozoology, and works all of these elements into his adventure fiction.

A proud member of International Thriller Writers and David co-hosts ThrillerCast, a podcast about writing and publishing in thriller and genre fiction. When not writing, he can be found coaching fast-pitch softball or rooting on the Atlanta Braves. He lives in Santa Fe, New Mexico with his wife and children. Visit him online at www.davidwoodweb.com.

Made in the USA
Middletown, DE
22 March 2016